If you wish to keep track of
what books you've read,
please indicate below.

MORE DEATHS THAN ONE

Constable Thorny Deepbriar can't resist trying his hand at a little detective work ... even if he is off-duty. Convalescing in the seaside resort where he was stationed during the war, Deepbriar starts looking into a case that the local police are treating as a joke, but when a body is discovered on the beach he is forced to wade into the murky waters of his past. Deepbriar must uncover the truth of events that took place over a decade ago ... unless he solves the mystery, he could be facing a charge of murder.

MORE DEATHS THAN ONE

MORE DEATHS THAN ONE

by

Jean Rowden

Magna Large Print Books
Long Preston, North Yorkshire,
BD23 4ND, England.

British Library Cataloguing in Publication Data.

Rowden, Jean
    More deaths than one.

    A catalogue record of this book is
    available from the British Library

    ISBN   978-0-7505-3431-4

First published in Great Britain by Robert Hale Limited 2009

Published in Large Print 2011 by arrangement with
Robert Hale Limited

Magna Large Print is an imprint of Library Magna Books Ltd.

Printed and bound in Great Britain by
T.J. (International) Ltd., Cornwall, PL28 8RW

Chapter One

'None of the pieces fit.' Detective Constable Thorny Deepbriar glowered at the man who sat across the table from him. What he most wanted at that moment was to rise to his feet and kick something, hard enough to hurt. His guiltless companion made a tempting target.

'I agree it's quite a complicated puzzle,' Cyril Byforth agreed timidly, unaware of Deepbriar's inner struggle as he concentrated on the scrap of card he held in his hand. 'I'm sure we'll get it sorted out eventually.'

The young man's tendency to agree with everybody was annoying Deepbriar almost beyond endurance. He considered making some truly outlandish statement to see if he could provoke Byforth to honesty. Unfortunately, he was stuck with Cyril for the moment, and he didn't want the youngster to turn sulky.

Deepbriar's forbearance only made him more irritable; he had been a member of Falbrough CID for seven weeks, yet there was no prospect of getting stuck into any decent detective work for another month at least.

'These things are always a bit slow to start

7

with,' Byforth warbled happily, turning the scrap of card through ninety degrees and squinting at it.

Deepbriar took a deep breath and resisted the temptation to punch him on the nose. 'It's impossible. I hate wasting time, and if there was ever a bl–'

'Now then, Mr Deepbriar, mind your language please.' Sister Davies came bustling into the room, carrying a tray. 'It's a good job Mr Byforth's the patient sort.'

The young clerk blushed. 'Don't say that Sister, Mr Deepbriar's got a lot to put up with; it's bad luck his leg has to stay in plaster for so long.'

'Well, only another week, with a bit of luck, though I find that a sour temper often slows down a patient's recovery. Time for your pills, Mr Byforth. Do you need something for the pain, Mr Deepbriar? Or maybe you're due for a tonic, since you're obviously feeling liverish.'

'I don't need anything,' Deepbriar growled, adding 'except to get out of here,' under his breath. He pushed to his feet and his plaster cast hit the table, sending a dozen jigsaw pieces cascading to the floor. The room he shared with Byforth seemed smaller than ever when he was standing up. Deepbriar had tried going to the common room once or twice, but the wireless was always on; the Light Programme reminded him of his wife, and how much he missed her, which made him even more miserable.

'Careful.' Sister Davies retrieved the pieces and put them back in the box. 'I've always rather liked that picture of Nelson's flagship.'

Deepbriar bit his tongue to stop himself telling her what he thought of Nelson, with or without his flagship.

'Oh, and somebody's dropped their book. You're in the middle of this, aren't you, Mr Deepbriar?' She moved towards his bedside locker, holding the battered copy of *Escape From Stalag 9* at arm's length as if it harboured something contagious.

'No, I've handed it on to Mr Byforth.' He'd abandoned the POW story when the bad dreams began. In the first of them he had been shoring up a crumbling tunnel, trying simultaneously to dig his way out of a hospital bed, held back by a plaster cast the size and weight of a baby elephant. Once he woke up he decided he had no wish to finish the book, and did his best to persuade himself that the dream had been amusing. Since then the nightmares had become so bad that he was reluctant to fall asleep.

After the incident which had left him trapped under a collapsing roof with his leg bent in quite impractical directions, Deepbriar had barely been able to recall how it happened, thanks to the concussion he'd suffered at the same time. Now, his brain seemed intent on filling the gaps in his memory and each improbable adventure was worse than the last.

Deepbriar grabbed his crutches and hobbled from the room, finding a window that looked out over the moorland surrounding the county convalescent home. There wasn't so much as a bird or a sheep to be seen. He stared at the lashing rain. The weather had been dismal all week, more like January than August. Water washed down the glass in solid sheets, leaving the gravel drive awash. The cast on his leg must on no account be allowed to get wet, which was doubly frustrating. If the rain would only relent he might have been allowed outside, if only to the bench by the front door.

A large grey car turned into the drive, and Deepbriar craned forward to watch as it drew up outside the front of the house, welcoming any distraction. When he'd been transferred from the hospital to the convalescent home it had seemed like an improvement, but after eight days the place felt like a prison.

The rain was beating down so hard that the vehicle was hardly more than a blur. He rubbed the condensation from the glass and watched as the driver jumped out to open the rear door, bending to help his passenger. Deepbriar felt something leap within him, an actual physical lurch of the heart.

Deepbriar had always had strong shoulders, and long acquaintance with the crutches had given him a fair turn of speed. Despite the cast he reached the front door as it flew open, thrown wide by the gusting wind. A woman dashed in, her head down as she clutched at her hat.

'Mary!' He took the crutches in one hand and flung his arms around his wife. Startled by his sudden appearance and his enthusiastic embrace, she took a step back, and they would have toppled to the floor if they hadn't made contact with the wall first. Having recovered from the shock of this unaccustomedly emotional greeting Mary returned her husband's hug, then stepped back, her face flushed.

'Goodness.' She looked pleased, if a little embarrassed, as she attempted to straighten her hat. 'Well, I can't say you're not pleased to see me.'

'I'm going stir crazy,' Deepbriar grumbled. 'And even if I wasn't I'd still be pleased to see you. But what are you doing here?'

She smiled, glancing conspiratorially down the corridor before she replied, keeping her voice low. 'Major Brightman had an idea. I think it was because of that book he saw you reading. We've formed an escape committee. We're planning a breakout.'

Deepbriar was following her towards a bench across the hall, but this brought him

11

up short. 'What do you mean, a breakout?'

'The major thought you were pretty miserable last Wednesday, and after I got home on Saturday he popped round to ask if you were feeling any better. I told him you'd practically bitten my head off several times, and how grumpy you were because they won't even let you go for a walk until the plaster's removed, not while the weather's so wet. He decided we had to get you out of here.' Her cheeks dimpled. 'He says time's running short. His best man has to be fit and healthy on the big day, in case he finds himself in need of support.'

'But the doctor said I couldn't go home yet,' Deepbriar protested, easing himself down on to the polished wooden seat.

'We're not going home. A bit of sea air will do you good, and if the rain stops you'll be able to go for walks without the risk of breaking your neck by falling into a bog. It's all arranged.'

'That's all very well, in fact it sounds fine, but they said I have to have medical care available, because of the concussion.'

'That's what I told Charles, but he's fixed it all. He'll explain when he gets back; he and Elaine will be along in a few minutes, they've just driven down to the garage in the village. They said they needed petrol, but I think Elaine decided we should have a little while on our own.'

'She's a very nice lady,' Deepbriar said, reaching to pull Mary down into the bench beside him. Having checked that nobody was in sight, he kissed her on the lips.

'Thorny,' she protested, glancing anxiously around. 'Do I gather that you're feeling better?'

'Never mind me, how are you two?' He nodded in the general direction of her stomach.

'Oh.' Her eyes widened in apparent enlightenment. 'All this affection is for Deepbriar junior, I might have guessed.'

Deepbriar was still trying to persuade her otherwise several minutes later when the front door crashed open again. Major Charles Brightman and his fiancée, Elaine Barr, came bowling in, to the accompaniment of a howling wind and a shower of wind-tossed spray.

Deepbriar settled back against the musty leather and sighed contentedly.

'It's lucky the old man insists on keeping this museum piece,' his friend said, turning out of the drive on to the road that twisted down to the valley. 'I'd never have fitted you into my car with that monstrosity on your leg.'

'I am truly grateful,' Deepbriar said. 'Sister Davies was more than I could handle, and I still don't know how you got round matron.'

'I pulled rank,' the major replied cheerfully. 'The chap who's going to be looking after you at the cottage hospital in Bradsea used to be a bigwig in London, before he decided his wife and children needed some healthy sea air. When matron looked like cutting up rough I dropped a hint that he'd attended at Buckingham Palace once or twice, and that he was going to be very disappointed if they didn't release you into his care. After that, the old dragon practically curtsied when she saw me out.'

'He's quite shameless,' Elaine said equably, giving her fiancé's arm a squeeze. 'One of these days he'll encounter somebody who sees right through him.'

'Nonsense, everybody loves my lord of the manor act.' Brightman replied, grinning briefly. 'Seriously, Thorny, you'll be well looked after, I went on a recce yesterday, and the hospital's only a hundred yards from where you'll be staying.'

Deepbriar nodded absently. Since Charles had mentioned their destination he'd completely lost track of the conversation. It was sixteen years since he'd been in Bradsea, and a flood of memories came washing through his mind. There had been good times, and bad. In six short months he'd learnt a great deal, about friendship and about betrayal. He gave an involuntary shudder. And about death.

'I didn't tell you, did I, Thorny?' Mary was saying. 'We're taking you to cousin Vera's.'

Deepbriar shook off the memories, reminding himself that he was free of the convalescent home; no more Byforth, no more Sister Davies, and no more jigsaw puzzles. 'You're sure she doesn't mind?' he asked, glancing at his wife.

'No, she's glad we're able to come. Luckily, one of her guest rooms is on the ground floor, and there's the scullery for you to wash in, and facilities just outside the back door. Even if the weather's bad, at least there's a view of the sea. I'll be able to make myself useful too, because the lady who helps with the cooking four days a week is poorly. It couldn't have worked out better.'

'You didn't think to mention that you were staying too?' Deepbriar stared at her, pleased that he'd be enjoying his wife's company, but irritated to hear that her cousin was planning to make use of her. 'I might have guessed. Vera never does anything for anybody unless it serves her own purpose.' He nodded delicately towards her slightly swollen figure. 'Does she know about you know what?'

'Yes, of course she does. And you needn't worry, I'm quite capable of helping out in the kitchen now and then. It's not good for me to sit around doing nothing.'

'Maybe not, but you mustn't overdo it,'

15

Deepbriar said, feeling unaccountably cross-grained. 'The only good thing about being stuck away in that place was knowing you could get plenty of rest, since you didn't have me to look after.'

Mary Deepbriar sighed, and from the front of the car Elaine Barr made a sympathetic sound.

'What have I said now?' Deepbriar demanded. 'I thought you liked having a break from all the cooking and housework.'

'I did,' his wife conceded. 'Until I'd cleaned the whole house from top to bottom, made about fifty pounds of jam and another twenty of chutney. After that I got bored. Anyway, I'm quite looking forward to using Vera's kitchen, she's got a brand new cooker, and a refrigerator. It'll be a nice change.' She patted Deepbriar's hand, like a mother comforting a fractious child. 'Don't worry, I shan't stop you going for a beer now and then.'

'Once this plaster's off I'll be out walking,' Deepbriar replied gruffly. 'The sooner I'm fit and back at work the better.'

'Oh yes, that reminds me,' Mary said. 'One of Vera's neighbours is hoping to have a word with you. Evidently there's been some sort of trouble in Bradsea, but she can't persuade the police to take it seriously. She's hoping you might look into it, since you'll have a lot of time on your hands.'

'What sort of trouble?' Deepbriar fidgeted,

wishing for the thousandth time that he could scratch his leg beneath the plaster.

'She didn't say. I gather Vera's arranged for you to meet this friend tomorrow morning, once you've been to the hospital.'

'I expect it'll be some nonsense,' Deepbriar said disparagingly. 'Anyway, I can't go upsetting the lads at the local station.'

'I thought you'd be glad of something to do,' his wife replied, a little tartly.

The major laughed. 'If you'd rather I turn round and take you back, Thorny, then say so now.'

For the briefest moment, gone so soon that he hardly acknowledged its existence, Deepbriar might even have astounded them all by telling him to do it. 'Not on your life,' he said. Bradsea was waiting for him. He would stroll on the promenade and bury his memories, despatching them to the past, where they belonged.

Deepbriar rolled out of bed. He was careful not to disturb Mary, breathing slow and steady at his side; with the baby to think of she needed rest far more than he did. He'd lain awake since the early hours, afraid of slipping back into the nightmare that had interrupted his sleep.

Awkward with the weight of the cast, he eased on to the crutches and manoeuvred himself to the door. When the hinges

17

squealed he held his breath until he was sure Mary hadn't stirred. As if the recent bad weather had been no more than a reflection of Deepbriar's mood, his first morning in Bradsea was dawning fine and sunny. Once he'd been to the outhouse he hobbled into the scullery, where he washed his hands and face in cold water. Reluctant to return indoors, delightedly breathing in great gulps of sea air, he hitched himself across the garden and peered over the side gate.

No evidence of the rain remained except the puddles that shone on the promenade. The sea was so bright Deepbriar had to squint through eyes half-shut to see the gentle waves curling on to the shingle beach. The front stretched away in both directions, inviting him to the pier or the putting green. Beyond that, a level path would take him all the way to Whellow. Deepbriar looked hungrily at the distant view; he could picture himself, striding out on a succession of beautiful mornings, getting his strength back. His injured leg twitched, as if it shared his enthusiasm. Wrinkling his nose, Deepbriar relished the scents of saltwater and seaweed, feeling a great lift of his spirits; from now on he'd surely sleep like a log.

There was nobody about except a solitary figure sweeping the paved area in front of Bradsea's diminutive bandstand. The man was tall, but he was stooped, and very thin.

There was something about the way he wielded his broom that suggested a deep melancholy. Reluctant to surrender his cheerful mood, Deepbriar began to turn away. As he did so, the man lifted his head to stare along the promenade towards the beach huts.

The constable let out a muted gasp; he recognized the man's profile instantly, despite the many lines drawn on it by the passage of time. Yet the unlikelihood of seeing that face in such circumstances made Deepbriar doubt his sanity for a moment. He blinked, looked again, and knew his first instinct was right.

His hand was on the latch and the gate open, before he remembered that he wasn't dressed. Early though it may he, he couldn't risk being seen on the promenade in his pyjamas. Cousin Vera would turn him out, and he'd be sent back to the mercies of Sister Davies at the convalescent home. Deepbriar flung himself back to the door. The plaster cast caught on the inch-high doorsill. He tumbled headfirst into the room, his involuntary yell of pain cut off abruptly as his chin struck the end of the metal bedstead.

'Damn and blast and hell's–'

'Thorny!' His wife's reproach silenced him, but she was all concern when she sat up and saw the blood pouring from his chin.

She hurried to kneel at his side. 'What on earth were you doing?'

'I have to get some clothes on,' he replied urgently, trying to push her away. 'It's nothing serious. Let me up.'

'No, wait. Look at you.' She pressed down on his shoulder with one hand, the other holding her handkerchief, soon soaked with blood, to his face. 'You'll ruin the mat. You'd better stay on the lino a minute. Don't move. I'll fetch some water.'

'There's no need for that. If I can just put my shirt and trousers on,' he suggested, trying to evade her grasp, 'I'll go and bleed outside, then you won't have to worry about Vera's furniture.'

'Nonsense. You can't go anywhere looking like that.' Mary Deepbriar sighed. 'Of all the things to do, I don't know how you're going to make yourself presentable. That cut will make it very hard to shave. We're seeing that London doctor today; whatever is he going to think?'

'With this on it's a wonder I'm not covered in bruises,' her husband replied, giving the plaster a whack with his fist. 'D'you reckon Vera's got a saw out in her shed?'

'If she has, you're not to go near it,' she said sharply. 'Oh, listen, that's Vera coming down now. You've probably woken the whole house.'

At that point Deepbriar admitted defeat.

With two women ganging up on him there was no chance of escape. The mystery of the sweeper on the promenade would have to wait.

Chapter Two

The so-called London doctor was not what Deepbriar had expected. Dr Torden turned out to be a small, rotund and ruddy-faced man, who rushed to greet his new patient like an old friend.

'I hear you play the organ in your local church,' the doctor said enthusiastically, once the preliminary introductions were over. 'If you want to try your hand up at St Giles's once you're out of plaster, the vicar is always keen to find new blood, if you'll pardon the expression. He organizes little informal evening concerts now and then. You'd be more than welcome, if you're willing.' He chuckled. 'It would be good exercise for that leg.'

'I'd need a bit of practice,' Deepbriar replied. 'It's been a while since I played, what with one thing and another. But let us know the date of the next concert and we'll both come along.'

'Of course. It's kind of you to mention it,' Mary said. With these social niceties out of the way she began to apologize for Deepbriar's appearance, but Dr Tordon cut her short, laughing as he leant forward to peer up at the fresh cut on the constable's chin. 'The major told me what to expect, Mrs Deepbriar. He warned me your husband is the sort of man who can get himself into trouble just about anywhere.'

'He's a good one to talk,' Deepbriar replied, slightly miffed.

The doctor smiled at Mary, ignoring her husband. 'Don't worry, Mrs Deepbriar. I served with Major Brightman's regiment during the war, I dare say I can deal with anything your husband throws at me.'

Mary returned the smile. 'I'm afraid we're putting you to a lot of trouble.'

'Not at all.' He turned back to Deepbriar. 'I suppose we'd better get down to business. I've read through your notes, and studied the X-rays. You managed to do yourself quite a bit of damage. Still, I'm hopeful we'll be able to take that cast off for you very soon. What do you say to Friday morning?'

Deepbriar beamed. Only four days. 'If you'd said I had another week to wait, I was thinking about raiding somebody's garden shed to find a saw, or taking a walk to the nearest ironmonger's shop,' he confessed.

'Can't say I blame you. I hope you realize,' Dr Tordon added, suddenly serious, 'that you can't expect to be handing in those crutches, not for a few days.'

'As long as I can get out and walk–' Deepbriar began.

'We'll see, once we get a proper look at your leg again.' The doctor wrote a few words on Deepbriar's record. 'Ten o'clock Friday morning we'll cut the cast off and have a new X-ray taken. If everything's all right, then we'll talk about what happens next.'

'I'm sure it won't take me long to get fit again,' Deepbriar said.

Dr Tordon gave him a piercing look. 'I must say, you don't appear as well as I'd hoped. Are you sleeping properly?'

'Not too badly,' Deepbriar lied.

'Hmm. What about the concussion?' He peered down at the notes again. 'Any recent headaches or blackouts?'

'No.' Not a direct lie this time, Deepbriar consoled himself. He wouldn't count three days ago as recent.

'How about your memory? Can you recall what happened to you?'

'Yes.' Deepbriar said no more. He didn't think anyone, even the doctor, needed to know how those memories had turned themselves into nightmares. 'I'll be fine once I can move about more, especially if I can get outside. Plenty of fresh sea air, that's all I need. Doing nothing has never suited me.'

'Hmm,' Dr Tordon said again. 'let's hope it's only a matter of exercise, though I must offer a word of caution. You won't be taking part in the annual beach games on Saturday.

Oh, and don't go dashing after criminals either, not for a few weeks. Take a bit of care and you might be back on the beat by the beginning of October.'

'That long!' Depression settled upon him like a cloud. He might otherwise have told Tordon that he was a member of the CID, which meant he never expected to walk a beat again, gammy leg or no.

'No time at all,' the doctor replied breezily, rising from his chair and going to open the door. 'With a bit of luck we'll have you good as new.'

'That was good news,' Mary said bracingly, once they were back outside. 'You only have to wait until Friday.'

'If you say so,' Deepbriar replied sombrely. 'I think I'll go for a little walk, love. Get a bit more fresh air while the weather's dry.'

'You can't, not now, that friend of Vera's is coming,' Mary reminded him. 'You know, the one who wants your help because the police won't listen to her. Vera promised you'd be here. Please?' she added, as he hesitated.

They sat in the tiny parlour which Vera kept for her own use. The room was crammed with too much furniture and hundreds of knick-knacks, presided over by a grandfather clock with a somnolent tick. The room looked as if it belonged to an earlier century; there were still gas mantles instead of electric light bulbs, although the rest of the house

25

had been modernized.

What with the plaster cast, the lack of space, and the tiny china cups Vera was handing out, Deepbriar felt like Gulliver in Lilliput as he eased himself down on an upright chair, brought in specially for his use and placed against a wall; he could never have extricated himself from the depths of the worn leather armchairs. He kept very still, half listening while Mary and her cousin chatted to Miss Caldwell; the main purpose of her visit was being postponed until the serious business of tea drinking was out of the way.

Deepbriar put in the odd word when necessary, but he allowed his thoughts to drift as Mary told the story of the case that had led to his injury; the saga had grown stale, and he was thoroughly sick of being seen as a hero. There was nothing heroic about having a roof landing on your head, and as the weeks had passed he'd become increasingly inclined to consider himself a fool for not having found a way to avoid the ton or so of wood and tiles that had rained down on him.

It was stuffy in the little room, and Deep-briar's eyes jolted open as Vera gathered the cups and picked up the tea tray. 'I'll leave you in peace, now you've had a chance to get acquainted,' she said. 'I'd better make a start on tonight's vegetables.'

'I'll come and help,' Mary offered. 'No, don't move, Thorny, I can step over your cast.'

Deepbriar glowered at the two women as they left him alone with Miss Caldwell. She wasn't quite what he'd expected; despite her attempts to hide it, he knew Vera had already celebrated her half century, but her friend appeared to be at least ten years younger, and from the snatches of conversation he'd heard before he dozed off she seemed quite sensible.

'Maybe I shouldn't be troubling you,' Miss Caldwell began apologetically as the door closed. 'It sounds as if you've had quite a hard time of it recently.'

'The tale gets taller every time it's told,' Deepbriar said. 'A roof fell in and I was unlucky enough to be underneath, that's about it. I'm not going anywhere for a while thanks to this leg, so it won't hurt me to sit and hear what you've got to say. It's not as if I've got anything else to do.'

The woman bit her lip. 'I don't know. You're bound to think I'm just a silly female making a fuss over nothing.'

Deepbriar roused himself, aware that he'd been bad mannered. 'I'm sorry, that was rude of me; I didn't intend to be offhand. I shan't know what to think if you don't explain. Just as long as you realize I don't work in this part of the county, and I mustn't interfere with

27

police business while I'm on sick leave, or I'll be in trouble.'

'I appreciate that. But nobody at the police station is prepared to take the matter seriously. They think it's a joke.' She gave a rueful smile. 'I can see why, to be honest.'

'Well, right now I could do with cheering up,' Deepbriar said. 'A good laugh might be just what I need. Tell me what's been going on, then I'll see what I think.'

'Right. I'll try not to be long-winded, but I need to explain how I came to be involved. I work at the library, as assistant to Mr Brown. It isn't an official part of my job, but two evenings a week I take books to some of our older residents, mostly those in the bungalows along North Terrace and High View. I realized something was going on about a month ago.'

Miss Caldwell offered him a small smile. 'Sometimes the old dears haven't had any company all week, so they like me to stop for a chat. Mrs Guest told me that something had gone missing from her front garden, but she hadn't bothered to report it to the police. She thought some of these teddy boys had wandered in looking for mischief; they can get a bit rowdy when they've had a drink or two.'

'Yes, we've had our share of bother too,' Deepbriar said. 'Go on.'

She nodded. 'The same thing happened

again, about a week later, but it was Mr Morrowby this time, and he was very cross. Of course, the poor man's housebound, so he couldn't go to the police himself; he asked me to call and tell them what had happened. As a result, a young constable called on him, but Mr Morrowby said he never even bothered to get his notebook out. He didn't seem to think it was worth pursuing the matter.'

There didn't seem to be much air in the room. Somewhere at about this point Deepbriar's thoughts began to drift again; there was mention of a man called Jack, and maybe a Mrs Rayner, who was worried about her cat cutting its claws. He gave himself a mental shake. That couldn't be right, it must have been paws.

'You can see why I'm concerned,' Miss Caldwell said at last. 'These old people have as much right to enjoy their gardens as anybody else, don't they. Strictly speaking it's probably criminal damage or something.'

'Damage.' Deepbriar forced his eyes wide open. 'Exactly what are we talking about here? Has somebody been trampling on people's plants? Or digging them up?'

'Oh no, it's not their plants. It's their gnomes.'

Deepbriar lifted on to his elbows to bring his head off the pillow. 'You might have warned me!' he said, looking balefully up at his wife.

'What do you mean, warned you?' She looked puzzled. 'What am I supposed to have warned you about?'

This Caldwell woman. I know what Vera's like for gossip; you can't tell me she didn't talk all this over with you first.'

'She didn't,' Mary protested. 'Well, except that it was something to do with gardens.'

'Then why are your cheeks all pink?' Deepbriar shot back, seeing her flushed face as a sure sign of her guilt.

'Because Vera's got some bread baking and it's warm in the kitchen.' She sat gingerly on the side of the bed, fanning herself with her hand. 'And if we're going to talk about red faces, what's you're excuse for getting so hot and bothered? If Miss Caldwell is making a fuss about nothing then all you have to do is say you agree with the local police, and that they were right not to investigate.'

Deepbriar said nothing, glowering at her suspiciously.

'Come on, Thorny,' she prompted, looking at him with the fond but slightly exasperated expression of a mother faced with a sulky child, 'it's no use putting on that face. I'm your wife, not one of your suspects. What's the matter? Is this still about what the doctor said this morning? He was just being cautious.' She gave his plaster cast a friendly pat. 'Sister Davies was sure you'd be fine as soon as you were rid of this old thing.'

'It's not that,' he replied grudgingly. 'You really don't know? You're sure you and Vera haven't been having a good old giggle out there while you were shelling the peas?'

Mary was beginning to look less than amused. 'What is it that makes grown men behave like children? I've told you, I have no idea what Miss Caldwell wanted to talk to you about, and even if I did, I can't see why you're making such a to-do about it.'

'Gnomes!' He burst out. 'She wants me to find out who has been going around stealing garden gnomes.'

'Gnomes?' She stared at him, her mouth dropping open a little.

He nodded. 'Those little beggars with pointy hats, sitting on toadstools or whatever it is they do. Somebody has been taking them. Except for one or two that have been smashed and left in bits on the garden path. Honestly! And I'm supposed to go round and make a few unofficial enquiries, chat to the neighbours and ask if they've seen anything suspicious. You can imagine the sort of answers I'd get. And what the heck do I say if anybody back home hears about it? I'll be the laughing stock of the whole force.'

Mary was trying very hard not to laugh. 'Vera did hint that you might be reluctant to get involved once you'd talked to Miss Caldwell.'

'She was right there! I mean, it's hardly the sort of stuff Dick Bland investigates. Can you see anyone asking a proper detective to look into a thing like this?' He scowled at the thought of this insult to his fictional hero.

'Oh, I don't know, I expect he'd find it interesting. Though I think it's even more suitable for your other favourite,' Mary said, her lips twitching uncontrollably. 'It's perfect for a hard-bitten New Yorker.'

Deepbriar's scowl vanished. 'There's a thought. *Mitch O'Hara and the Case of the Headless Gnome.* Imagine the picture on the cover; you'd be able to tell it was really scary stuff.'

'I've got some more titles for you. *Gnome-where to Run,*' Mary suggested, beginning to laugh. *'Murder on the Gnome Front.'*

Her laughter was infectious, and despite himself Deepbriar found himself joining in.

'How about *Death Gnomes no Mercy?*' he suggested. 'Or *High Gnome.*'

She gave an unladylike snort. 'Now you're just being silly.'

By this time they were both laughing so much that the bed shook beneath them.

'Shh!' Mary gasped a few minutes later, tears running down her cheeks. 'What on earth will people think?'

'There's no law against having a good laugh,' Deepbriar said, 'though it's a bit painful.' He rubbed his face; it ached from the unaccustomed exercise. 'Look out, I'm going to get up. I need a bit of room.'

Mary rose to her feet, one hand on the slight bump at her waistline. 'It's a good job you'll be rid of that cast soon. If you were still wearing it in a few months time, neither one of us would find it easy to get out of bed. We might get stuck and just roll about in the middle.' She began to giggle again, then hiccupped.

Deepbriar was instantly sobered. 'Steady on, love,' he cautioned, 'you'll be upsetting the baby.'

'Nonsense,' his wife replied, wiping her eyes and giving him a light-hearted kiss. 'I'm sure it would be far worse for him if I was grumpy like his father. Come on, we'd better tidy ourselves up; it's nearly time to eat.'

As she combed her hair, Mary watched Deepbriar in the mirror. He heaved himself to the side of the bed and reached for his tie, his lips pursing unconsciously as they always did when he tied the knot. She smiled as he met her eyes. 'So, what did you tell Miss Caldwell?'

'I didn't. And before you ask, I wasn't rude to her. Well, not very. I don't think I said anything much, I was a bit flabbergasted.' He sighed. 'It makes sense, I suppose. So much for being a detective. Dick Bland and Mitch O'Hara investigate bloodcurdling murders, but a case of vanishing garden gnomes is all a middle-aged copper can expect. It's about what I'm fit for.'

'Am I supposed to argue?' Mary asked fondly, her eyes bright. 'You forgot to mention that this particular copper has been acting the hero lately, and he got himself a commendation for it. Though despite that I'm afraid he's been feeling very sorry for himself.'

'Maybe I have at that.' Deepbriar came to stand beside her, balancing uneasily on his good leg and one crutch so he had a free hand to put round her thickening waist. 'Sorry, love.'

She gently disengaged herself. 'Time enough for that when you're back on two legs, we don't want you falling over again.' She turned to face him. 'Don't tell me you're really going to look into the case of the disappearing gnomes.'

'Why not? I'll wander round and take a look at the crime scenes tomorrow morning. It'll help pass the time until this dratted thing comes off.' He glared at the hated plaster cast. 'But I'm only doing it on one condition. If anybody breathes a word to the blokes at Falbrough station about gnomes, I'll go straight back to the convalescent home and get the gruesome Sister Davies to swear I never left.'

'I shan't tell if you don't. Though if Charles asks what you're doing to keep busy I shan't know what to say.'

'I don't mind him knowing,' Deepbriar said. 'We've shared each other's secrets since we were knee high to a grasshopper; he won't give me away.'

Chapter Three

Bradsea police station didn't seem to have changed much. Deepbriar knew of old how heavy the front door was and he juggled awkwardly with his crutches so he could get a firm grip on the handle. As it turned beneath his grasp he pushed against the solid oak with his shoulder. When it began to shift he leant his whole weight on the door, and without warning it swung wide, pitching him into the front office.

Deepbriar was saved from falling on his face by a pair of uniformed arms. 'Good morning, sir,' the young constable who'd pulled the door open greeted Deepbriar respectfully, unfazed by this sudden entry. 'I thought I could hear somebody struggling out there. Is there something I can do for you?'

'I was hoping to talk to somebody I used to know,' Deepbriar replied, once his crutches and his composure were back under control, 'but I'm not sure if any of them are still here. Constable Lumley perhaps?'

'Constable Lumley.' The young man looked thoughtful. 'The name's familiar. Oh yes, it came up last week when we were talking about the coronation. He's long gone from here, sir, I imagine he must have retired. Perhaps you'd like to tell me what the problem is, and I'll see if I can deal with it.'

'There's no problem,' Deepbriar replied. He hadn't been sure he wanted to talk about vanishing gnomes before he came in; he was quite sure he wouldn't be confiding in this youngster, who barely looked old enough to be wearing the uniform. 'This is more like a social call than business. My name's Deepbriar. I worked here once, during the war.' He nodded towards a plaque on the wall. 'I was one of those drafted in after the bomb.'

'Bomb?' The smooth-faced constable looked baffled, then his face cleared. 'Oh, that.'

'Yes, that,' Deepbriar said sourly. It might be over a decade since the war ended, and he knew things had to move on, but he hadn't expected Bradsea's infamous visit from the Luftwaffe to he forgotten so soon.

A German bomber, crippled by fighters before it reached its target, had dumped its deadly cargo as it crossed the coast, then run for home. One bomb had fallen in the sea and two others left huge craters on the beach, while the fourth scored a direct hit on Bradsea police station.

Bad luck had made things worse. It was time for a change of shift, so there were far more men in the building than at any other time, though if the air-raid siren had gone off a few minutes earlier they would have been scattering to the various posts assigned to them during emergencies.

The explosion killed four officers outright and injured five others, depriving the town of half its law officers at one blow. Deepbriar had been one of the men brought in temporarily to fill the gap. He recalled the macabre jokes that had done the rounds at the time; the front of the building had suffered hardly any damage, the oak door standing firm, along with the four main offices. The greatest devastation had been in the locker room, where the men gathered before they went on duty.

'How about Constable Hobday?' Deepbriar asked, though without much hope.

'He's Sergeant Hobday now,' the constable replied. 'But I'm afraid he's off on his holidays this week. If you want to call in again on Monday, he'll be here then.'

'He'll have gone fishing,' Deepbriar hazarded, a half grin on his face. He was surprised Hobday had made it to sergeant; the man must be close to retirement, he hadn't been young when Deepbriar knew him. A huge lumbering man, Hobday had seemed older than his years, stolidly plodding his same old beat. To a young bobby, only a few months out of training, he'd been an enigma, a man without ambition, showing no animation except on the rare occasions when he spoke about fishing. With hindsight, his weary defeated look probably owed much to the sudden loss of so many of his friends and colleagues.

'Detective Chief Inspector Vorrman was here during the war,' the constable said, breaking into Deepbriar's abstraction. 'He's in charge at Whellow now.'

'Chief Inspector, eh?' Deepbriar's eyebrows shot up. Vorrman had done well for himself. He'd been a sergeant when they'd last met, another of the original Bradsea team who'd escaped injury when the bomb fell.

'Yes. He lives in town, you might catch him at home over the weekend.' There was something unreadable in the constable's tone; it made Deepbriar wonder if Vorrman was still unpopular. 'He's got a house up Wellington Rise.'

This was another surprise, though maybe it explained the youngster's attitude. Deepbriar could only recall one member of the force who lived in Bradsea's most exclusive road during the war, and that was the superintendent. Even for a man of that rank it was a smart area, but then Superintendent Ruggles was said to have married a very rich woman. How could Vorrman afford to live there?

The telephone rang, and the young man darted back behind the counter to answer it.

As he did so, the door from the back of the building opened and a woman came in, carrying a tea tray.

'Rosie!' Deepbriar was relieved to see a familiar face. 'You're still here!'

'Gor bless us, it's young Thorny Deepbriar!' The old lady set the tray down on the high wooden counter, beside the constable. She tilted her head back and looked Deepbriar up and down. 'What brings you here after all these years?'

'I thought I'd look up old friends,' he said, 'but they've moved on.'

'Only me and Jack Hobday left now, since old Vermin's working in Whellow most of the time,' she replied, nodding. 'Not that he was any loss.' Rosie gave Deepbriar a wicked gap-toothed grin when the young constable sent a scandalized look in her direction; she was evidently enjoying the privileges that forty years as the station's cleaner and tea lady granted her. 'Come through to me little cubby-hole, Thorny, and we'll have a cuppa. It'll be just like old times.'

An hour later Deepbriar left, his stomach full of tea and fruit cake, and his head filled with news of the men he'd known at Bradsea station during the war. True, he had been the youngest by several years, yet still it depressed him to find they had nearly all left the force. It would have been good to see one familiar face, even Vorrman's, though Rosie had been scathing about the man; he'd been right, he still wasn't popular. 'Heaven knows how he bought that house,' she said. 'There was rumours he'd been left a tidy sum by an uncle, but you know how things get exaggerated.'

'I never thought he'd make chief inspector,' Deepbriar commented, 'and in the CID at that.'

'Good at creeping, he is,' Rosie replied with a disparaging sniff. 'And he's not slow to take the credit for other folks' efforts, neither. Superintendent Ruggles never saw through him, not right up till he retired.'

'When was that?'

'Must be two years back. Time don't half fly.'

'So, I gather they're neighbours now, Vorrman and the super.'

'No, Mr Ruggles moved. Funny that, he's in Whellow now, which is where old Vermin works, lucky for us. Maybe the superintendent finally got tired of the high life, eh? He lost his wife, of course, maybe it wasn't the same once she'd gone. He don't get written about in the paper every week, neither, not like he did then.' She gave a shrug. 'Everything changes if you wait long enough.'

'That reminds me, Rosie,' Deepbriar said. 'What happened to Bob Houghton? I've got an idea I saw him. Is he back in Bradsea? I never heard a thing about him after he went

41

off like that in '41.'

'He's back,' she said shortly, but she volunteered nothing more. Recalling his own mixed feelings about his old friend, Deepbriar didn't pursue the matter. Sergeant Bob Houghton had been on leave when the bomb struck, returning to find himself dealing with a crisis. Unlike Sergeant Vorrman he'd been popular with the other men, and he'd been kind to the youngest of the officers who'd been sent to help tide the regulars over the worst of the confusion. It had come as a shock when he'd suddenly resigned in favour of the local regiment, vanishing overnight, but if there was a mystery involved then it seemed that Deepbriar was going to have to fathom it out for himself.

'If you come in next week you can have a nice chat with Jack Hobday,' Rosie suggested. 'I remember how you and him used to natter on about fishing.'

'We did more than natter. I brought you a nice pollack more than once,' Deepbriar reminded her, a smile coming to his lips at the thought. 'Talking of fishing, have you heard anything about disappearing garden gnomes?'

The drone of the aircraft's engines was loud in his ears, rising and falling yet getting no closer. Deepbriar stood in the police station corridor, the brown lacquered walls seeming to close in around him. He had a sudden overpowering impulse to run, but when he tried, his feet refused to obey. Looking down, he saw that his legs were encased in concrete from the knees down, a great slab of it, stretching into the darkness.

Panic descended as the sound of the diving plane filled his head, the roar so loud that it was painful, his whole skull throbbing with it. Deepbriar looked up. Seeing rotten wooden beams overhead instead of the old stained plaster, he reached to grasp hold of them. Inch by inch he raised himself up; for a few ecstatic moments he thought he would escape, although his shoulder muscles were tearing under the strain. Then the timbers above him splintered, cracks running out like spiders' webs as the ceiling inexplicably reappeared.

As the roof disintegrated and fell in, burying him deep, Deepbriar's scream was swallowed up in the deluge that filled his mouth with dust. Then there was only pain, and darkness.

His heart pounding, the constable lay staring into the light of dawn which was creeping round the edge of the curtains. He was drenched in sweat, and his injured leg was aching. Beside him Mary lay on her back, a faint rhythmic snore coming from her open mouth; she had been the unwitting cause of his nightmare, her soft breath the beat of the distant aero-engine.

With the terror still fresh upon him Deep-briar eased his body from the bed, sitting still and taking long slow breaths until he felt calmer, then pulling on his clothes, offering his wife a silent word of gratitude; as soon as he was allowed out of bed Mary had adapted an old pair of trousers, so he could dress himself without help.

Clean air laced with salt embraced the constable as he hobbled out of the door, and by the time he had crossed the promenade to stand looking out over the sea the nightmare was all but forgotten. He leant his back against a convenient street lamp. After a while he fumbled in the pocket of his jacket and pulled out a notebook, not unlike his police-issue pad. Miss Caldwell had brought it round the evening before, having written in details of everyone who had complained of a lost or damaged gnome.

It was the first time he'd made any attempt to study what had been happening, and despite himself he found the notes quite interesting. Some people had been targeted more than once. The names of the roads where gnomes had been stolen or broken were all familiar to him, from his old days on the beat, and he mapped out a route in his head before he set off to visit the first of them, thinking with longing of his bicycle, languishing behind the police house in

Minecliff. On cold wet days when he pedal-
led his way around the villages he hadn't had
much affection for the machine, but suddenly he was filled with nostalgia.

By the time he reached the furthest point
from the promenade, Deepbriar had seen a
great deal of Bradsea's streets and he was
tired. His leg ached and his head was throbbing; it was a good job he was no longer
under the eagle eye of Sister Davies.

He had looked over walls and hedges at
half a dozen gardens, and seen little in the
way of evidence. Here and there a few
scraps of broken plaster told him he was in
the right place, but he could see no real
pattern to the attacks; some gardens hadn't
been targeted at all. One corner plot had a
positive infestation of gnomes, six of them,
but they were intact. As he approached for a
closer look, Deepbriar saw a kennel beside
the house. A bulldog lay half in and half out,
his head on his paws, keeping a watchful eye
on this possible intruder, a little growl
starting up in his throat. There was a sign on
the gate that read BEWARE OF THE
DOG. Withdrawing a little, Deepbriar made
a brief note in his hook. It just proved what
a good defence a dog was against burglary,
even if the thief's target was nothing but a
garden gnome.

The first bus of the day came along.
Deepbriar watched it, tempted to leave the

rest of the houses for another time. Then he remembered the nightmare. Maybe he'd sleep better if he exhausted himself; once Mary was up and about it would be harder to escape, so he might as well make a proper job of it while he had the chance. The strength of his resolve carried him back down the hill to the seafront; a strong breeze was blowing up and he began to feel better, despite his various aches and pains.

It was still over an hour before he could expect any breakfast back at cousin Vera's. He made his way across the promenade to the shelter overlooking the sea and eased himself down on to the bench inside, his mind occupied with nothing more taxing than the prospect of a plateful of bacon and eggs, followed by plenty of toast and marmalade.

A black dog came trotting along from the direction of the pier. It veered off to leave its mark on a lamppost, then came directly towards the shelter. Deepbriar reached for his crutches which were leaning against the seat, but as he put his hand out they slid to the ground. They weren't going to be easy to recover, and the animal was heading purposefully for his cast.

The dog hesitated.

'Don't you dare,' Deepbriar growled, fixing the dog with a glare. The animal gave him a sidelong glance then with a half-hearted whisk of its tail it moved on. Grunting with the effort, the constable retrieved the crutches and made sure they were within easy reach.

Deepbriar was in a comfortable drowse when something tapped against the wall at his back. He was awake enough to recognize the sound; it was the sweeper's broom knocking on the bricks as he worked. With careful haste, Deepbriar pushed upright and hitched the crutches under his arms. He stood for a while, listening, then hobbled out of the shelter and around to the back. The man was bending down to pick up a newspaper that still held the remains of somebody's fish supper.

'Hello, Bob,' Deepbriar said, hiding the shock he felt as the man straightened and he could see his features at close quarters. As he'd suspected the previous day, the years hadn't been kind to his old friend. 'It's been a long time.'

The man's lined face remained hard and unwelcoming. 'Not long enough,' he replied. 'I've got nothing to say to you, Deepbriar. Leave me alone.' Flinging his broom haphazardly on to the top of his barrow, the man turned and hurried away.

'Bob!' Deepbriar hirpled along the prom-enade after the sweeper. Houghton increased his pace. Swinging his crutches precariously far on each stride, Deepbriar followed, ignoring the ache in arms and shoulders, keeping his balance only by strength of will.

Ahead of Deepbriar the tall lean figure was trying to run while steering the ungainly handcart. Occasionally he had to grab the handle of the broom as it threatened to bounce off the top when the wheels hit a crack in the pavement. The constable brought up the rear, ungainly on his crutches, the plaster cast awkward to manage and likely to bring him crashing to the ground at any moment. If he'd had any sense he would have stopped then and there; his breathing was laboured and his limbs were trembling with effort, and despite his irritation at his old friend's irrational behaviour, a laugh was bubbling up in his throat. He couldn't help thinking how ridiculous they must look. Seeing that his quarry had left the pavement to cross the road, he followed, hoping to cut a corner. That was his undoing.

Chapter Four

The right-hand crutch caught in a drain cover. It stopped. Deepbriar didn't. His momentum took him into a spectacular somersault, his hat taking off as if it meant to fly out to sea, while the heavy cast encasing his leg went wheeling up behind him. Instinct saved his skull, an old skill coming to him when he needed it; he'd never thought his training for a place in the junior school gymnastics team would come in handy. He tucked his chin down so he flipped right over on to his back. It wasn't a neat landing; the impact when his body smacked into the ground was enough to drive the air from his lungs. A dazzling display of fireworks flashed across his vision, followed by a brief moment of darkness before he found himself staring up at the clear blue morning sky.

'I'd forgotten what a clumsy oaf you were,' Bob Houghton growled, bending over him. 'You all right?'

'Give us a hand,' Deepbriar gasped, swivelling to see if there was anybody in sight. 'If my missus hears what happened there'll be hell to pay.'

Houghton helped him to his feet and over

to a nearby bench. Deepbriar ran anxious fingers over the cast; much as he longed to be rid of it, he didn't want to offend Dr Tordon. Meanwhile Houghton went down on the beach to fetch his hat, which had almost reached the water's edge. Then he recovered the crutches from the gutter. 'I'll say this for you, Thorny, when you make a hash of things you do a proper job of it.'

'I wouldn't have needed to if you hadn't run off,' Deepbriar said. 'What's the matter with you? I never saw a poacher caught in the act take off so fast.' He gestured at the plaster cast with a rueful grin. 'And I'm not even in uniform.'

'Once a copper always a copper,' the other man returned, a slight quirk of his lips suggesting that he hadn't entirely lost his sense of humour. 'OK, I'll come clean, guvnor. I got no brakes on me barrow.'

'Very funny. Look, Bob, all I wanted was a chat.'

'What, about old times?' Houghton said, his face regaining its sour expression. 'It was all too long ago, there's no point going over what might have been. Maybe you don't even remember the bad turn you did me. Perhaps it didn't seem very important at the time.'

'Bad turn?' Deepbriar was mystified.

'I said let's forget it.' The other man began to turn away.

Deepbriar got to his feet and went after him. 'Be blowed if I will. This needs sorting out. Is there anywhere we can get a cup of tea at this unearthly hour? I need one after that flipping hundred yard dash, my throat's parched.'

Houghton hesitated for a long time, then he shrugged. 'Same old Thorny, if you're not chasing the local villains you're thinking about your stomach. Come on, then, there's only one place open for a brew-up this early in the day, I hope you still like it strong.'

Coming to a little shed behind the bus depot, they stepped into an atmosphere redolent of hot fat and tobacco smoke. Houghton went to the counter while Deepbriar eased into a rickety seat, the cast stuck out across the room. 'Watch out for that chair, it's got a dicky leg,' Houghton cautioned, putting two steaming brown mugs on the table.

'I know how it feels,' Deepbriar replied.

Houghton grimaced. 'So, what did you do to yourself this time, trip over a cat?'

'No, not even a cat burglar,' Deepbriar said. 'I just got in the way when a roof fell in.'

'Might have guessed it was something like that.' Houghton nodded. 'Too bloody big and slow, that was always your trouble. Did you say you were still in uniform? I always thought you'd be in the CID by the time

51

you reached twenty-five.'

Deepbriar grimaced. 'I've tried a few times. I thought I was going to be a village bobby for the rest of my days, but I finally made it this year. The transfer didn't come through until after this happened,' he said, tapping the plaster. 'I'm hoping to be back at work in a month. What about you? Nobody seemed to know why you decided to resign.' Recalling the hurt he'd felt at the time, Deepbriar tried to keep the resentment out of his voice. 'It came as a bit of a shock. You didn't even give me a chance to wish you good luck.'

Houghton was silent for a while, staring at the thick brown liquid in his mug. 'You don't know?' he said at last. 'So, I got it wrong. You didn't give them what they wanted.'

'Give who? You've lost me. Was there something going on that I was supposed to know about?'

Suddenly Houghton smiled, and for the first time he looked like the man Deepbriar had known during the war. 'Blimey, Thorny, I know you were a mite green back then, but I didn't realize you were such an innocent.'

'I'm not too innocent to punch you on the nose if you don't get a move on and tell me what the blazes you're talking about,' Deepbriar retorted.

'You really thought I went into the army because I wanted to?'

Deepbriar studied Houghton's face; he knew the man was in his late forties, but he looked ten years older. 'Well, I said I was surprised. I mean, everybody had you tipped to be made up to inspector in a couple of years.'

'Me included.' Houghton sighed. 'Some bastard put paid to that. I'm sorry Thorny, I should have known you wouldn't have gone along with it. It sounds as if you got tarred with the same brush. I can't think of any other reason why you'd still be a constable after all this time; you were by far the brightest of that bunch they sent us.' He seemed to be deep in thought, taking a long swallow from the mug. 'Have you been happy stuck out in the sticks?'

'It's been pretty good,' Deepbriar confirmed, after giving the question brief consideration. 'I always hankered after doing something more, but I've got no complaints.'

Houghton nodded. 'Then you've been lucky, it didn't ruin your life like it did mine.

Deepbriar stared at him. 'What the heck are you talking about?'

'The Greensall affair. You can't have forgotten.'

He wasn't likely to forget. It had been his first sight of a body that had spent two weeks decomposing in water. 'Sidney Greensall. All-round villain and nasty piece of work. Reckoned to be responsible for more than half the black market trade hereabouts during the war. Until he vanished.'

'Only to be found dead in very suspicious circumstances,' Houghton said, nodding. 'Everyone knew he'd been giving back-handers to somebody in the local force, probably for years. When he turned up in the river it was thought he'd sailed too close to the wind. Somebody chose to get rid of him, and there were those who reckoned it had to be this copper, whoever he was. It was a nasty business.'

Houghton looked up, his expression bleak. 'Superintendent Ruggles called me into his office, two days after Greensall's body was found. He showed me a note in Greensall's writing. It was addressed to me. He said it had been found on the floor under my locker.'

'That's crazy.' Deepbriar stared at the older man in disbelief. 'You were the one responsible for finding the evidence that was going to put Greensall away.'

'You know that, because you were with me the night I finally persuaded young Hatherly to talk, but Superintendent Ruggles thought the record of that interview was phoney. Evidently, Hatherly denied our meeting ever took place.'

'But I was there, writing down every word Hatherly said! You worked by the book.'

Houghton nodded. 'Yes. But Hatherly

never signed an official statement. The way the superintendent saw it, I manufactured evidence against Greensall, presumably because I was under pressure to show some results for all the work we'd put in, but since I was on Greensall's payroll, I wanted any proceedings against him to fail.'

'So I was implicated too?' Deepbriar asked incredulously.

'I thought they'd spoken to you. Super-intendent Ruggles never put it in so many words, but he made it sound as if you'd ad-mitted you only went along with me out of loyalty.'

'That's nonsense.' Deepbriar protested. 'Nobody ever talked to me about the Green-sall case, or about Micky Hatherly's evi-dence, not after Greensall's body was found. Are you saying they decided you were bent without giving you the chance to prove them wrong?'

'Bradsea was in a mess, the whole lot of us working long hours. I suppose nobody else on the local force really got to know you. They must have reckoned you were in it with me.' Houghton sighed. 'I could have insisted on having my day in court, but I didn't have any solid proof. With Greensall dead, how could I prove I hadn't been taking backhanders? There was the note. It was faked, it must have been, but who was going to believe me?'

'You say it was found under your locker, but did it directly implicate you?'

'It had "Bob" written in pencil on the outside, though the note itself wasn't addressed to anyone. It gave the date and time of a shipment being delivered by lorry at a pull-in on the coast road just outside town, and asked that the police patrol should be delayed for an hour that night. The place was on my beat.'

Deepbriar stared at the man who had been his mentor and hero during his brief spell as a beat officer in Bradsea. 'You'd never have got involved in a thing like that. You wanted to break that black market outfit. It was all you ever talked about.'

Houghton shrugged. 'I *was* delayed the night that was mentioned in the note. A woman ran out of an alleyway behind Bridge lane, claiming she'd been attacked. Hysterical, she was. She said a bloke had tried to grab her, and she'd fought him off. Reckoned when she fell to the ground she got her hand on a brick, and used it to hit him on the head. He went down and didn't get up again, and she said she thought maybe she'd killed him. Before I could stop her she went dashing off, but she hadn't told me where this attack was supposed to have taken place. She climbed over a fence into a garden, and made a run for it. I went after her, which seemed like the thing to do at the time.

56

'I never even thought it might be a pack of lies. She led me a hell of a dance, then suddenly she vanished, in that maze of alleyways to the south of the town. You know what it was like in the blackout. There wasn't even a moon that night.'

'You were set up,' Deepbriar conjectured.

I couldn't prove it. By the time I'd wasted half an hour trying to find this woman again, and her mysterious attacker, I was late reporting in. I was told to resume my beat. A couple of lads were sent to look for this injured man, but of course they never found him. Superintendent Ruggles decided I'd made up the whole thing. Of course, bloody Vorrman didn't help, maybe if he'd squeezed Micky Hatherly a bit harder he'd have got something out of him.' Houghton pulled a face. 'We'd never seen eye to eye. I think Vorrman was glad of the chance to get rid of me.'

'The note could have been written to somebody else,' Deepbriar said thoughtfully. 'Greensall wasn't stupid. He wouldn't have identified his accomplice by putting a name on it. That must have been added later.'

'That's the way I saw it. Three little letters.' Houghton drank the last of his tea. 'As for who it was, God knows. I'm no nearer finding an answer now than I was all those years ago. Vorrman was certainly keen to get me out of the way, but that could have been because he wanted a clear run when it came to promotion; everybody knew there'd be a lot of changes after the bombing, and I'd been a sergeant longer than he had.'

'Vorrman wasn't an easy man to like,' Deepbriar mused.

'No, but if he was bent then he hid it well. Still, I couldn't help wondering, when I came back and found he'd bought a house in Wellington Rise. A bit of black market money would have been quite a help to a man with big ideas.'

'I heard he bought the place with a legacy.'

'So they say.' Houghton looked defeated. 'I don't know who set me up. There was a time I even suspected Ruggles, but it was a bit unlikely, a super going bad! He'd married money. You must remember that bloody mansion he and his wife lived in; we patrolled past it often enough, even when every other beat was being squeezed through shortage of manpower. A man like that's got too much to lose.'

'What did you mean about Vorrman? Why did he talk to Micky Hatherly?' Deepbriar queried.

'That was on Ruggles's orders, or so he told me. He swore that no matter how hard he pushed, Hatherly denied he'd ever said anything against Greensall.' Houghton stopped to take a mouthful of tea and the silence stretched to several minutes before he sighed and went on.

'I didn't have a leg to stand on. As you know, I set up a trap on Micky Hatherly's say-so, and unlike the one the day I was an hour late on my beat, that delivery never happened, which made it look as if I'd either invented the whole thing, or made a massive cock-up. Then Greensall turned up dead in the river, and there was talk that I might have been the one who put him there. I was finished.'

'I don't know why you didn't tell me about all this,' Deepbriar said. 'Maybe together we'd have persuaded him.'

Houghton shook his head. 'Whatever happened I was finished. I told you, I thought Vorrman or Ruggles had persuaded you to go along with their version of events. I'm sorry, I should have had more faith in you. As it turned out, you were made a scapegoat too. Vorrman wouldn't have had the necessary seniority to do it, so it must have been Ruggles, but whose idea it was I couldn't say.'

Deepbriar looked at him in puzzlement. 'What are you talking about?'

'Come on, Thorny, didn't you ever wonder why you got shunted off to be a village bobby? You were too bright for that. All it needed was a note on the bottom of your record, a niggling doubt about whether you'd lied to back me up, or maybe even taken money from Greensall. Nothing concrete, not enough to get you pushed out of the force, but just a hint that would keep you from getting promotion.'

'You honestly think Superintendent Ruggles did that?'

'He didn't want a court case and a lot of fuss, with the newspapers writing stuff about bent coppers, so he took the easy way out. I got the blame, and you got a black mark to prevent you from rising too high. Vorrman came to me with a message from the superintendent, telling me to volunteer for the war effort, and fast. I'm sorry about not saying goodbye, lad. I should've known you wouldn't have been so flipping weak-kneed.'

'So, you went off to join the local regiment.'

'It was a bad choice. I was just in time to get shipped out to North Africa, and like a good many of our lads I spent the next three years in and out of hospital.' Houghton stood up, picking up the empty mugs. 'Want another?'

Deepbriar nodded, feeling in his pocket for coins. Sitting at the table alone, he stared unseeingly at the condensation running down the window, lost in thought. He'd never considered that there might be some reason for his failure to win promotion or a transfer to CID. Even now, he wasn't sure he quite believed Houghton, not on that score.

'What did you do once the war was over?' he asked, when his old friend returned with a fresh brew.

'Knowing I'd never get taken on again here after what happened, I applied to join the police down on the south coast, then when that didn't work I went up to Scotland. I soon discovered there wasn't a force in the country that would take me.'

Houghton didn't seem to notice Deepbriar's shock. 'I never found anything much worth doing since then, but last year I finally drifted back here and went to the council. They'd got vacancies in the parks department, and the highways, but all they'd offer me was a broom and a barrow. Reckon they thought I'd refuse and clear out.' His mouth twisted in a wry smile. 'It wouldn't take much to make them give me the sack, so I have to watch myself. I don't want to move on again, Thorny. There comes a time when a man has to return to his roots.'

Deepbriar stared at him, not knowing what to say. With a sense of outrage he thought back over his own career, wondering if it was true, if Superintendent Ruggles had blocked his attempts to gain promotion within the uniformed branch, not to mention the move to the CID he'd wanted so much. It was ironic that he'd finally made it, long after he'd convinced himself that he simply wasn't good enough.

'You ought to rest,' Mary said, a worried frown creasing her brows. 'I don't know what sort of time it was when you went out, but you can't have had much sleep.'

'I felt like getting some fresh air,' Deepbriar replied. 'I didn't miss breakfast.'

'If you had I'd really be worrying about you. But what were you doing?' Her sharp gaze roamed over the tear in his jacket and the scuff marks from his fall.

'I fell over when the crutch slipped, but I'm fine. It was a nice morning, so I decided to take a look at the houses on Miss Caldwell's list.'

'Are you going on with that? Maybe you shouldn't. The doctor noticed how tired you're looking. Why didn't you tell him you're not getting much sleep?'

'There's no point; he can't do anything about it,' Deepbriar said. 'You know how much I hate taking pills. I'll be fine once the plaster's off and I can get some proper exercise. Look, if you don't think I should do any more this morning I'll buy a paper and take it over to the shelter. I can look at the sea and watch the people go by. That's better than lying in bed being bored.'

'If you feel like reading why don't you go

to the library?' Mary suggested.

'What, and join all the other old crocks in the reading room?'

'No, you can bring some books home. Miss Caldwell said you could get temporary tickets. One fiction and one non-fiction. We're so close to the library, you could change your books every day if you wanted.'

Deepbriar sighed. 'All right, anything to keep you happy. We could both go. You're supposed to put your feet up for a while in the afternoon. You could find something to read too.'

'Vera's saved some magazines for me,' Mary said. 'And if you hadn't been off gallivanting round town yesterday you'd have known that she settled me down in her best armchair with a rug over my knees for two hours. Stop trying to change the subject. You're the one who has to take more care of yourself.'

'First you want me to go chasing after lost gnomes, and now you don't,' Deepbriar grumbled. 'Make up your mind.'

Her expression softened and she sat down beside him. 'I'm a bit worried about you, that's all. I didn't mean to nag. Did you discover anything?'

'A bit. It's odd the way most of the gnomes were stolen, but two were smashed. And not everybody who owns a gnome has been a victim. I found one house with lots of gnomes that haven't been touched, but they also have a dog.'

'That could explain it,' Mary replied, smiling a little. 'Anything else?'

'I've hardly got started yet. Anyway, it's motive that's really got me baffled. I doubt if it's teddy boys, and younger lads are more likely to go scrumping.' He was silent a while, staring into space, thinking hard. 'Do you think it might be the people who make the things, breaking people's favourite gnomes so they go and buy some more?' he suggested facetiously.

Mary looked sceptical. 'You'll tell me next the gnomes are at war, the blue hats against the red hats.'

'It's about as likely,' Deepbriar admitted. 'Anyway, I shan't do any more investigating today, so you can stop scolding me.' He would go to the library as she suggested, and while he was there he'd see if Miss Caldwell had any more information for him.

Chapter Five

It was lucky the weather was fine; even at five in the morning it wasn't too cold to sit in the shelter on the seafront. The dream had woken Deepbriar long before dawn, and he hadn't wanted to sleep again, lying wakeful in the dark until the first light appeared. He was so tired his eyes felt full of grit, and his whole body was aching from lack of sleep.

Deepbriar tried to focus on the notes he'd written the previous day, after a second talk with Miss Caldwell. She had assured him that the victims whose gnomes had been stolen or damaged were not only willing but positively eager to see him, and she had added two more names to his list. Deepbriar had one reservation about making these calls; he feared the woman had exaggerated the story of his sufferings in the line of duty, and that her friends were expecting to meet some kind of hero.

The constable gave an audible groan at the thought as he stared out across the sea. He heartily wished he could spend the whole day right where he was, though if somebody had offered him three wishes at that moment, getting rid of the plaster cast would have been at the top of his list. Slowly the minutes passed and Deepbriar's mind drifted, going back over the winter he'd spent in Bradsea. Bob Houghton had been good to him. Along with another officer who had lived in the station house, Houghton's quarters had been wrecked by the bomb, and on his return from leave they had all been billeted in the same miserable digs.

Within days Deepbriar had discovered the sergeant's hatred of those who made an illegal profit from the war. 'In my book they're no better than the Jerries,' he'd said vehemently, 'worse even. If I had my way men like Greensall would go to the gallows.' With the CID in even greater turmoil than the uniformed branch, Houghton had been given charge of the investigation into the black market although he wasn't a detective. He'd enlisted Deepbriar's help when he went to interview Micky Hatherly, convinced that the youth was the weak link in Greensall's organization.

Their enquiries had been going well, until Greensall vanished. The discovery of his corpse in the river two weeks later had pretty much put an end to the case, though a few members of the gang had been charged with minor offences.

There had been no proof that the man had been murdered, cause of death being impossible to discover, but the circumstances suggested it hadn't been a natural death. Deepbriar recalled his own small part in the investigation. He had conducted a house-to-house check in the street where Greensall lived, and he'd turned up nothing of any value. He'd learnt that Greensall hadn't been a popular man, but that didn't mean some of his neighbours hadn't had dealings with him; with even basic essentials increasingly hard to come by as the war effort intensified, many people succumbed to temptation and obtained goods on the black market.

Sergeant Bob Houghton had told Deepbriar why he was so determined to bring Greensall to book, as they walked home to their dismal lodging house late one night. 'It's not just the unfairness of it,' he said. 'There was a case a few months ago where a farm was raided. Thinking they'd cover their tracks the gang set fire to the barn. The farmer had gone to the pub that evening, but he didn't stay long enough, poor devil.' Houghton's face was grim. 'I was there when they found his body in the ashes the next day; if the bastards hadn't hit him hard enough to crack his skull before they threw him into the flames, we wouldn't have known it was murder. I was pretty sure Greensall was involved, but we never got anything concrete on him, though two of the men were caught. Even with the threat of a death sentence hanging over them, they were too scared to turn King's evidence against him.'

Recalling the sergeant's expression as he told that tale, Deepbriar was certain Houghton hadn't been in Greensall's pay. He had been triumphant when Micky Hatherly agreed to spill the beans, giving them information that should have led to the black-marketeer's downfall. 'We'll take care of you,' Houghton had promised the young man, as Deepbriar jotted down details in his notebook. 'Greensall won't get a chance to do you any harm. We'll lock him up and throw away the key.'

But nothing went as planned. The delivery they hoped to intercept had never taken place. Only days later Greensall vanished, and they could only assume that whoever got rid of Greensall had also frightened Hatherly into retracting his statement. Had that really been a member of the police force, covering his tracks before the gang was split wide open? The thought brought a sour taste to the mouth. At the time, one or two people had wondered aloud if Houghton had killed Greensall, but knowing the man, Deepbriar was sure that wasn't so.

Soon after Bob Houghton volunteered for the army, Deepbriar's temporary assignment had come to an end, and he'd returned to Falbrough. As for Hatherly, he'd never heard what happened to him. With Greensall dead, perhaps the young man had given up his criminal career and gone straight. He'd probably been called up within the next few months anyway; perhaps a spell in the army had straightened him out, if he'd survived the war.

'I thought you might be out here.' Mary appeared as if from nowhere, to stand between Deepbriar and the wide expanse of sea. 'It's breakfast time.'

'Is it?' Deepbriar hadn't realized he was hungry. He reached for the crutches and rose stiffly. 'I was waiting for Bob Houghton. You know, the chap I told you about last night. I thought he came along here with his barrow every morning.'

'You can't have missed him,' Mary said, glancing at the rubbish lying behind the shelter. She came to take Deepbriar's arm, looking worried. 'Thorny, I know you're hardly getting any sleep. You have to tell the doctor.'

'Stop fussing,' he replied shortly, slipping away from her hold. 'You'd do better worrying about yourself, coming out here in your condition before you've had anything to eat.'

The Bradsea council depot was nearly a mile from the seafront, and Deepbriar was weary by the time he stood outside the high wooden gates. He was in a black mood, for

Mary had taken umbrage and refused to talk to him over the breakfast table; he had escaped from the house as soon as he could.

'You want something, mate?' A man wearing a shiny suit appeared from the office to challenge the constable as he entered the yard.

'Are you in charge here?' Deepbriar asked.

'I'm the foreman. Superintendent's out.'

'You'll do. I was looking for Bob Houghton.'

'He didn't turn up for work this morning.' The man's face went from uninterested to distinctly unfriendly.

'You couldn't tell me where he lives?' Deepbriar asked.

'No, I couldn't.' He began to turn away.

'Look, I'm an old mate of his,' Deepbriar persisted, following a few steps behind as the foreman headed back to his office. 'I bumped into him on the promenade yesterday, I just want to be sure he's all right. He might be sick or something.'

'I can't say that bothers me.' The man turned to face Deepbriar as he reached the doorway. 'I don't know where Houghton lives, and if I did I wouldn't tell you. He's not the sort to make friends, and nobody here would want him as a pal, even if he was. The council never should've taken him on. Now clear off, you're trespassing.'

Deepbriar was tempted to blow caution to

70

the winds and bring out his warrant card, but he knew it would be unwise. He didn't belong in this part of the county, and there was nobody in the Bradsea and Whellow constabulary who could be relied on to back him up.

'Well?' the foreman demanded, planting his feet a little apart and glaring up into Deepbriar's face. He was a small man, and even with one leg in plaster Deepbriar was sure he could have flattened him. In fact, he would have quite enjoyed it. The thought came as a shock and Deepbriar turned away; first young Byforth at the convalescent home, and now this jumped-up official. Mary was right, the lack of sleep was beginning to tell.

His route back to cousin Vera's took him past the bungalows in High View, and there was somebody in the garden of number seven. As he hobbled by the woman looked up and smiled, as if in recognition. She was small, grey-haired and rather bent-backed, but the eyes scanning him showed little sign of age. With an internal sigh Deepbriar came to a halt. 'Mrs Guest, isn't it?'

'Yes, that's right. And you must be Constable Deepbriar. Miss Caldwell said you might call on me. Imagine, a real hero, she told me you'd been in the paper...' she broke off, her enthusiasm quelled a little by the look on his face.

'There are a couple of questions I was hoping you might answer for me,' Deepbriar said. 'Where did you buy your gnome? Was it from a shop in town?'

'I bought it from Henwick's, the iron-mongers in Whellow. If you want to know where Mr Henwick gets them, I can tell you that too. They're made in a village called Dummel's Bottom. Do you know where that is?'

Deepbriar nodded. 'Up in the hills. Were you planning to buy yourself a replacement?' he asked, looking around at the garden. It was very tidy, and somehow he couldn't picture a gnome amongst the regimented rows of sweet williams and asters.

'I don't think so,' she replied. 'I bought a windmill instead, a wooden one.' She smiled, seeing his evident confusion. 'Didn't Miss Caldwell tell you? The gnome was in my back garden, not the front. The side gate is locked at night. Would you like to come and see?'

With some reluctance, Deepbriar followed her. The gate was solid wood and six feet high. It wouldn't be easy to climb, and there were two heavy bolts on the inside. 'I doubt if anyone would have got in this way,' he commented.

'No. All I can think is, they must have come along the footpath and climbed over the fence next door. The gnome was just there.' Mrs Guest pointed at a corner beneath a flowering bush. A model of a windmill with white painted sails stood in the sheltered spot, where it had no hope of ever feeling a breath of wind. 'I think that's much better, so maybe losing the gnome was blessing in disguise.'

'Very nice,' Deepbriar said, trying to work out how the thief had made his entrance. An impenetrable hedge flanked two sides of the garden, so that only left the fence belonging to the next house as a means of entry. Number nine was the last in the row, flanked on each side by a fence made of wooden palings about four feet high. There were some gaps between the uprights, but only a small child could have squeezed through them. Beyond the farther fence an alley ran down towards North Parade.

'Reckon a man could get in here if he was set on it, but that's a lot of trouble to go to just to steal a gnome,' Deepbriar said.

The old lady nodded. 'To be honest, that's what I thought. I can't imagine why anybody would want the thing anyway. I bought it on an impulse, because I'd been looking for something to put in that corner. The gnome was sitting down, pulling on its boots. I found it amusing at first, but after a while I wasn't sure I liked it.' She gave a little laugh. 'Silly of me, of course, but it seemed to have a nasty expression on its face.'

Deepbriar couldn't help recalling Mary's flight of fantasy about the gnomes being at war. Before he could stop himself the question was out. 'This gnome of yours, what colour was its hat?'

Back on the seafront some time later Deepbriar knew he'd got a visitor long before he reached cousin Vera's door; the big grey Humber standing by the kerb was hard to miss.

'Here he is!' Mary sounded relieved. 'Charles and Elaine have been here for nearly an hour, Thorny; we didn't know where you'd got to.'

'I was looking up an old friend,' Deepbriar replied, once the greetings were out of the way. 'What brings you two back to Bradsea?'

'It was Elaine's idea. She thought you might be getting bored,' Major Brightman said. 'We borrowed the old man's car again so we can take you both for a little run in the country this afternoon. Mary's told us you're due to get shot of that cast tomorrow, so a trip out might help pass the time.'

Deepbriar opened his mouth to refuse, but then he saw the look on Mary's face, like a child hoping for a treat. She loved a car ride, especially in the Colonel's old Humber. 'That's nice, it's very good of you to think of it.' A sudden inspiration came to him. 'I've got an idea where I'd like to go, too, unless you've already made plans.'

'You can't really miss it,' Major Brightman said, turning off the car's engine and putting on the handbrake as he stared at the sight before them. They had stopped in a narrow lane. About a hundred gnomes, all painted in bright colours, stood along the top of a brick wall. Three dogs milled in the gateway to the cottage and barked until a young woman came out, smiling a welcome.

'Hello. Did you want to come in? We have lots of people stopping, so we do a sort of informal tour. You don't have to buy,' she added quickly, 'not unless you want to. It gives me a bit of a break, having visitors. Don't worry about the dogs, they're quite friendly, really.'

'The car's blocking the lane,' the major said, opening the door and helping Deepbriar out. 'Shouldn't I move it?'

'Oh, nobody's likely to come along, the milk lorry's been and gone. If they do, they'll hoot.'

The gnomes were made in a barn. Elaine and Mary exclaimed over the moulds, dozens of them, waiting to be filled with plaster. As the various stages of manufacture were explained, Deepbriar lagged behind; he'd long since abandoned his silly theory about the makers of the gnomes being involved in the thefts.

'My husband sees to all that part of the

process,' the woman explained, leading them into a small room alongside the barn. 'I do the painting.' There were rows of gnomes already made, looking strangely featureless without their coat of paint. Deepbriar could see why she might like an excuse to escape from the monotony of her work.

'There are factories that turn out gnomes much quicker, of course, but they aren't handmade. We pride ourselves on the number of different designs we do.' She moved on to the shelves of completed gnomes, picking one up to show them. 'We've just brought out a new design.' The gnome – complete with red hat, Deepbriar noted – was carrying a bucket and shovel. 'Some people like to collect different characters,' the woman said. 'We've got a few regulars who'll be coming to fetch one of these.'

'I heard you had one that was pulling its boots on,' Deepbriar said.

'Mmm. Here we are.' She reached across and lifted down another model. 'It's not been very popular. It's a funny thing, but no matter how I paint it, this one always seems to have an odd expression.'

It was true. The gnome stared back at him with a decidedly unpleasant leer on its face. He wasn't surprised Mrs Guest hadn't liked it much.

'Charles, I think we should buy a gnome,' Elaine said, her eyes twinkling.

'I hope you aren't thinking of the one with the squint,' the major replied, sending Deepbriar a look somewhere between despair and amusement.

'No, that one at the end. With the fishing rod.'

'That's one of our most popular designs,' the woman replied. 'Two and sixpence to you. Shall I wrap it up?'

'I'm not sure where you're planning to put that,' Major Brightman said, as they got back in the car.

'It's all right, it's not for us,' Elaine replied. 'It's for old Mrs Tucker, the lady who helps out with the flowers at the Manor. She's going to be eighty soon. Only last week I heard her telling somebody how much she liked garden gnomes. She'll love it.'

Mary laughed. 'I think you had him worried. I'd love to see the Colonel's face if one of those appeared beside his fishpond.'

'Apart from getting my little present, that was a very interesting place,' Elaine said, as the car pulled away down the lane. 'What made you want to go there, Thorny?'

Deepbriar put away the list the woman had given him, showing which shops sold the gnomes, and explained. Charles and Elaine were highly amused, and some of the suggestions they volunteered about the reason for the thefts made Mary's idea of a gnome war look almost sensible. The laughter lasted all the way back to Bradsea. It wasn't until Charles Brightman was opening the car door to help Deepbriar out that he became suddenly serious.

'I've just remembered something I read in the newspaper, Thorny. Wasn't there a case where china ornaments were being used for smuggling?'

'There was,' Deepbriar agreed. 'Though I think you'll find it was fiction, not fact. Anyway, I don't think it's likely here. It would be different if the gnomes were being shipped in from overseas, or if they were being exported, but as far as I can discover, none of them has travelled further than the other side of the county.'

Chapter Six

At Vera's insistence, Charles and Elaine stayed for a meal and the evening passed quickly. Deepbriar felt pleasantly tired and once the wearisome routine of getting to bed was over and done, he closed his eyes, and fell instantly asleep. Although he had a feeling of unease when he began to dream, he didn't find himself in an enclosed space; there was no roof waiting to fall on him, or even anything to keep him from running away. On the contrary, he looked down and saw with delight that he was wearing his uniform trousers and boots.

He was walking along a narrow country lane, the sun was shining and flocks of birds, many of them too brightly coloured to be believable, were singing from the hedgerows. When the first few gnomes appeared amongst the exotic wildlife, Deepbriar wasn't concerned. But then the hedges gave way to walls, and the walls were lined with small plaster figures, thousand upon thousand of them. Instead of fishing rods and spades, they were carrying guns and spears, and every painted face was twisted into an evil leer.

Deepbriar wanted to turn and run, but now when he looked down at his feet he saw that both his legs were once again encased in concrete. The gnomes grew, swelling until they were human sized. They filled the lane, an army of smirking monstrosities, advancing on him in a menacing silence. Panic seizing him, Deepbriar struck out wildly, but he was falling, their weight bearing him down, down into the dark.

'Thorny!' Somebody was gripping him by the wrist. 'Thorny, for heaven's sake, wake up!'

Mary must have switched on the light. As Deepbriar came to his senses the first thing he saw was her face. Tears were streaming from one eye, the flesh around it reddened where he'd hit her.

'My Lord, what have I done.' Deepbriar threw his arms around his wife and clung to her, so full of remorse it almost choked him.

'It's all right, it was an accident,' she said, hugging him tightly in return. 'You poor thing, that must have been quite a nightmare.'

'Never mind the nightmare, I hit you.' He pulled free and stared at her in horror. 'I could have hurt the baby!'

'Well you didn't,' she soothed. 'Come on, settle down again. I'll go and make a cup of Horlicks, shall I?'

'I don't want any Horlicks.' He rolled away

from her and struggled to get off the bed. 'I'll not risk anything like this happening again. From now on I'm sleeping on the floor. Don't waste your breath,' he added, seeing that she was going to argue. 'Just give me my pillow.'

'All right,' Mary said, coming to put a blanket down on top of the rug, 'but if you don't tell the doctor about these had dreams when you see him tomorrow, Thorny Deepbriar, then I shall!'

Deepbriar turned the page of the newspaper, trying to concentrate on the closely printed columns of Women's Institute reports and local events. He hadn't slept much; he'd been up before dawn and yet again he was sitting in the shelter on the promenade. As he left the house, the paperboy had been about to put the new edition of the Bradsea and Whellow Gazette through the letter box. Deepbriar had taken it from him; anything to help the time to pass. He didn't think he'd want any breakfast.

A description of a cricket match played the previous Sunday kept him occupied for several minutes, but finally there was nothing left unread but the little *STOP PRESS* box at the bottom of the page. Deepbriar drew in a sharp breath. *'DISAPPEARANCE OF LOCAL MAN'*, it said. *'Michael (Micky) Hatherly, hasn't been seen since he left his home to go to work, a week ago last Wednesday. His wife and family are concerned for his safety. Hatherly, age 33, is 5 ft 6 in tall, and was last seen wearing a brown check sports jacket and green cap.'*

Deepbriar was still lost in thought when his wife came to find him. 'We have to go to the hospital soon,' she scolded, 'and you've had nothing to eat.'

'I'll just have a bit of toast,' Deepbriar said. 'Don't fuss, there's a good lass.' He grimaced as he looked at the beginnings of a black eye she was sporting. 'Whatever that doctor wants to give me I'll take, but if he can't promise I won't go thrashing about in my sleep again, then I'm staying on the floor from now on.'

'I'm terribly sorry. Dr Tordon asked me to apologize.' The nurse offered them a smile that was almost as stiff as her starched uniform. 'There was an emergency. He had to go to the city, and he isn't likely to be back today.'

'But it's only a matter of taking off the cast,' Deepbriar protested. 'Surely there's somebody here who can do it.'

'Dr Tordon particularly wanted to see to it himself. He did say he could squeeze you in at around ten o'clock tomorrow morning, if you don't mind coming on a Saturday. If that's not convenient for you then it will have to be Monday afternoon.'

'Tomorrow will do nicely,' Deepbriar said

quickly. One more day was bad enough; if Dr Tordon didn't remove the thing in the morning he really would be looking for a saw in Vera's shed.

'Thank you, nurse,' Mary Deepbriar said, taking her husband's elbow, 'we'll be back in the morning.' Outside, she led him straight past cousin Vera's to head along the promenade.

'Where are we going?' Deepbriar asked, following her unwillingly.

'I thought we'd go to the tea shop and have an early elevenses,' she replied, 'to see if it will stop you looking so grumpy. At the moment your face is about as cheerful as a week of wet Mondays.'

An hour later, Deepbriar hobbled up the Hill towards the middle of town. The hated cast felt heavier with each stride. He was heading for the council yard once again; the foreman might not be willing to talk to him but he hoped he might find somebody there who knew where Bob Houghton lived.

Deepbriar didn't get as far as the depot. In the little park, halfway up Victoria Road, he saw an old man pushing a big square handcart identical to the one Houghton used. He watched for a moment then went to sit on a bench and waited for the sweeper to reach him.

'Morning. Pleasant spot to work, this.' Deepbriar said.

'Not bad,' the sweeper agreed, propping the broom under his arm with the ease of much practice, looking more comfortable leaning there than Deepbriar had ever felt with his crutches. He took the makings of a cigarette from his pocket. 'You on holiday?'

'Sort of,' Deepbriar replied, tapping the plaster cast with his fingers. 'I'm convalescing. It's a nice town, Bradsea.'

'I've lived here all my life,' the old man said. 'I used to be caretaker at the school, but this is easier. They wanted me to do the promenade, but it's a bit breezy on the seafront when you get to my time of life.'

'Funny you should mention that. I knew the chap who sweeps down there, I bumped into him the other morning. Bob Houghton. We were friends during the war. I was hoping to see him again, but he's not been about these last two days. You might be able to help me, if you're willing?'

The old man didn't answer, apparently intent on licking the cigarette paper and sealing it, fumbling a little. 'If I ain't careful I spill half me baccy,' he said. 'Can't afford that, the price you have to pay these days. Bloomin' rheumatics. Slows a man down summat cruel.'

But it doesn't make you deaf, Deepbriar thought sourly. He took a half crown from his pocket, holding it between forefinger and thumb. 'Do you know why Bob hasn't been at work? Or maybe where I can find him?'

Lighting his cigarette and shaking out the match before he flung it into his barrow, the old man drew in smoke a couple of times before he replied. 'Haven't seen him meself, not since Wednesday. He'll likely come to the depot for his money tomorrow, be a fool if he don't. We get paid at five, when we finish for the week. Short day Saturday, see. If you want him quicker nor that you might try askin' up Waterloo Road. Could be he was took sick. He's got a room in that big old house with the stairs going up the outside.' He gave a derisive snort. 'Clifftop View they call it. Only thing you can see from there is the gas works. You know it?'

'I know it,' Deepbriar replied. He handed over the money, and the man's fingers seemed quite nimble as he tucked the coin out of sight.

'You must pick up all sorts of rubbish in your job,' Deepbriar said. The sweeper seemed in no hurry to leave; he might as well get his money's worth.

'I do that,' the old man agreed.

'You didn't ever come across a garden gnome, did you? Broken, maybe?'

The old eyes narrowed in the wrinkled face. 'Not me, but one o' the blokes who does the bins, he found one, down near the pier. It was in two pieces. He took the bits

85

home to his missus and she stuck the head back on. Funny thing was, she put it out in their garden and the bloomin' thing went and vanished. One day it was there, next it was gone.' He chuckled. 'Swearin' fit to bust he was, reckoned the person who threw it out must've pinched it back once it was fixed.'

'Whereabouts does he live, this chap?' Deepbriar asked.

'No idea,' the old man said, stubbing out his cigarette and jerking his head towards the south. 'His name's Fred, if that's any help.'

Once the sweeper had moved on, Deepbriar got to his feet and set off for Waterloo Road. It was strange to walk the familiar route again, and even stranger that Bob should be living in the same run-down boarding house where they'd both been billeted all that time ago. Clifftop View still had the same faded paintwork, the same streaks down the walls where the gutter leaked, and a garden that had grown out of hand long before the war. There was a narrow path chopped through the rampant privet hedge to allow access to the peeling front door. Next door's garden was neat and trim, and he was interested to note that a gnome holding a fishing rod was stationed next to a tiny pond. Deepbriar's lips twitched, recalling Mary's fantasy. The wilderness surrounding Clifftop View would hide a whole gnome army. They could venture forth at night to wage guerrilla warfare, without ever being seen in daylight.

A slovenly young woman answered Deepbriar's knock, her head covered by a ragged head scarf, tied like a turban, and her overall spotted with stains. A cigarette end dangled from her lips. There was something familiar about her; she had slightly protruding eyes, and an expression of dumb resignation that stirred Deepbriar's memory. Then he realized this was Myrtle, the granddaughter of old Ma Jessup. She had been a little girl, tanglehaired, barefooted and neglected, when last he'd seen her.

'I'm looking for Bob Houghton,' Deepbriar said, setting one crutch just inside the door as if by accident.

'He don't live 'ere no more,' the woman said. 'Lef' six weeks ago. Dunno where 'e went, 'e di'n't say.'

'Maybe there's somebody else here who would know,' Deepbriar suggested, reaching into his pocket. He brought out a florin, reflecting gloomily that he would soon be out of money. Myrtle's eyes lit up, and he could see her struggling to think of something that might earn her this largesse. 'Ain't never 'ad no friends 'ere,' she said, staring at the coin. 'Used to see 'im 'angin' around at the station, watchin' the trains.'

Deepbriar didn't think the information was worth much, but he handed over the money. 'Your grandma still here?' he asked, turning back when he was halfway down the garden path.

'Nah, she died,' Myrtle looked hard at him then, recognition dawning on her face. 'You was one o' them coppers, like 'im. You was 'ere in the war.'

'That's right.'

A sudden smile transformed the thin face. 'You was the one wot give me apples. An' you used to save me a bit o' toast from your breakfast.'

He nodded, half smiling in return. 'I didn't think your grandma fed you very well. Come to that, she didn't feed any of us very well, but we got some of our rations down at the station.'

'She was a mean ol' cat,' Myrtle agreed, nodding. 'Sorry I can't 'elp. What if I sees 'im?'

'Tell him Thorny's looking for him. He knows where I'm staying.'

There was still a fish and chip shop down the road from Clifftop View. With a newspaper parcel tucked awkwardly under one arm, Deepbriar hobbled on to the railway station. Here too, time had wrought few changes. Only the garden looked different. During the war it had been extended beside the line to grow vegetables; now it had shrunk back to its former size and was filled with flowers.

Deepbriar recalled his first sight of the place, with its sodden rows of Brussels sprouts and cabbages. He had stepped off the train late in 1940, along with five other officers gathered from various parts of the county, all of them strangers to him. They had been met by Constable Jack Hobday, who escorted them to the police station, where they started their first turn of duty immediately, helping to rescue records and equipment from the dusty shambles that had been left behind by the bomb, while the local officers tried to maintain the normal order of the day, patrolling the beats of those who had died as well as their own.

Ten hours later, long after darkness had descended, the new men had been told they could go to their digs for the night. Sergeant Vorrman gave them the address, reminding them with relish that they were to report again at seven. One of the newcomers, older than the rest, had the temerity to suggest they could do with a guide, since they were all strangers in town.

The blackout was in force and it was a moonless night, but Vorrman had replied that if they weren't capable of finding their way from one end of Bradsea to the other they were bloody useless as coppers and might as well leave on the next train.

As they made their way to the door Bob Houghton had come in, his face drawn and his eyes dark-rimmed with exhaustion. The same bombing raid that had caused such havoc in Bradsea had cut the railway line further south, and it had taken him two days to return from a visit to his family, but despite having had no sleep he'd come back intent on returning to duty that night. Hearing of the newcomers' plight, though, and not bothering to hide his opinion of Sergeant Vorrman, he'd taken time to show Deepbriar and the other constables to Clifftop View before he started work.

A goods train rattled through the station as Deepbriar approached, its long tail of coal trucks clanking as it slowed to wait for the signal. He breathed in the smoke and steam belching from the engine, enjoying the smell; that had been one of the things he and Houghton had often talked about on their walks through the unlit streets all those years ago. They'd shared a fondness for steam engines, swapping memories of childhood days spent hanging around the level crossing gates, putting farthings on the line in the hope of seeing them flattened, and consequently being chased by irate crossing keepers.

Deepbriar bought a platform ticket and settled on a bench to eat, offering the porter a few chips. The man accepted, keeping a wary eye on the stationmaster's office, willingly answering Deepbriar's questions, but he didn't recognize Bob Houghton from Deepbriar's description.

Trains came and went. Deepbriar found his eyelids drooping and fought to keep them open. He accepted a cup of tea from the porter, who evidently thought he was a suitable case for charity. When the shadows grew long Deepbriar left, his muscles stiff and aching, and headed back towards the seafront and cousin Vera's shepherd's pie.

It was a quiet meal. Mary was annoyed with him because he hadn't returned for lunch, and to make things worse he'd arrived as the dinner gong sounded, barely having time to wash the sooty smudges from his face and hands in the scullery before he sat down. Seeing the dark swelling around her eye he felt his guilt anew, and after an hour of frosty silence in the lounge, he followed her meekly back to their room to find that she and Vera had rearranged things in his absence. The double bed had been pushed against the wall to make room for a mattress on the floor, all made up ready for him.

'Thanks, love,' he said, leaning towards his wife with the intention of kissing her cheek, but she turned away. Deepbriar sighed. The mood would pass, but he felt rather lonely as he settled into his makeshift bed.

Deepbriar came groggily to the surface and stared up at the rusty springs above his head; somehow he'd slid half off his mattress and landed under the bed. Mary's even breathing told him she was still asleep. He'd had a bad dream, but he couldn't remember what it was about, and that was a big improvement. It was very early, but he decided not to try to sleep again, in case the nightmare returned. Only a few hours now and he would be seeing Dr Tordon; perhaps once he was rid of the cast the dreams would stop.

The sea was so bright it made Deepbriar squint. As he crossed the promenade there was nobody in sight, but something was moving over by the railings that topped the sea wall. It took him a moment to realize it was a black dog, probably the one that had nearly christened his plaster cast a few days before. The animal paused for a while as if looking through the railings at the sea, then it went purposefully on, trotting down the nearest set of steps and out of sight.

Although there was a stiff breeze it wasn't cold. Deepbriar went first to the shelter, but he felt restless, willing the time to pass so he could be rid of the plaster cast. Too impatient to sit and wait in the hope that Bob Houghton would appear, he made his way slowly along the promenade. He drew level with the steps where the dog had descended to the beach. The tide was coming in; there was only a narrow strip of shingle waiting to be covered by water. A waving black tail showed him where the dog was, only yards away, intent on something close against the sea wall.

Idle curiosity took Deepbriar on to the first step. The dog was sniffing at a little heap of what looked like the pieces of a brightly painted toy. Deepbriar almost moved on, but then something about the colours struck him as familiar. He looked for an easier route to the beach, not sure that he was ready to tackle steps, but the slipway was almost half a mile away.

Deepbriar hesitated for only a moment. The treads were uneven, worn away in places where the shingle had been tossed up by high seas, and it was nearly twelve feet to the bottom, but he decided not to let that deter him. Clutching the crutches very firmly, he made his way down, one careful step at a time, leaning his buttock against the rail for support.

Chapter Seven

Deepbriar reached the beach safely, one eye on the advancing water. He calculated that he'd be safe enough for half an hour or more; it would only take a few minutes to reach the thing that had aroused his curiosity and get back to the steps. The dog lifted its head and looked at him, then turned and ran off, as if it had urgent business at the pier.

Shingle is hard to walk on, without the added complication of crutches and a plaster cast. The stones lay in ridges, which made matters worse, and Deepbriar was breathing hard by the time he arrived at the thing that had caught the dog's attention.

The animal had apparently been trying to bury this new plaything, for some pieces were almost hidden by the shingle, but Deepbriar could see that his hunch was right; the scraps of broken plaster had been a gnome. He sat down heavily on the damp stones to examine the evidence. Both the gnome and the wheel-barrow it had once pushed were broken, but they didn't look as if they'd been there long.

Deepbriar picked up the two largest shards and struggled to his feet with the help of the sloping concrete beside him.

Balancing precariously on one crutch he found he could just reach to push the fragments on to the top of the sea wall; he would recover them from the promenade later. He had a vague idea that it would be worth trying to trace the owner; he must consult with Miss Caldwell.

Along the beach the dog had reached the pier. As Deepbriar turned towards the steps the animal gave a sharp bark. It made to move into the shadows beneath the pier, then backed into the daylight again, barking incessantly now, the sound it was making becoming ever more frantic. Deepbriar hesitated. He tried telling himself that the dog had probably cornered a cat, but some innate policeman's instinct told him something was wrong.

The tide was advancing, but it wouldn't be high for a while. With sudden determination Deepbriar set off along the narrow band of shingle. From his days in Bradsea during the war he knew there were more steps on the other side of the pier; he could get back to the promenade there. Still, he had to hurry if he wasn't going to risk getting the bottom of the cast wet. That would doubtless upset Dr Tordon, though as he lurched along, Deepbriar was more concerned about Mary's reaction if he went back to Vera's with his shoe and socks soaked in sea water.

The dog was barking frantically, still showing the same interest in whatever it had found, yet reluctant to go any closer. As he drew near, sweat pouring from his face, Deepbriar's feeling of unease grew.

An indistinct shape lay at the base of the sea wall, right under the pier where the morning light couldn't penetrate. Even before he stepped into the shadows a chill struck the constable and he suppressed a shiver. There could be any number of perfectly innocent objects of that size and shape, yet he knew this was no child's Guy Fawkes abandoned here out of season, no discarded shop dummy or bundle of old clothes. The cause of the dog's agitation was human. Or it had been.

The man lay on his front, so close to the wall that his right arm was lifted awkwardly by the curving concrete of its base. It was a wholly unnatural position. Deepbriar bit his lip and waited a second for his eyes to accustom themselves to the comparative darkness in the dank space under the pier.

Apparently reassured now that somebody had come, the dog retreated a few paces, fixing its doleful gaze on Deepbriar. The water was lapping ever closer as the constable made his way awkwardly between the great metal girders, green slime transferring itself to his sleeve in a messy smear when he slipped and half fell against one of them.

The clothes the man wore were dry; he hadn't been in the water. Deepbriar dropped one crutch and lowered himself gingerly to his knee, reaching to touch the man's neck above the collar of his shirt, already sure he would find no sign of life. There was something slightly odd about the texture of his flesh, though Deepbriar was too preoccupied to think what it was.

'Cold as the grave,' Deepbriar commented, glancing at the dog. The animal's tail gave a half-hearted wag, as if it too felt the need to hear a human voice at that moment. Deepbriar turned his gaze back to the body. He reached to roll it over.

The constable stared into the dead face. His heart, already pounding after his exertions, thudded loudly against his ribs, and the dark world beneath the pier reeled and shimmered.

'That's impossible,' he breathed. 'That's bloody impossible!'

A wave swept in and splashed icily over Deepbriar's foot, wetting his toes in their protective sock and dampening the end of the plaster cast. The constable roused himself with an almost physical effort, and looked around. Something felt wrong. His limbs and neck were stiff as if he'd been in the same position too long, and the tide was higher than when he first stepped out of the sunlight, although surely that had been only a moment ago.

If he'd lost consciousness he would have fallen. He was still balanced on one knee. His foot and leg were almost under water. How could time have passed by unnoticed? Fighting down the panic welling in his throat, Deepbriar drew in a gulp of air. He was afraid the nightmares were beginning to seep into his waking life, and he shuddered as he looked down at the body of the man lying on the shingle. How long a time had passed since he looked into the dead face and thought he recognized it?

The years of discipline came to his aid. Deepbriar battened down the terrifying thought that he was going insane; there was a job here that had to be done, and with the tide rushing in there was nobody but him to do it. He told himself his imagination had played a nasty trick, that was all. What he thought he'd seen had to be an illusion, an hallucination no more founded in reality than those that disturbed his sleep.

When he'd released his grip on the dead body it had rolled back into its original position, lace down. Now, with his face grim, he took a fresh hold and turned the corpse over again.

There was no mistake. The unusual texture of the neck where Deepbriar had touched it to check for signs of life was due to the large strawberry birthmark that blossomed above the collar of the white shirt. Nor could he have forgotten those features, even though he'd last encountered them sixteen years ago. But if there was one certainty, it was that he'd never expected to see this man again, dead or alive.

It wasn't the time to worry over the mystery of the man's reappearance. In normal circumstances the local CID would want the body left exactly where it was found, in case there was vital evidence to be gathered there, but he had to act soon or the corpse would be swept away by the tide. This was surely a suspicious death; the man hadn't drowned, and it seemed unlikely he had simply taken a walk under the pier during the hours of darkness and died of natural causes. And, unless the years had brought about a total change of character, Deepbriar couldn't believe this man had committed suicide. That left murder.

Fit and unhampered, the constable would have heaved the body on to his back and carried it to the steps, even though the man must have weighed more than his own fourteen stones. He gave a mental shrug; no good thinking that way, he had to work out some alternative.

Deepbriar gave an experimental pull at the man's jacket, wondering if he could drag the corpse to the steps. The body shifted an inch, then settled back on to the stones. He admitted defeat before he'd even started; walking with crutches or crawling on one knee, he couldn't hope to move the man far enough before the tide overtook him. With a gargantuan effort he pushed the corpse further up into the curve of the sea wall; it would be out of the water there for a few minutes more. It was time to fetch help, and quickly.

His actions had at least brought the plaster cast a little further from the water's edge, but it was still in danger of getting a thorough wetting; he'd had a dozen lectures about the absolute necessity of keeping it dry. It was no use dwelling on the bad luck that had prevented Dr Tordon being available to remove the thing the previous day.

Though Deepbriar no longer cared about keeping the cast in good condition, it would weigh him down even more if it got soaked. Grasping the crutches firmly, he attempted to climb to his feet, but his good leg had sunk into the wet shingle almost to the knee, and the wooden shafts couldn't find a decent purchase. The shifting stones chuckled vindictively as the water swirled them from beneath his boot and piled them ever deeper around his leg. They seemed to be trying to suck him down and bury him, just a yard away from dry land.

Abandoning the attempt to rise, Deepbriar tossed the crutches towards the girder closest to the wall, where the concrete base was still clear of the water, then began to crawl after them. The rusty metal would provide support; once he was back on his feet he'd be away up the beach in no time.

There were unexpected currents running beneath the pier. Another wave came, the largest yet. The spray damped his hair and he felt himself being dragged sideways. He'd been right about the cast, it was soaking up moisture, and the lower part of his leg felt most peculiar, as if it was being ground between the icy cold gums of some massive fish. When the undertow released him he had to make a wild grab at the crutches or they'd have been swept out of his reach.

Deepbriar caught sight of the black dog, which had retreated further along the beach where there was still a narrow hand of shingle untouched by the advancing tide. The animal gave a slight wave of its tail and barked, as if in encouragement.

'I'm blowed if I'm going to crawl along the promenade on my hands and knees,' Deepbriar told it, regaining the ground he had lost, keeping hold of the crutches in one hand and trying to keep the top of the cast free of water. 'Don't just stand there,' he went on, torn between frustration and amusement at the sheer absurdity of his predicament. 'Haven't you ever been to the pictures? Lassie goes for help when some-body's in trouble.'

The dog wagged its tail again, its tongue lolling.

A larger wave gave the cast another soaking. For the first time Deepbriar felt a stir of real fear. He had a vision of drowning in a few inches of water, and being found dead, floating alongside the corpse. Either that or he'd be swept headlong into deep water, or get his head bashed in as the waves pounded the supports beneath the pier.

The plaster had become very heavy, and almost the whole of his leg felt damp and clammy. If he didn't get himself out of this mess soon things were only going to get worse. He waited for the moment when a wave receded, then lurched towards the nearest girder. The concrete base connected hard with his shin and he swore, but before the next wave swept in he managed to get his foot on it and push himself upright. A moment later, with the crutches in place cradling his elbows, he launched himself up the beach. It was a relief to join the dog on dry ground; the animal celebrated by coming to offer Deepbriar's hand a salute with its wet tongue.

It felt good to be out in the sunlight. Deep-briar set off hastily along the ever-narrowing strip of beach, heading for the nearest steps. They were set behind a concrete bulwark, no more than ten yards away.

Memory told him there was a telephone kiosk at the very end of the pier. All he had to do was get off the beach. Deepbriar glanced back into the shadows to reassure himself that the body was still clear of the water. Waves were splashing at the foot of the sea wall in places, and he increased his pace, coming breathless but triumphant to his goal.

The steps had gone. He stared at the bent pieces of wrought iron protruding from the sea wall above the level of his head, all that remained of the old stairway. Too late, he remembered something cousin Vera had said about a recent storm. If he'd paid more attention he would have known this was one of the places where the high seas had wreaked havoc the previous winter.

Up above, on the promenade, a length of chain had been stretched over the gap to keep people from trying to come down this way. It was a shame he hadn't walked a little further on his morning excursions.

The dog ran past Deepbriar. Obviously accustomed to the obstacle, it gave a great bound, leaping to the last fragments of a top step that hung over the gap, and from there it soon gained the safety of the pavement. With a cheerful whisk of its tail it vanished from view.

Deepbriar had seen how the suspended

remnant of concrete shook under the dog's weight; the step would never support fourteen stones, even if he could reach it. He turned away to stare further along the beach. The slipway that allowed boats to be launched at almost any state of the tide looked impossibly distant, and water was lapping at the base of the wall most of the way. That left the option of going back the way he'd come, but that looked no better. He would have to negotiate those ridges of shingle, most of them under water by now.

'Hey,' he shouted, facing the steps again. 'Anybody up there?' There was no answer. Bob Houghton should have been sweeping the promenade around the shelter by this time, Deepbriar reflected, if he hadn't so inconveniently chosen to vanish two days before. It might be another hour before anyone came along.

During the day the pier was popular with fishermen, but the gates were locked overnight, to prevent vagrants from sleeping in the booths, or thieves from breaking into the café and the theatre at the far end. Deepbriar had no idea what time the man came with the key, but he guessed it was too early to expect help from that direction.

He turned to face the long haul to the slipway. The cast was a problem. Perhaps it would fall off once it was thoroughly soaked, which might be helpful, but he daren't waste time trying to remove it.

No matter how quickly he made the trip, he doubted if he'd he able to prevent the body from being washed into the sea. He gave one last despairing glance back at the pier, and that was when he caught sight of a possible alternative. A rusty metal ladder hung from the safety rail up above, attached to one of the supporting girders only a few yards from the spot where the body lay. True, the bottom of the ladder was already under water, but at least it wasn't far away.

The weeks spent with his leg in plaster had strengthened Deepbriar's arms and shoulders. All he had to do was stay upright. At each step the tide did its best to sweep away the crutches, but he planted them with great care before trusting his weight to them, moving on only during the seconds when the water was slack. The cast grew heavier with every passing moment, and the powerful tug of the undertow snatched at him, but he slogged on, gasping at the chill of the water, which splashed to the top of his thighs.

With a final gargantuan effort Deepbriar took a last long stride on to the base of the pillar alongside the ladder, sighing with relief when he felt something solid beneath his foot. He flung one arm thankfully around the weed-covered girder. He lifted the crutches as high as he could and hitched them on one of the supports holding the ladder.

From there it was simple. He pulled himself up, taking his weight on his arms until he could bring his foot to the first rung. Then he only had to repeat the manoeuvre another dozen times, the plaster cast a dead weight, his shoulders and arms protesting painfully. Deepbriar was mouthing an audible prayer when he finally squeezed beneath the railings and on to the sun-warmed wooden planks. He lay on his stomach for a few seconds, thankful to be alive, then some sixth sense made him lift his head. A pair of bright dark eyes were watching him from across the pier.

The boy was about ten years old, his grey knitted jumper a little too small for him, while the home-made fishing rod he carried was twice his own height. Deepbriar met the child's gaze and the youngster turned, sensing authority and ready to flee.

'Don't go, I'm trespassing too,' Deepbriar said urgently. The boy hesitated, watching warily as Deepbriar sat up and felt in his pocket, producing a coin. 'You want to earn this thruppenny bit?' he asked.

The boy nodded, still cautious.

'There's two crutches stuck just down there,' Deepbriar said, 'I can't reach to pull them up, and I can't get far without them. Do you think you could get them for me?' He held out the coin. 'Be a good lad, eh?'

A few minutes later they were heading for the entrance, side by side, the boy confiding that he'd had no luck with his fishing. When they reached the gates they were locked, as Deepbriar had expected; he was still trapped, and no nearer calling the local force for assistance.

'Reckon you've got a way of getting through here,' Deepbriar said, breaking off a conversation about lugworms and winking at the boy. The lad grinned and went to the side of the gate, where an array of spikes fanned out from the railings. Agile as a monkey, he swung himself round them, then squeezed through the gap behind the telephone box which stood just beyond the barrier.

'Listen, son,' Deepbriar said, 'You're the right side of the gate now, so nobody can say you did anything you shouldn't. I need you to give me a hand again.'

With the youngster holding the door of the phone box open, handing him the receiver and dialling 999, Deepbriar finally called for help. A few minutes later bells jangled through the morning calm, as a police car swerved round the corner from the High Street, followed by a fire engine.

Chapter Eight

The thin man in the dark suit wiped his fingers on his handkerchief and looked with obvious displeasure at the damp stains around the soles of his shoes. Turning, he leant down to speak to the firemen who were still on the beach. Deepbriar pushed the side of his face against the railing and craned his neck a little further, but he couldn't quite see the top of the ladder they had put down just beyond the pier. It seemed to take a long time to bring the body up, but at last it lay on the promenade, being inspected by the plainclothes man and a uniformed constable. Despite his best efforts, the corpse had obviously got wet, since a damp patch was spreading away from the lower half of the body.

Deepbriar was so intent on what was happening that he hardly noticed the arrival of the second police car.

'Ain't this a turn-up!'

Deepbriar jumped, leaping back to find himself face to face with a grinning council worker. 'Bin a while since anybody got stuck in 'ere, an' I can't figure out 'ow you did it neither,' the man said, sorting through a bunch of keys. He paused to stare at Deepbriar's plaster cast and crutches. 'Blimey! Now that's what I call magic. Don't tell me you was in there all night?'

'I came off the beach a few minutes ago, up the ladder,' Deepbriar replied, half his attention on the constable who had brought the man. He had joined the other officers by the body, and was scribbling down notes at the direction of the man in the suit.

'Wonder you wasn't drowned,' the council worker went on cheerfully, swinging the gate open and standing aside to let Deepbriar pass him. 'I didn't know what the 'eck was going on, getting dragged away from me breakfast by a copper. We don't often get bodies washed up at Bradsea, the current usually takes 'em further north, or into the estuary.'

The plainclothes man detached himself from the small group gathered round the corpse, his long bony face drawn into a scowl. 'That will be all, Mr Johns, you can go.' He waited for the council worker to leave, then turned to Deepbriar. 'I'm Inspector Prout, Bradsea CID. I need you to answer a few questions.'

Deepbriar drew himself upright, coming as close as he could get to standing to attention while he needed the support of the crutches. 'Detective Constable Deepbriar, sir,' he replied. 'From Falbrough. Anything I

109

can do to help. I'm sorry I didn't manage to get to the phone before the tide came in. It looks as if the body got a bit wet.'

'You say you're a DC?' Prout glared at him. 'Got any identification with you?' he barked.

'No, sir. I'm here on convalescent leave, my warrant card is at my digs. Sergeant Hobday can vouch for me, though. I was stationed in Bradsea for a while during the war, he knew me then.'

'Hobday's away.' Prout's scowl deepened and he looked pointedly at the crutches and cast. 'How did you get on the pier? And what on earth were you doing on the beach in the first place?'

Deepbriar began to tell him about the dog's persistent bark, deciding it wasn't necessary to bring up the business of the gnomes. Before he'd got very far they were interrupted by one of the uniformed constables, hurrying across looking pleased with himself.

'Inspector,' he said, 'the man was staying at the White Swan Hotel, there's a room key in his pocket.' He offered Prout a wallet. 'I found this too, we've got identification. He's from Manchester. He's called Hubert Masters.'

'What?' Deepbriar exclaimed. That's not his right name.'

'You want to explain yourself, Deepbriar?' Prout asked, a mounting suspicion on his face. 'This is all starting to look decidedly fishy to me. You've got your leg in plaster, yet you go wandering about on the beach when the tide's almost in. Lo and behold, you find a corpse. And now you're telling me we've got his name wrong. Did you know the dead man? Perhaps I'd better read you your rights before you say anything more.'

Deepbriar was almost rendered speechless, so unexpected was the inspector's hostile reaction. 'I don't think that's necessary, Inspector. I wasn't exactly wandering about the beach; I told you, the dog led me to the body,' he said. 'And I know the man's identity because I've seen him before, a long time ago. I assure you his name wasn't Masters then. But I don't see how that makes me a suspect.'

'Most murderers know their victims,' Prout replied grimly. 'So if the dead man isn't Hubert Masters then who is he? Friend of yours perhaps?'

'No, not a friend. I saw him quite a few times, during the war,' Deepbriar replied. 'That birthmark...' he broke off, still hardly able to believe what he'd seen.

'Yes?' Prout prompted.

'Well, it's distinctive. There can't be two men with marks like that.' Then Deepbriar dropped his bombshell. 'The trouble is, the man who had that birthmark died sixteen years ago. His name's Sidney Greensall.'

Deepbriar's feet were cold, the plaster cast felt heavy and clammy, he hadn't been offered so much as a cup of tea, it was nearly ten o'clock and his stomach was growling emptily. Twice he had told Prout about his appointment with Dr Tordon, but the detective refused to allow him to leave.

'So, what else can you tell me about the dead man?' Prout demanded, leaning forward over the desk.

'Sidney Greensall,' Deepbriar said wearily, 'ran the local black market. We spent most of the months I was in Bradsea putting together a case against him.'

'Who's we?'

'Me and Sergeant Houghton, though Detective Chief Inspector Larch was officially in charge. After the bombing, the CID were even more short of men than the uniformed branch.' He was reluctant to explain further; the explosion that destroyed half the police station had killed two of Larch's best friends, one of them his brother-in-law.

When Deepbriar knew him, Larch had been a broken man. Like most of those who survived, or who hadn't been there that night, Houghton had done his best to protect the senior CID officer from censure when his work suffered. They had all worked extra duties in an attempt to cover his cases. Al-

112

though he was a uniformed sergeant, Houghton had been given responsibility for pursuing the Greensall case, and having taken a liking to the youngest and greenest of the constables sent to Bradsea during the emergency, he had asked that Deepbriar be allowed to help him.

'All right, so maybe it is Greensall, it's easy enough for a man to change his name. But what's this about him being dead already?' Prout demanded.

'I told you, he was supposed to have died in 1941,' Deepbriar said, rubbing at his wrist where a patch of dried salt was beginning to irritate his skin. He sighed, guessing how the inspector was likely to react as he went on. 'I was the one who found the body.'

'You what?' Prout's slightly protruding eyes looked about ready to leap out of his head. 'And you still expect me to believe this is all above board?'

Deepbriar made a helpless gesture with his hands. 'I've never believed in coincidences, either, Inspector, but all I can do is tell you the truth.' He explained that the river bridge had been on his regular beat, and that some boys playing down by the water had called his attention to the bundle of rags caught up against the central pier.

'All right, we'll let your part in all this wait for the moment. Tell me the rest.'

'The body had been in the river for two

weeks, according to the doctor, which tied in with the last time Greensall was seen alive. By the time the fish and the rest of the wildlife had finished with him there wasn't a lot left to identify, not as far as his features were concerned, but the clothes and watch were definitely his.'

'What about dental records?'

Deepbriar shook his head. 'Apparently Greensall had never been near a dentist in his life. Looking back, you can see how it was. Sergeant Houghton was building a case against him and he must have realized he couldn't avoid arrest much longer. He found a man about his own height and weight, and made the substitution. What better way to disappear when things became too hot for him?' He pulled a wry face. 'Whether the bloke he used as a decoy was alive or dead when Greensall got hold of him I wouldn't like to guess. Greensall was a nasty piece of work; he'd been known to turn violent. He was suspected of having something to do with the murder of a farmer a few months before he disappeared, but there was insufficient evidence to bring a charge against him.'

'So, you're suggesting this man, this Greensall, got away with faking his own death by drowning, sixteen years ago? And now, here he is, drowned all over again, and both times you were the one who found the body.' Prout fixed the constable with a sceptical look. 'I don't know what game you're playing, Deepbriar, but none of this rings true.'

'You'll find it all in the records, Inspector. Greensall had a couple of convictions for receiving stolen goods. He died, or we thought he had, before we got round to making the more serious charges stick.'

'I don't suppose he had any close relatives?' Prout managed to make even this sound like an accusation. 'Anyone we can ask to identify him?'

'We didn't find anybody last time,' Deepbriar replied, 'He didn't seem to have any family. There must be plenty of people in Bradsea who'll remember the man, though, and there'll be a photograph on his file. As for him being drowned this time, he was high and dry when I found him, and his clothes weren't even damp. I don't think he'd been in the water.'

'So in your expert opinion he didn't drown.' Prout was sarcastic. 'Perhaps you'd like to tell me exactly how he died? A blow to the back of the head with a blunt instrument perhaps?' He gestured at Deepbriar's crutches.

'I didn't see any outward signs of injury, but it was a bit dark under the pier.' Deepbriar returned the inspector's gaze, refusing to be cowed. 'I don't doubt the surgeon will be able to tell you more about that than me, sir. I'm only the man who *found* him,' he concluded, with emphasis.

'And who failed to get help before the body had been immersed in water.'

'I've explained how that happened.' Deepbriar was extremely hungry by this time, and his leg was feeling very strange. The cast was drying out. He wondered if it might damage the newly mended bones.

Deepbriar knew he shouldn't do it, but he picked up the crutches and offered them to Prout. 'If you'd like to see how hard it is to walk on the beach using these things then feel free to borrow them. Sir.'

The uniformed constable who sat by the door taking notes made a slight sound, and Prout rounded on him angrily. 'Have you got something to say, Norris?'

'No sir,' the man replied, hastily wiping the remnants of a smile off his face.

'Good. Right then, Deepbriar, let's go back to the beginning. You say you're with Falbrough CID, yet the identification my man fetched from your digs tells me you're in the uniformed branch. You want to explain that to me?'

'I've been based in Minecliff for quite a few years. I only heard about the move while I was in hospital,' Deepbriar said. 'I won't be starting in my new post until I'm passed fit.'

116

'You see, that's where I'm having problems with your story,' Prout said, his lips curling up at the ends in an unpleasant smile.

'Village bobbies don't get moved to CID, not at your time of life. You must be knocking forty. How do I know you haven't pinched this?' he asked, waving Deepbriar's identification at him.

'If that's all you're worried about there's a simple enough way to find out,' Deepbriar said, a grin breaking out on his face in spite of himself. 'Get Rosie to bring us a cup of tea.'

'What?' Prout looked about ready to explode. 'You've got the nerve to sit there–'

'And ask for a cup of tea,' Deepbriar broke in. 'Yes, I have. For two very good reasons. First, even a suspect, if that's what I am, has some rights, and I'm parched. Not to mention starving hungry. And second, Rosie knows me; she'll tell you who I am, and we can both stop wasting our time!'

The plaster cast was off at last. Deepbriar sat down on the bed, giving a sigh of pleasure as he wiggled his toes. Dr Tordon had made him wait while the X-rays were developed, but when they arrived the results had pleased him; the bones had knitted well. Now it was just a matter of building up his wasted muscles.

'Don't forget what the doctor said about

overdoing things,' Mary cautioned, watching him from the doorway. 'Do you really have to go back to the police station later? I almost said something to that young constable who came round this morning, when he said you were helping Inspector Prout with his inquiries. You're here to convalesce. It was bad enough getting your cast all wet like that; did you see the nurse's face when she saw it? I didn't know where to look. I suppose somebody had to go down on the beach, but I don't understand why it had to be you.'

It had been idle curiosity, and the remains of a gnome, that had led him into the whole mess, but that wasn't the thing to say when Mary was in this mood. Deepbriar sighed. 'I was the only one around. I couldn't leave the body on the beach or it would have been washed away.'

'I still don't think they should expect you to spend all day working.'

'It's not exactly work.' Deepbriar would prefer not to tell her that Inspector Prout was treating him as a murder suspect, but unless he could prove his innocence it was only a matter of time before she would have to know. 'I'm a witness. And since the man turned out to be somebody I knew when I was serving here in the war, I can hardly refuse to give the inspector a bit of help.'

She sighed. 'Well, I'm going to have a lie

down. Are you off to see the inspector again now?'

'No. He didn't exactly say I had to go today, just that I ought not to be too far away if he wants me. I don't think it'll hurt if I go for a little walk.' He hurried on before she could protest. 'Dr Tordon said it was a good idea. I'll take the crutches. I know I'll need them for a couple of days yet. My leg won't get better if I don't give it something to do.'

She gave him an old-fashioned look, then suddenly smiled. 'I'm being cranky again, aren't I? Sorry, love. But when it comes to you looking after yourself—'

'I'm not very good at it,' he finished, returning her smile. 'I don't get much practice, when you do it so well.'

'That's just flannel, Thorny Deepbriar, and you know it,' she exclaimed. 'Well, go on then, take your walk. But see if you can stay out of trouble!'

Quite willing to obey, for the moment at least, Deepbriar didn't go far, but settled down in his favourite spot in the shelter to watch the sea, waiting until it was time to go the council depot and see if Bob Houghton turned up to fetch his pay. He half dozed in the warmth of the sun, wishing he didn't still feel like an invalid; getting about was only a little easier without the cast, as his leg was very stiff and weak.

119

At last he went hobbling up through the town. He couldn't help worrying about Prout. The inspector had made his suspicions very clear, and by now he was probably looking into Deepbriar's record. If Bob Houghton was right, then Deepbriar's name had been connected with Greensall's nefarious activities during the war. He had no idea what Ruggles might have committed to paper, maybe he had even suggested that he had joined Houghton in taking bribes from Greensall. But if what he'd written was that bad, wouldn't he have been turned out of the force when he returned to Falbrough, or, like Houghton, quietly invited to resign?

He thought he knew the answer. It had been wartime, and it was possible the comment had gone unnoticed. Latterly, perhaps, the passage of time had reduced the potency of Ruggles's accusation, but it could still have been sufficient to prevent his promotion. Deepbriar made up his mind not to dwell on something he couldn't change. Until a couple of days ago he'd never questioned his lack of advancement, there was no point agonizing over it now.

Deepbriar turned his thoughts to the events of that morning. Perhaps there was something he'd missed. Greensall's body had been cold, but it couldn't have been on the beach during the last high tide. He was hardly likely to have met his murderer under the pier by chance, so it had to have been an assignation.

Perhaps Greensall had arranged to meet an old acquaintance, but hadn't wanted to risk being seen in the town in case he was recognized. After so many years he wasn't being sought by the law, but his resurrection might have led to awkward questions being asked. Maybe Greensall killed the man whose body had been mistaken for his back in 1941; if that was the case, some of his old pals could have known about it.

Deepbriar considered Greensall's closest associates. There had been an ex-boxer, Pug Parry; a huge gorilla of a man. He was hired muscle, slow-witted but devoted to his employer. Greensall's second in command had once been Parry's trainer, another ex-boxer but a far brighter type, quite capable of trying to squeeze money out of his former boss if he had a hold over him. No, he'd got this backwards. If blackmail was involved then surely Greensall was the blackmailer, not the victim. A 'mark' couldn't pay up once he was dead.

It was no use; he didn't have enough facts. He didn't even know if Greensall had been killed by a blow to the head, though Prout had hinted that was the case. Deepbriar tried to imagine himself standing under the pier, balancing himself on one crutch as he brought the other down on Greensall's head. If the inspector really suspected him of murder, was that the way he saw it?

He stopped in his tracks, blocking the pavement. Holidaymakers flowed round him as if he was a traffic island, but he didn't notice them. A chill swept through him, dowsing him more thoroughly than the rising sea that morning. He recalled the strange hiatus when he'd knelt on the shingle by Greensall's body, the way the tide had rushed in without him noticing, his body growing stiff and cold. For a few frightening moments, crouching there on the beach, he had doubted his sanity.

Was it possible he was guilty? Was there a chance, no matter how slight, that he really had committed murder? With a shiver, he acknowledged that he couldn't be absolutely certain. To his eternal shame, while he was immersed in a nightmare, he had hit his wife and left her with a black eye.

It didn't seem impossible. He could almost picture himself, venturing out during the night, striking a man over the head with deadly force while he was sleepwalking, then going calmly back to his bed.

Chapter Nine

The council depot was busy. Deepbriar stood outside the gate and stared in, looking for the familiar thin figure among the men gathering around the office, but not seeing him. He noticed the old road-sweeper he'd met in the park, and when the man looked his way he beckoned. The sweeper came, looking smaller and rather frail without his barrow and broom.

'You got rid o' the plaster, then,' the old man commented. He took a tin of tobacco from his pocket, extracted a generous pinch and a paper and gave the whole of his attention to rolling a cigarette.

'I'm still looking for Bob Houghton.' Deepbriar said, once the man had taken his first long draw.

'I've not seen 'im.' He pointed. 'See the chap in the black hat? That's the boss. If anybody knows what's happened to Houghton he's the one. Not likely he'll tell you, mind, he's a bit of a toffee-nosed beggar.' The sweeper turned to go back into the yard, tossing a parting shot over his shoulder. 'Wait till he's finished handin' out the pay before you ask, there's a good lad.'

'I'll do that,' Deepbriar replied. He limped across the road, where a low wall provided him with a seat. An orderly queue formed, snaking into the office and around the yard. A few minutes later individual men began to reappear through another door with their pay packets in their hands, some scattering to fetch bicycles, others walking straight out through the gate. Within a short time the last member of the queue vanished inside, and in due course came out again.

Deepbriar rose to his feet and went to meet the works superintendent, who emerged a few minutes later, accompanied by the surly foreman and a woman carrying a wooden tray which bore a single small brown envelope; presumably she was a clerk from the accounts office. Deepbriar wondered if the pay packet was the one that should have been collected by Bob Houghton.

'Excuse me,' Deepbriar said, hobbling across the now deserted yard. 'I'm sorry to bother you, but I was hoping to see Bob Houghton. Somebody told me I'd find him here.'

'He didn't turn up,' the woman said, 'I hope–' she broke off as the superintendent frowned at her.

'What did you want with him?' the man asked.

'I'm an old friend. I met him on the promenade the other morning, but he hasn't been about since. To be honest, I was a bit worried. I thought he might be ill.'

'If so, he hasn't had the courtesy to inform his employers,' the superintendent said shortly. 'I'm sorry, I'm afraid I can't help you.'

Deepbriar turned away, retreating to his post on the wall once again. He had a feeling the clerk might be more forthcoming, if he had the good luck to see her alone. It was worth the wait. The superintendent drove out of the depot in an Austin 7, not deigning to notice Deepbriar as he swept past. The woman followed on foot a few minutes later. She looked across at Deepbriar and smiled. He took that as an invitation, going over the road to join her.

'I don't think there's anything I can tell you,' she said, though she sounded a lot less unfriendly than her boss. 'We're not supposed to give out the addresses of our employees.'

'I know Bob was living at Clifftop View, in Waterloo Road,' Deepbriar said. 'But he's not there now.'

'Really?' She looked concerned. 'That's the only address we have for him. If he's moved he hasn't let us know.'

'He left a few weeks ago.'

She smiled ruefully. 'You see, I was right, I can't help you. I hope he's not ill. He's the quiet sort, he doesn't seem to have any friends among the men here.'

'He wasn't like that when I knew him, during the war.'

'Folk change. I'm sorry, but I can't think where he might have gone. The only time I ever met him, other than at work, was in the little ironmonger's shop near the railway station. He was buying some paraffin.'

'When would that be?' Deepbriar asked.

'Oh, only a couple of weeks ago. Is that any help?'

'Possibly,' he said, though he wasn't sure how, 'Thank you.' Deepbriar fumbled the crutches into one hand and touched his hat to her. Once the woman had gone he stood hesitating for a moment. Prout might be wanting to see him again, but he wasn't far from the shop she'd mentioned. He could spare a few minutes more, and the trail was getting warmer; Bob Houghton was probably living near the railway station.

Deepbriar's thoughts returned to the past as he limped along the quiet back streets. This had been part of his beat so many years ago; the river wasn't far away, he recalled his first sight of the decomposing body, lodged under the bridge where High Whellow Road crossed the river. It had been in the water quite some time. The face was swollen and unrecognizable, nibbled away in places so it didn't look remotely human, but the expensive gold watch and the flashy snakeskin shoes had been enough to identify the missing Sidney Greensall. Deepbriar had hurried to the nearest telephone box, and another constable had been sent to his assistance. They'd waded into the water to pull the corpse to the bank and heave it on to dry land. They had then both retreated among the bushes to be sick.

All these years, everybody had thought that Greensall was dead. So where had he been? Presumably in Manchester, masquerading as Hubert Masters. And how had he made his living since 1941? There was a good chance Inspector Prout already knew the answers to those questions. True, the body had got wet, but only below the waist, thanks to the way Deepbriar had wedged it higher up the wall. The contents of his wallet had looked dry, and since it had provided a name and a location, more information shouldn't have been too hard to find.

Despite his shock and that weird hiatus he'd suffered as he knelt by the body, Deepbriar hadn't wasted those few moments of lucidity before he realized he had to get off the beach. Greensall had been overdue for a haircut. And, true to form, he'd been wearing expensive shoes, but the soles were almost worn through, and there were metal tips nailed on to the heels, also well worn. His suit had the look of being made to measure by a good tailor, but the ends of the cuffs had been frayed. All those things led Deepbriar to suppose that the man was down on his luck. Was that what had brought him back to Bradsea?

Deepbriar had a sudden vision of Bob Houghton, bent backed, dressed in the shapeless overalls issued to him by the council. The collapse of his case against Greensall, and the suspicion that he'd tried to manufacture false evidence, had ruined Houghton's career. If he were to come across Greensall, would he be capable of wreaking vengeance on his old enemy?

But it hadn't been Houghton accepting bribes from Greensall during the war, Deepbriar was sure of it. At the time there had been whispers, rumours, that somebody in the force must be protecting Greensall in return for a share in his ill-gotten gains. He couldn't recall anybody suggesting a name for this hypothetical bent copper. Maybe he was still around; certainly he would have a powerful motive for wanting Greensall out of the way.

Deepbriar went over what he'd learnt from Rosie. Of the officers who'd been in Bradsea during the war, very few were left. There was Jack Hobday, and Sergeant Vorrman – Chief Inspector Vorrman now, Deepbriar corrected himself. That was it. Except Superintendent Ruggles, who had retired and now lived in Whellow. None of them seemed likely murderers. Perhaps Greensall's death had been nothing to do with his reappearance in Bradsea. Maybe some underworld rival had followed him from Manchester.

With a sigh, Deepbriar acknowledged that he had too little information. He was working in the dark, and that was unlikely to change, because one thing was sure; Prout wasn't the sort of man who'd take him into his confidence, even if he stopped seeing him as a potential murderer.

When he reached the ironmongers the shopkeeper was busy removing his stock from the pavement to store it inside. He paused briefly when Deepbriar asked about Bob Houghton, but he wasn't much help.

'I sell a lot of paraffin,' he said, bending to pick up some galvanized buckets and a basket full of clothes pegs. 'I'm blowed if I could tell you the names of more than a dozen of my customers, even the regulars. As for what they look like, I never did have much of a memory for faces.'

Reluctant to have wasted the journey, Deepbriar consulted his watch, wondering if Inspector Prout had sent an officer to summon him. He would be annoyed to discover that his prime suspect wasn't available for questioning. Deepbriar felt a stir of rebellion; he decided he didn't much care. At the moment, finding Bob was more important.

At the railway station he dug out two

129

halfpennies for a platform ticket and took the same seat as before. The porter remembered him and came across for a chat, but he shook his head when Deepbriar reminded him of his search. 'No, sorry. What do you want him for?'

'Nothing important,' Deepbriar replied, though maybe that was no longer true. He had to face facts. Bob Houghton could have been involved in Greensall's murder.

'It's a shame you haven't got a photograph, that would make it easier.'

Deepbriar agreed, he'd thought the same thing. It was possible somebody might have an old photo tucked away somewhere. During the war, Constable Hobday had sometimes brought a box Brownie to work, but the intervening years had wrought a lot of changes on Bob Houghton. A photograph that was more than sixteen years out of date might not be much use.

A long line of trucks rattled through the station, then a slow passenger train wheezed in, bringing people from Whellow, most of them holidaymakers with faces reddened by the sea breeze, their hands full of beach balls and buckets and spades. Among the general atmosphere of jollity, one man stood out. Dressed in a grubby boiler suit and with dirt on his hands and face, he looked about fifty-five, with a craggy face set in lines of permanent discontent. There was something about him that was instantly familiar. Deepbriar craned to keep an eye on the man as he threaded through the crowds, then on an impulse he rose to his feet, adjusted the crutches and followed.

They were almost at Cockle Close before Deepbriar remembered who the man was; his instincts had been right. He was trailing Joe Hatherly, the father of the missing Micky.

'Pretty sure of yourself, aren't you, coming after me on your own? In broad daylight too,' Joe Hatherly said. He had waited until he reached the entrance to Cockle Close to force a confrontation. As he rounded on Deepbriar his fists were bunched and there was a clear threat in both his voice and his aggressive pose. He'd chosen his spot well; large shrubs hung over the pavement from an overgrown garden, and the houses nearest to them showed windowless side walls to the road.

'I'm not here looking for trouble,' Deepbriar said.

'Reckon you're likely to get it just the same.' Hatherly rocked gently from one foot to the other. He seemed to notice the crutches for the first time, and looked perplexed. 'Looks like I'm odds on. I'd like to meet the bloke who did the damage. Got his own back, did he?'

'I think you've got me confused with

somebody else, Mr Hatherly, I'd like a word, that's all,' Deepbriar replied placidly, though he curled his fingers more tightly around the right-hand crutch, just in case.

Still looking a little puzzled, Hatherly studied Deepbriar, taking in both his size and his features, and maybe deciding that it wouldn't be an uneven match in his favour after all.

'I've not been in Bradsea for a good few years. No reason why you should remember me, but we met during the war,' Deepbriar prompted. 'I visited your house with another police officer, at least three times, as I recall. You'll not have forgotten Sergeant Houghton, him being a local man like yourself. We came to talk to your son, Micky.'

'You're a copper. I might have known.' Hatherly was still surly, but the constable thought he saw relief on the man's face, which struck him as a little odd. Deepbriar's mental cogs were whirring. Joe Hatherly's son had gone missing, just when Sidney Greensall had turned up again, dead for certain this time. Added to that, it seemed Joe had mistaken him for some sort of strong-arm bully. Deepbriar wondered if there was a connection between all these apparently unrelated facts.

'You've put on a bit of weight,' Hatherly said disparagingly, looking Deepbriar up and down, 'You was a long thin streak back then.'

'It's been a few years,' Deepbriar agreed. 'It took me a moment to recognize you, too. I saw you get off the train. Are you still working at the gasworks?'

'It's a job.' There was a brief pause, then Hatherly sneered. 'You're as nosy as ever, so I'd guess you're still a copper.'

'I am, but I'm in Bradsea to convalesce. I'm not here on official business. Let's call this a chat between old friends. I saw the stop press item in the local paper and I was wondering if Micky had turned up yet. Seeing you at the station, it seemed like a chance to renew our acquaintance.'

Hatherly didn't reply for a long moment. An expression of doubt resurfaced for a moment, then the lines on his face seemed to deepen and he looked suddenly old. His shoulders sagging, the man turned towards his front door. 'No, he hasn't,' he said. 'You'd best come inside.'

Like its tenant, the house had aged, and not in a dignified way. The same wallpaper, stained brown by several decades of cigarette smoke, was still curling off the walls, and a threadbare runner laid across the middle of the single living room threatened to trip the unwary. 'I'm on my own now,' Hatherly said. 'The council gave Micky and Susie a house in Dry Lane. Never did nothing like that for me,' he grumbled. 'I have to go on paying an arm and a leg for this dump.'

'They've got a family, haven't they?' Deepbriar asked.

Hatherly nodded. 'Council seems to think a couple of kids need a garden to run about in, but from what I've seen, their mother's letting them wreck it.'

Deepbriar looked at the wilderness outside the window and forbore to comment. 'He's doing all right for himself then, your Micky?' he asked, lowering himself into an upright chair without waiting for an invitation.

'Earns a fair wage. He's a plasterer. You said this wasn't official,' Hatherly objected, seeing Deepbriar take a notebook from his pocket.

'So I did,' Deepbriar replied calmly, 'but if you want help finding Micky there are things I'll need to ask you. I don't suppose you know why he left.'

'Haven't got a blinking clue.' Hatherly's answer came so quickly, Deepbriar was inclined to suspect it wasn't quite true, but he didn't pursue the point, merely raising his eyebrows and waiting for the man to go on.

'Been gone nearly three weeks, he has, and his boss was round on Saturday saying he won't keep the job open if he don't come back soon. Susie hasn't said much but I reckon she's going frantic. I've been giving her a bit of money to help with the kids, but I've my own bills to pay.' He paused. 'You may not be local, but you coppers stick together like bloomin' glue. What've you heard about my boy?'

'Nothing. Not about Micky.'

Hatherly scowled. 'Then what're you doing here? You wouldn't come just because you were curious about that bit in the local rag.'

'That's exactly why I came, Joe.' Deepbriar paused, watching the man's expression carefully. 'Do you remember Sidney Greensall?'

'Hardly likely to forget him, am I? He was the one got Micky into trouble with your lot. I reckoned when that bastard turned up dead it was the best thing that could have happened. Let my boy off the hook.' At that point Hatherly seemed to realize he might have said too much, and he glowered at Deepbriar 'Don't you go reading nothing into that; it wasn't none of my doing. You only got to ask around to know I steered clear of the likes of Greensall. I had more sense than to tangle with that mob.'

'They weren't very nice,' Deepbriar agreed. 'But Micky wasn't so careful. And when things turned nasty and people started getting hurt your lad got scared. That's when he decided to talk to us. He gave us information that would have delivered Greensall and the rest of the gang on a plate. We'd have caught the whole lot of them red-handed.' Deepbriar fixed his eyes accusingly on

Hatherly. 'Trouble was, Micky changed his mind, and Greensall vanished.'

'That sergeant was bloody simple if he thought it was going to be that easy. He must've known Greensall wouldn't sit back and let a kid like Micky shop him.' Hatherly was scornful. 'If it hadn't ended the way it did, I reckon the pair of you would likely have got the lad killed.'

'So you changed his mind for him,' Deepbriar said, finding it hard to hide his anger. 'You told him to clam up.' Thanks to this man, Bob Houghton had ended up sweeping the streets. And, though his own penalty hadn't been so severe, if Houghton's suspicions were correct, he'd got a black mark against his name that wouldn't easily be wiped out. All Superintendent Ruggles had needed to do was add a scribbled note to his record, accusing him of lying, at Bob's instigation, about the statement they'd taken from Micky Hatherly. Even worse, he could have hinted that both officers were on Greensall's payroll.

Deepbriar suppressed a twinge of fear. Circumstantial evidence was quite capable of convicting an innocent man. That untruth would look like a very good reason for them both to want Sidney Greensall dead. He'd been a police officer long enough to know that even the best detectives made mistakes, and he'd seen enough of Prout to know he wasn't the best. He couldn't leave the case in the inspector's hands; he needed to prove his innocence, and the first step must be to root out the truth about what had happened in Bradsea sixteen years before.

Chapter Ten

'It wasn't me who told Micky to keep his mouth shut, I swear,' Hatherly added, seeing the look on Deepbriar's face. 'Not that I didn't try, but he'd never listen to me.'

'Why should I believe you, Joe?' Deepbriar demanded harshly.

'I'll tell you what I know, though it's not much. That night, when Micky spilled what he knew about Greensall, I saw you and the sergeant leave the house. You never saw me because I dodged down the alley. I heard that sergeant crowing. From what he said I guessed what had happened. When I got in, Micky wouldn't talk to me, but that was nothing unusual. In the early hours I heard the boy leave the house. I got up and looked out of the window. He met somebody down the road, and they went off together. It's no good asking me who it was, because I couldn't tell.'

'You must have seen something.'

'A shape, that's all. There was a war on, you couldn't see nothing in the bloody blackout. It was a man, and he was wearing a hat. There, does that help you?'

'Was he small? About Micky's size? Skinny?'

'He was heavy built. It wasn't Greensall though, this bloke was taller.'

'You're sure?'

'Yeah, I'm sure. But whoever it was, the next time I saw Micky he was scared out of his wits, wouldn't hardly open his mouth. During that twelve hours somebody had put the fear of God into him.'

'You reckon it was the man who met him that night?' Deepbriar asked. The man who came for Micky could have been Pug Parry, but the description was far too vague to be useful.

'He never told me, so how would I know?' Hatherly scowled. 'Anyway, next we heard, Greensall was dead, and it was all over. If there was any of his gang left they must've found things too hot for 'em. Micky was glad to be out of it. And if you reckon my boy had anything to do with Greensall ending up in the river you can think again. What chance would a lad of seventeen have against a man like that? Anyway, Greensall went nowhere without Parry or Thwaite on his heels. Look, you said you'd come because Micky was missing, but all this old stuff was over and forgotten years ago.'

'Everybody thought so, but maybe we were wrong.' Deepbriar couldn't tell the man about Greensall turning up dead for the second time; if he did, and it got out, Prout would lock him up and throw away the key. 'Have you been to the police to report Micky missing?'

'No.' Hatherly looked uneasy again, his gaze drifting to the door. 'Susie wanted to, but I told her to try the paper first. I don't want the cops round here. See, Micky plays for the local cricket team, scored a hundred twice last season. I thought they'd write him up a bit, maybe ask people to come forward if they'd seen him, not put that little scrap in a corner on the back page, where nobody would notice.'

'But why didn't you want her to go to the police? Has the boy got something to hide?' Deepbriar hazarded. 'Or maybe you've been up to your old tricks. Still like to gamble, do you? Out in the street just now, who did you think had sent me? Somebody's been leaning on you, haven't they? Was that to do with Micky, or are you running an illegal book again?'

'If I've had a bit of trouble, that's none of your business,' Hatherly said, his face suddenly ugly. 'Bloody coppers, you're all the same, you got no interest in finding what happened to my boy, not unless there's something in it for you. I don't need your help. I'll take care of my own.'

Deepbriar rose to his feet, but on his way out he stopped and rounded on Hatherly,

140

staring down into the older man's face. 'I'm right, aren't I? There was somebody else asking questions. Maybe he came mob-handed. Did he go to Micky's wife too, or was it just you?'

'I've got nothing more to say.' Hatherly dragged open the door. 'Clear out, and don't go bothering Susie neither, or I'll give you something else to bloody convalesce over.'

Deepbriar considered this rather ill-defined threat as he left Cockle Close behind. He would have to speak to Micky's wife sometime, but there was no rush. It was good to be back in the fresher outside air and he walked slowly, thinking about what Joe had said, and, more particularly, what he hadn't.

There was a policeman patrolling the end of the pier, and a few sightseers remained, scanning the sea as if they expected another body to be swept in on the tide. Further along the sea wall, a small patch of colour reminded Deepbriar about the broken gnome he'd found early that morning. He'd almost forgotten about his enquiries into the vanishing gnomes. There were more important puzzles to solve now, but he went to fetch the pieces, pushing them into his jacket pocket. The sharp edge of the gnome's broken head tore a hole in the lining and he grimaced, thinking that Mary wouldn't be pleased; he wished that was the worst of his worries. Sometime soon he must admit that he was Prout's prime suspect for the murder of Sidney Greensall.

Staring out to sea, Deepbriar was blind to the bright glitter of the white horses, and deaf to the cry of the gulls as they followed a fishing boat towards the shore. He neither heard nor saw the holidaymakers on the shingle below. Once, he'd thought getting rid of the plaster cast would be a huge step towards a return to normality; now it hardly seemed to matter. In just a few hours his life had been turned upside down.

Now he was alone again, worst of all was the fear that had been growing in him all afternoon. He was disturbed by that strange moment on the beach, when he realized the time had passed unnoticed while he knelt by the dead man's side. If he couldn't trust his own mind not to play tricks on him, then nothing was certain. Was it possible he'd left his bed in the middle of the night? He hadn't been able to recall his most recent nightmare. Had he dreamt he was facing the ghost of a man supposedly dead and buried for sixteen years?

With sudden decision Deepbriar turned and headed back over the road, and up to the cottage hospital. It was nearly six, but a harassed nurse reluctantly admitted that Dr Tordon hadn't yet left the wards. When Deepbriar insisted it was urgent she showed him in to an empty room, where the doctor joined him a few minutes later.

Dr Tordon stroked one finger across his top lip, his normally cheerful face creased into a slight frown as Deepbriar explained why he was there.

'I'm not sure I understand. Are you saying you think you've lost your memory?'

'I don't know.' Deepbriar's heart was pounding as he went on. 'It's not exactly a gap in my memory, more like ... I don't know, it was as if time had slipped by without me being aware of it. I didn't lose consciousness, I can't have done or I'd have fallen over. It's crazy. One second the tide was a foot or two down the beach, the next it was over my feet.'

'I gather we're talking about the circumstances which led to your plaster cast getting into such a state. I think you'd better tell me what you were doing on the beach. Going for a stroll on crutches when the tide was coming in hardly seems a sensible thing to do.'

Deepbriar hesitated. He'd been warned not to talk about what had happened that morning. Prout had been quite emphatic on the subject.

'Well?' the doctor prompted. When Deepbriar had turned up for his appointment that morning, late, wet and dishevelled, Dr Tordon had been far from his usual friendly self. Deepbriar squirmed in his chair.

143

Without the doctor's help he might never get the answers he needed. He had to know that he wasn't a danger to Mary – or to anybody else. Whatever the consequences, he had to be assured that he hadn't killed Greensall.

'I'm not supposed to talk about this, but unless I tell you what happened you're not going to understand what's worrying me. There's something I have to ask you.' Deepbriar told the doctor how he'd discovered the body on the beach.

Dr Tordon steepled his fingers and leant across the desk, his expression serious. 'As a police officer you should be less shockable than most. I wouldn't have expected you to react in that way, even in those circumstances. However, bearing in mind your recent injuries, you may be in a slightly fragile state of mind. There is even a possibility that the gap in your awareness could have been caused by the concussion you suffered at the time of your accident.'

'It was quite a shock,' Deepbriar admitted, 'but I've dealt with a few deaths in my time. I think it must have been when I turned him over that my brain went haywire.' He hesitated, then went on. Hang Prout, he had to make the doctor see why he was so concerned. 'The fact is, the man was somebody I knew, a long time ago. But he'd been dead for years.'

The constable wiped a hand over his forehead, surprised to find that his face was damp with sweat. 'I'm not making sense.' He swallowed hard, and tried again, going on to explain how the first body had only been identified by the clothes it wore.

When he'd finished Dr Tordon sat back in his seat. 'So, you came across a body, and when you examined it you found yourself looking at a man who'd been presumed dead during the war. Only that time the body had decomposed to an extent that made certain identification impossible.'

'That's right,' Deepbriar breathed out a sigh of relief, glad he'd finally got it straight enough for Tordon to understand.

'Then I'd say my first analysis was correct. This was a case of shock. There are many things about the human brain which are not fully understood, Constable. Faced with something that appeared to make no sense, I would say your mind couldn't cope. It therefore took a brief respite from reality. The fact that you had suffered a severe concussion within the last two months could have contributed to your reaction.' He gave Deepbriar a penetrating look. 'When you were here earlier with your wife I believe she mentioned something about you having trouble getting to sleep, but we were interrupted by the nurse at that point and nothing more was said.'

'I've not been sleeping well,' Deepbriar admitted.

'That would be a contributory factor to your condition. When a man becomes sufficiently tired he may suffer from delusions, and begin to see things that aren't there. I doubt if you've quite reached that stage, but I shall give you some pills to assist you to sleep, and I strongly advise you to take them. Your wife was quite right to want to bring the matter to my attention.'

'It's Mary I'm worried about, more than anything,' Deepbriar confessed. He stared at the desk between them as he went on, feeling a flush rise in his cheeks. 'You guessed she wasn't telling the truth about that black eye.'

'I've heard too many women claim to have walked into an open door or fallen down the stairs,' the doctor replied grimly.

Deepbriar's chin came up. He was horrified. 'Did you think I'd hit her? Well, I suppose I did, but I was asleep at the time.' It all came out then, the whole story of the increasingly horrific nightmares that had him so scared that he dreaded falling asleep.

'I'm so tired I'm hardly sure what I'm doing,' he admitted. 'That's why...' he spilled out the worst of his fears at last. He told the doctor how it had occurred to him that he might have killed Greensall, though he had absolutely no memory of seeing him until he found his body lying on the shingle.

146

Dr Tordon sat silent until Deepbriar was done. 'You should have told me about these nightmares when we first met,' he said sternly. 'As for killing a man while you were in some kind of altered mental state, I would say it's highly unlikely. It's one thing to lose track of a few minutes, but that hardly suggests that you could have left your bed, met up somehow with this man, killed him, and returned, without any knowledge of it whatsoever. Even for a man with a severe mental illness that would be exceptional. I can assure you unequivocally that you aren't as sick as that.'

'Lord, that's a relief,' Deepbriar breathed, slumping back in his chair.

The ready smile reappeared on the doctor's face. 'I'm glad to find I wasn't wrong about your character. You would have done better to explain your wife's black eye honestly when you were both here earlier.' He fetched a bottle from a cupboard. 'I was going to prescribe something fairly mild, but I think we'd better try these instead. You're to take two pills when you go to bed tonight. You'll sleep like a log, and probably not wake up until midmorning. You may take one pill on subsequent nights. You're to come and see me on Monday anyway. That reminds me, there's an organ recital at the church on Monday evening, I hope you'll be joining us.'

147

'I hope so too,' Deepbriar replied, unpleasantly aware that he had disobeyed Inspector Prout's injunction to silence.

'And try not to worry, Constable, a few nights sleep and you'll be your old self again.' Deepbriar nodded. He already felt a little better, but as he rose to leave he reflected that he was still a suspect in a murder case. Maybe if he'd known about Inspector Prout, the doctor wouldn't have been so sure about his speedy recovery.

On Sunday morning the weather changed. The brief dry spell that had lasted since Deepbriar's arrival in Bradsea came to an end. Dark clouds were sweeping in from the sea and as they had breakfast – a little late because Deepbriar had slept until nine – the first heavy drops of rain began to fall.

By the time they were ready to go to church, the streets were awash, and the downpour showed no signs of relenting. Mary was wearing her raincoat, and Deepbriar noticed that it was tight around the middle; her condition was beginning to show. The realization plunged him into gloom. If Prout had his way, his child might grow up without a father.

'At least we don't have far to go,' cousin Vera chirped happily, picking up her umbrella and opening the door. 'Thorny, do you want–' she broke off. A uniformed constable stood on the doorstep, his hand lifted to the knocker. He was taken aback for a second but he soon recovered.

'Thomas Deepbriar? I'd be obliged if you'd accompany me to the station, sir. Inspector Prout wants a word with you.'

'I don't think you've been entirely honest with me, Deepbriar,' Inspector Prout said, an unpleasant smile on his lips. 'You didn't tell me you'd been consorting with Houghton during your stay in Bradsea.'

'Well, if you call having a chat and a cup of tea consorting, then I suppose I have,' Deepbriar acknowledged, 'but I don't see what that's got to do with Greensall's death.'

'Don't you? Well, maybe that's why you've never been anything but a clod-hopping village bobby all these years. You don't think it looks a mite suspicious, the two of you meeting up for a nice friendly chat only days before the man who ruined Houghton's career is found murdered?' He tapped one of the folders on the table.

'There's a note in here. Houghton was suspected of taking bribes, and fabricating evidence. In short, he was bent. Nobody likes a dishonest policeman, Deepbriar. If I'd been in charge I'd have seen him tried for what he did. But I gather Superintendent Ruggles didn't want a scandal, not while the local force was still in turmoil after the bombing of this station, so Houghton was allowed to resign. You were involved in that little episode too. It seems to me you both had good reason for wanting to get rid of Greensall.'

'You've got it wrong,' Deepbriar shot back. 'Sergeant Houghton was never involved in any of Greensall's operations, and we had no need to fabricate evidence. We were getting close to nabbing him, until somebody put a scare into our prime witness.'

Prout shook his head, dragging another folder from the heap. 'This is the file on Sidney Greensall. There's hardly anything about the black market racket, and nothing at all about any witness.'

'That's not right,' Deepbriar protested. 'We'd been talking to a lad by the name of Micky Hatherly. We saw him several times, and in the end he agreed to cooperate. I took notes when the sergeant interviewed him, and I wrote a report which was given to Inspector Larch. It has to be there.'

Deepbriar stared back into the past for a moment, and when his eyes refocused he found he was looking at Sidney Greensall's file. It was very old, with dog-eared corners. As he studied the faded cardboard his eyes widened. 'I may be a clod-hopping country copper,' he said, 'but that file's been tampered with. It used to be twice that size.'

'Now what are you trying to pull?' Prout demanded irritably. 'You can't go making allegations like that and get away with it.'

Throughout the interview a young detective sergeant had sat silent at Prout's side,
taking no part in the proceedings apart from
jotting down notes. Now he leant forward.
'Hang on, sir. He's right. I did think it was
odd when I fetched the thing from records.
Look at the way the folder's bent out of
shape, as if it's been stretched round something. And there's the remains of an old rub-
ber hand, stuck on the other side. There'd be
no need of that, unless the file was full.'

'And,' Deepbriar said, heartened to think
he might have found an ally, 'you can see
where the photograph was clipped to that
side, the cardboard behind it isn't faded. So
what's happened to it?'

Chapter Eleven

Prout looked as if he'd just eaten a lemon. He examined Greensall's file, carefully avoiding Deepbriar's eyes. 'You brought this up from the basement yourself, Sergeant?'

'I did, sir.'

'You found it in the right place, I take it?'

'Yes, but I noticed it wasn't nearly as dusty as the rest of the files in that section,' the sergeant replied, 'it was a bit smeared, as if somebody had given it a quick wipe.'

'To remove their fingerprints perhaps,' Deepbriar muttered, unable to contain himself.

Prout shot him an angry glance before turning back to the sergeant. 'Anything else you need to tell me?'

'I don't think so,' the sergeant said, a frown forming between his brows as he thought about it. 'Though at a guess I'd say whoever had been handling the file, it wasn't within the last couple of months.'

Prout sighed. 'All right, I want a thorough search made for the other papers that should be in here. You'd better see to it yourself, just in case it's relevant to Greensall's death. We don't want any accusations flying about. I daresay the rest of the documents will turn up, it wouldn't be the first time a few bits of paper were put in the wrong file.'

The sergeant went to the door. 'Send a constable in here to take over from you,' Prout ordered, 'and hand him your notes.'

'Excuse me, sir, but at the same time, wouldn't it be worth checking whether any of the officers who were here in 1941 still have access to the files,' Deepbriar suggested.

'When I need your advice, I'll ask for it, Constable,' Prout snapped. He gave Deepbriar a jaundiced look once the sergeant had gone, then stood up, walking round the table to loom over him. 'You'll notice we do things by the book in Bradsea these days,' he said.

'As we did in the war, Inspector,' Deepbriar replied evenly, determined to keep his temper.

'I doubt that. I spoke to Inspector Stubbs at Falbrough, just for a friendly exchange of views, so to speak. He was quite concerned when I said you'd got into a bit of bother, he seemed to think it was out of character. According to him you've always been pure as the driven snow.' Prout's lips twisted, but the result could hardly be called a smile. 'I thought I'd ask him to take a look at your file, and see what Superintendent Ruggles had to say about your conduct while you were here in Bradsea. It seems he didn't like you much. Apparently you put your friendship for another officer before your loyalty to the force. You agreed to lie in an attempt to save Houghton from dismissal.'

'That isn't true,' Deepbriar said, struggling to keep his tone quiet and reasonable. So, Bob Houghton had been right, and the superintendent had indeed condemned him unheard. Prout had sprung it on him, maybe hoping to goad him into saving something he'd regret. He would need to keep his wits about him if he was going to clear his name and get that libel removed from his record. And it wasn't just for his own sake either; he owed a lot to Inspector Stubbs. He'd hate his new boss to regret finally securing his move to the CID.

'We interviewed Micky Hatherly,' Deepbriar said. 'And we obtained information that should have resulted in Greensall's arrest and conviction.'

'Come off it, Constable. At a guess, I'd say Sergeant Houghton was keen to show some visible sign of progress in the case, but at the same time he was desperate to avoid any real investigation into Greensall's activities, because he was on the man's payroll. So, he fabricated this story of a witness who changed his mind, and persuaded you to back him up. He was unlucky not to get away with it. If Greensall's body, or what was thought to be Greensall's body, had been found a little sooner he probably would have escaped scot-free.'

Deepbriar didn't reply. Prout had got it all wrong, but the man wasn't going to change his mind until he'd seen some solid evidence.

Prout bent so he was looking into Deepbriar's face, too close for comfort. 'Nothing to say? Look, why not come clean. It's not as if this makes any difference now. You were young, a bit wet behind the ears. Why not admit you made a mistake? You helped out a mate, that's all.'

'I did no such thing!' Deepbriar declared, half lifting from the chair, and fighting an overwhelming desire to punch Prout on the nose. He knew he wouldn't do it, but the conflict raging in his head reminded him that he probably needed a few more decent nights' sleep. 'With respect, *sir*, Bob Houghton was a good officer, and he wasn't involved with Greensall. And I'm going to find a way to prove it. I'll clear Bob's name and get that damned lie wiped off my record if it's the last thing I do!'

Prout gave an unpleasant laugh. 'If that's your attitude then maybe it will be, Constable. Your friend Inspector Stubbs won't like being made to look a fool. He said Ruggles must have made a mistake, but I reckon he'll be the one eating his words, not me. He may still think the sun shines out of your backside, but it's not an opinion I share.'

The young constable who had been on duty at the desk when Deepbriar first visited the station came in. Prout returned to his chair and the questioning went on.

'Tell me, Deepbriar, when did you last see Houghton?' Prom asked.

'Wednesday morning. I met him on the promenade. Since it was too early for anywhere else to be open we had a cup of tea at the place behind the bus station.'

'Perhaps you'd like to tell me why you've been looking for him ever since? Don't deny it, you've been all over the town making a nuisance of yourself.'

With an inward sigh, Deepbriar realized only the truth would do. He admitted that before they spoke on Wednesday he hadn't known that Bob Houghton's decision to leave the police force hadn't been voluntary. 'Until then I didn't know I was suspected of acting improperly, either. Once I'd had time to think about what I'd been told, I wanted to know more.'

'Was that all? I don't doubt you could have got some old crony back in Falbrough to bend the rules and check that for you. After all, I only had to ask your friend, Inspector Stubbs, to check the relevant page in your file.'

He met Prout's eyes. 'I suppose I could, but I didn't. And that wasn't the only reason I wanted to see Bob. There was something in the local newspaper on Friday I thought might interest him.' He told Prout about the STOP PRESS announcement concerning Micky Hatherly's disappearance. 'Before that, I hadn't really thought about looking into what really happened in 1941. And I suppose it struck me as a bit odd, him going missing just now. Anyway, I decided it would be worth having a word with Bob.'

Prout sent the constable to find a copy of the local paper. While he waited he flicked through the Greensall file. 'Why were you and Sergeant Houghton ever involved in this case? It was a CID matter and you were both in the uniformed branch.'

Deepbriar did his best to describe how things had been during the war, morale on the force at an all time low, with Chief Inspector Larch barely functioning. Some of the lower ranks, men like Houghton and Vorrman, had held things together, taking on cases that should have been dealt with by detectives, allocating manpower as best they could.

'The uniformed men were mostly working fourteen hours a day,' Deepbriar said, 'helping out the CID on top of their normal duties, because there hadn't been any replacements sent for plainclothes work.'

'So, who would have known about this case?' Prout persisted. 'If it was the major investigation you claim, it can't have been only you and Houghton.'

'It was Sergeant Hobday who first suggested that Micky Hatherly might know something useful,' Deepbriar said. 'Though he was Constable Hobday then. He'd lived in Bradsea all his life; I think he knew the family. He reckoned they were rogues to a man. Then there was Sergeant Vorrman; he got involved at the end. He was the one who spoke to Hatherly, on Superintendent Ruggles's orders, shortly after he'd agreed to help us. By then Micky Hatherly had changed his mind, though, and swore he'd never said a word about shopping Greensall.'

The constable returned with the newspaper. Prout read the relevant item, then he was quiet for a few moments, leaning back in his chair. 'All right, let's get back to what happened yesterday. You didn't search the body when you found it. Why not, when it was obvious that valuable evidence would be destroyed by the incoming tide? You may not have been on duty, but you're still a police officer.'

'I thought there was time to fetch help before the tide came in. If it hadn't been for the steps beyond the pier being missing, the body wouldn't have been left there long enough to get wet.'

'So it would surprise you to know the dead man had a hundred pounds hidden in his shoes.' Prout was watching him narrowly.

158

Deepbriar frowned, remembering the worn soles and the general down-at-heels look of Greensall's outfit.

'He didn't look as if he had that sort of money,' he mused. 'And why in his shoes? Was there any cash in his wallet?'

'I'm the one asking the questions,' Prout said. 'But I suppose it won't hurt to tell you he was carrying a ten bob note, and about a shilling in change. I think we can rule out robbery as a motive.'

'He was always a snappy dresser,' Deepbriar remarked. 'The body that was identified as Greensall in 1941 was wearing his gold watch, and there was a fair wad of cash on him too. He must have wanted to make sure people would believe it was him.'

'If all this isn't a figment of your imagination, I'd say his plan worked,' Prout said, tapping the file. 'So far, of course, we only have your word for it that the dead body belongs to Sidney Greensall. There's still been no formal identification.'

'What about the description in his record?' Deepbriar challenged.

'The birthmark does seem to make it fairly conclusive,' Prout conceded, with evident reluctance. 'One last thing. You claim to have made that emergency call from the phone box by the pier, but somebody from the council had to be called to let you out through the gates, which means you were the wrong side of them. Perhaps you'd like to explain that to me.'

Deepbriar told him about the boy who had opened the door to the phone box and handed him the receiver, then, at Deepbriar's instruction, dialled 999. He could see by Prout's face that he knew what was being left unsaid, and he did his best to look apologetic. 'The boy shouldn't have been on the pier, but he wasn't doing any harm, just fishing. I asked the lad for his address, if you want to confirm what happened, sir, but I told him he wouldn't get into trouble. If he hadn't helped me, the body could have been halfway across the North Sea by the time anybody else came by.'

'If I didn't have my hands so full I'd see the little beggar got what's coming to him,' Prout said sourly, 'but we'll let it pass. You'd better give the constable the boy's address before you go. That's all for now, Deepbriar, but I'll want to see you again, so don't go wandering too far. And if you manage to find your friend Houghton, or Micky Hatherly come to that, then you'd better get round here smartish.'

A few minutes later Deepbriar stood on the promenade, drawing in long breaths of sea air. He had never stopped to consider how it felt to be part of a police investigation from the other side, to know oneself a suspect in a case of murder. Almost the worst thing was being denied access to information which might help him with the case. Prout hadn't given away anything about the cause of death. And for all Deepbriar knew, by now the inspector had plenty of useful information about Greensall's life in Manchester.

Mary and Vera would be back from church and he knew he should go and reassure his wife, but he didn't want to be confined within four walls. He turned towards the pier, aiming to walk as far as the spot where the wrought-iron steps used to be, savouring the quietness; the rain had eased to a drizzle, but only the very hardiest of holidaymakers were out and about, the rest of them huddled into bus shelters and cafés, or wasting their loose change in the one-armed bandits on the pier.

Deepbriar stared past the loop of chain to the shingle below. A bright patch of colour caught his eye. There, apparently unbroken, lay a gnome in a red hat, its rosy cheeks glistening with rain, a broad smile on its plaster face.

A family came walking along the beach, Mum and Dad muffled up in thick coats and carrying umbrellas, the two children wearing raincoats and wellington boots.

'Excuse me,' Deepbriar called, 'I wonder if you'd be kind enough to bring that gnome off the beach for me? I think it might belong to a friend of mine.' He really didn't care if every gnome in Bradsea went missing; the investigation he'd taken on as a joke didn't seem funny any more, but he needed something to do. Thanks to Inspector Prout, his thoughts were running in circles inside his head, like mindless hamsters on a dozen spinning wheels. Thinking about gnomes might keep him from going insane.

'On the beach?' Miss Caldwell peeled off her gardening gloves and reached to take the gnome from Deepbriar's hands. 'How very strange.'

The earlier rain had drifted out to sea, but the clouds were thickening again, and Bradsea had descended into a state of gloom. However, Deepbriar's stomach was comfortably full of Vera's Sunday roast and two helpings of steamed pudding with custard, so he was feeling reasonably cheerful.

'Unlike the one I found yesterday, it hasn't been damaged, apart from those little gouges.' The constable pointed to a pair of marks on the back of the gnome's bright blue jacket.

'Do you think they're significant?' The woman's eyes lit up with a kind of fervour. 'If we can find the owner, we can check if these scratches were there before it was stolen.'

'Mmm.' Deepbriar stared at the two tiny

marks. There was something familiar about them, but he couldn't think what it was.

'I shall take a walk this very afternoon,' Miss Caldwell declared, 'and ask all the gnome owners whether this is theirs. Should I take it with me?'

'Best not,' Deepbriar advised. 'Ask them if they've lost another gnome, and if they say they have, then take down a description of it. Once you're sure you've found its proper home, we'll arrange to take it back.' He struggled to pull the remnants of the other gnome from his pocket. 'There's this as well, so if anybody mentions one that was pushing a wheelbarrow you'd better make a note of that too.'

'I certainly shall. I must say, this is all getting quite exciting. But why would anybody steal a gnome just to throw it away again?'

'Maybe they think it lowers the tone of Bradsea,' Deepbriar suggested, only half joking. 'There's nowt as queer as folk, so they say.'

'Very true.' Miss Caldwell suddenly looked awkward, twisting her gloves in her hands. 'I hope you won't mind me saying so, but you seem a little distracted. I know it's none of my business, but I couldn't help hearing all the gossip yesterday. People talk, even in the library, especially our regulars. I heard about that body turning up by the pier. You were there, weren't you?'

'Yes, I was the one who found him.'

She shook her head in evident distress. 'Oh dear, how unpleasant for you. People don't realize how dangerous the sea can be.'

'They certainly don't,' Deepbriar agreed, eager to get off the subject; he'd been trying to forget the Greensall business for a few hours. He put the gnome back in the shopping bag he'd borrowed from Mary, along with the remains of the other one, and shifted his weight from the single crutch he was using, on to his newly mended leg. It was beginning to feel as if it belonged to him again.

'You're getting along very well,' Miss Caldwell remarked, walking solicitously alongside as he began to manoeuvre his way out of her garden.

'It's certainly easier without the plaster cast,' Deepbriar said. He couldn't help it, try as he might, there was only one thing on his mind. 'Miss Caldwell, I was wondering if you could help me with something. You see a lot of people in your job. Is a man called Bob Houghton one of your regulars at the library? He works for the council. I knew him in the war, and he used to talk a lot about books. Not that we had much time for reading in those days.'

'Oh yes, I know Mr Houghton. He's a quiet soul, hardly says a word, but he's pleasant enough.'

'So would you know where he lives now?' Deepbriar asked eagerly. 'He moved a few weeks ago.'

'Did he?' She frowned little. 'He didn't tell us, which is rather naughty of him. Not that he's the sort to keep his books overdue. He's not a very communicative man. I understand he was greatly changed by the war.'

'You haven't seen him in the last few days, have you?'

'No. He's not been in this week. Oh, but I've just remembered. The last time I spoke to him we were talking about how noisy it is in Bradsea these days. He made some comment about being able to hear the mail trains going by in the middle of the night, but that he quite liked it. I thought it was odd, since he didn't live near the railway line.'

'I think perhaps he does now,' Deepbriar said thoughtfully.

Chapter Twelve

'You mustn't overdo things,' Mary cautioned.

'You're a good one to talk,' Deepbriar replied, pushing his chair back from the dining table. 'You were up and about long before me this morning.'

She smiled. 'Well, you did lie in until nearly nine again. The doctor's pills seem to have done the trick. You're much more like your old self.'

Deepbriar didn't contradict her. It was true the pills had made him sleep, but his head felt as if it was stuffed with cotton wool, and he was finding it hard to concentrate. He needed to get out of the house; the sea air might blow away the cobwebs in his brain.

'You have to see Dr Tordon again today,' his wife reminded him, whisking away the table cloth and folding it, before turning her attention to the tray of cutlery and condiments that would be needed for dinner. 'Once you've got that out of the way, I think you should take things quietly.'

'I don't need to go to the hospital for hours yet. Look love, I have to find Bob

Houghton. He's the only one who can help get to the bottom of the Greensall business.'

'You're on leave!' Mary rounded on him, a cruet in her hands and a touch of colour flaring in her cheeks. 'After that constable coming to fetch you yesterday, on a Sunday too, I'd have thought you'd have had enough of police work for a while. The idea is to get you fit and well. It was bad enough you taking on that business with the gnomes, but now you're behaving as if you were practically on duty. I could understand if we were in Minecliff, but this is Bradsea.'

'I know.' He looked up at her, realizing he'd have to come clean. 'Stop what you're doing for a minute, will you? Come and sit down. There's something I haven't told you.'

Mary stayed where she was, a dangerous light beginning to show in her eyes. 'I think I've heard enough about this old friend of yours. If I'd known what was going to happen maybe I'd never have agreed to come to Bradsea in the first place. You'd have been better off in the convalescent home with Sister Davies keeping you in order...' She broke off suddenly, as if noticing the expression on his face for the first time. Replacing the cruet gently on the tray she stood looking down at him.

'Thorny? What are you so worried about?' When he didn't answer, just pointing to the chair opposite his own, she sat down, reaching across the table to take his hands. 'You're scaring me now. Whatever's wrong?'

It was even harder than making his confession to Dr Tordon, staring at the bruise he'd left on her face and knowing what he was saying might cause her far more pain.

'It's all utter nonsense,' she said, as soon as he'd finished. 'Nobody would ever believe that you're a murderer.'

'You wouldn't,' he amended. 'But not everyone has your faith in me.' He had decided not to mention his rather crazy suspicions about his own guilt. Looking back on the episode after two night's sleep, he was sure the doctor was right; his encounter with Greensall's dead body had been the first time he'd seen the man in over sixteen years. The shock of discovering the corpse of a man whom he'd believed to be long dead, compounded by his exhaustion, was surely sufficient to account for his brief mental aberration.

'Prout's pretty much made up his mind; sending that constable and making it an order rather than an invitation was his way of letting me know he thinks I'm guilty. I can't sit on my hands and wait for him to solve the case, Mary. I've seen this sort of thing before. He's so sure it's me that he's not looking any further. In fact, I'd guess he's hardly bothering to consider the evidence.'

'Quite apart from knowing the sort of man you are, what about your leg?' Mary said sensibly. 'It was all you could do to get off the beach without drowning yourself on Saturday. How are you supposed to have killed a man while you were hobbling about on crutches?'

Deepbriar's lips twitched in a reluctant smile. He had always appreciated Mary's common sense. 'Prout hasn't told me that yet, but I'm sure he will once he's got it worked out.' He shook his head, sobering again. 'The trouble is, if he accepts that I'm innocent, he'll go after Bob instead, and in some ways that's even worse. At least I'm still a copper, and I've got friends in Falbrough who'll make sure I get a fair deal. Bob won't stand a chance if Prout decides he's the murderer.'

There were several streets of tightly packed terraced cottages built within earshot of the railway line, and Bob Houghton might be living in any one of them. Or he could be staying in one of the slightly seedy bed and breakfast establishments on Western Lane, some of them almost as dreary as Clifftop View.

Deepbriar limped along past yet another row of anonymous houses. He had knocked at the doors of several which displayed signs saying they had rooms to let, but he'd drawn a blank; nobody had recently taken in a lodger matching Bob's description.

Prout was almost certainly looking for Houghton too. Worried that the inspector might conduct a full house-to-house enquiry, Deepbriar was determined to find his friend first. He no longer cared what Prout thought about him. He doubted if the inspector would change his opinion even if he and Bob Houghton succeeded in solving the crime and presented him with a cast-iron case, served up on a china plate. There was another reason for finding his old friend quickly. If he ended up in custody, Deepbriar wouldn't even get the chance to talk to him.

Returning to Station Road, Deepbriar made a detour into a dingy shop which sold fishing tackle. He took an old tobacco tin out of his pocket, scrounged from one of Vera's guests, and came out a moment later to make his way to the address given him by the boy called Tom.

The door was opened by a youngish woman with her hair tied up in a headsquare. A strong smell of wet washing and soap powder accompanied her to the door, and her hands were wrinkled from long immersion in water.

'Sorry to bother you on washing day,' Deepbriar said, 'but I was wondering if I could see your son Tom. I'm a police constable, here in Bradsea on leave, and the boy did me a good turn the other day. We got talking about fishing and I promised to bring him a decent bit of bait.' He exhibited the tin. 'The least I could do, really.'

'You'll be the man who found that body,' the woman said. 'Tommy told us, though not till we'd heard most of it from the neighbours. It was all a bit of a shock.'

'Not a pleasant business,' Deepbriar conceded. 'Young Tom did very well; he seems a bright boy. Is he at home?'

'He'll be along at the railway yard. That's where he goes when he's not fishing. His Dad told him he wasn't to go to the pier any more.' A small frown formed between her brows. 'We didn't know he was breaking in, Constable.'

'Squeezing more than breaking. He didn't do any harm,' Deepbriar assured her. 'Don't be hard on him. He was quite a hero on Saturday, the local police never would have found that body before it was washed out to sea if young Tom hadn't helped me get to the phone.'

Her eyes widened. 'Our Tom a hero? You're kidding me.'

'It's true,' Deepbriar said. 'Even if you make him wait till the pier's officially open in the mornings, I think you should let him get back to his fishing. There's a lot of worse things he could be doing with his time.'

'Maybe you're right. I'll tell his Dad what you said,' the woman declared. 'Do you want to leave the bait with me? I'll see Tom gets it.'

'No, thanks. I'm going by the station,' Deepbriar said, slipping the tin back in his pocket. 'I'll give it to him myself.' He touched his hat. 'Sorry to have bothered you.'

He found the boy on a patch of cinders and clinker overlooking the goods yard, and handed him the till. 'Lugworms. Catch just about anything, they will,' he said. There was a handy pile of sleepers nearby and he sat down, leaning his crutch alongside. 'I told your Mum what a hero you were on Saturday, Tom, and she's promised to speak to your Dad. I reckon they'll let you go fishing again soon.'

'Really?' the boy beamed. 'Thanks.' He opened the tin to peer in, then pushed the lid on quickly.

'You have to store them in a tin with a few little holes in the lid,' Deepbriar pointed out, 'to keep them alive.'

'Right. Thanks,' Tom said again. 'You haven't got that thing on your leg any more.'

'No, the bones are mended. All I have to do now is build up my muscles again, then I can go back to work.'

The boy nodded. 'My friend Barry broke his arm once. He didn't stay off school the whole time, but he couldn't throw a cricket

172

ball for toffee, not for ages.'

They sat watching companionably as a goods train rattled by, followed a few minutes later by a local passenger service. 'I used to like watching trains when I was a lad,' Deepbriar said, staring at a pair of dilapidated old coaches on a neglected siding across the yard. Weeds grew high all around them; it was clear they hadn't moved for years.

'It's all right, but I like fishing better.' The boy's eyes followed where Deepbriar was looking. 'Me and Barry used to go and play in one of them, but there's an old tramp lives there now.'

'Chases you off does he?' Deepbriar asked idly.

'No, but he looks a bit odd. Sort of cross.'

Deepbriar was struck by a sudden thought. 'How long has he been there, this tramp?'

'I don't know. He wasn't there at Easter.' The boy was losing interest, gazing at the signal gantry outside the station. 'Look, there's another train coming. If we go up on the bridge we can get a better view. They don't let me go on my own, but it'll be OK if you're there.' He got to his feet.

'All right, I reckon I can manage the steps,' Deepbriar said, taking hold of the crutch. 'What does this tramp look like?'

'He's really skinny and he needs a hair cut.

173

And he's old.'

Deepbriar grimaced, knowing that to a boy of ten, his own sum of nearly forty years made him look ancient. It was a long shot, but nothing the boy had said ruled out Bob Houghton as the man living in the carriage. He'd seen tramps better dressed than his old friend. 'We don't want to get arrested for trespassing. How do we get to those carriages without being seen by the stationmaster?'

They lingered on the footbridge, getting covered in smuts when an express roared through, much to Tom's delight. Finally the boy was persuaded to show Deepbriar the way round the back of a row of dilapidated houses and through a bramble patch. A worn path proved somebody was still coming this way fairly frequently, though wild roses and nettles caught at their clothes and stung their hands as they pushed through.

'There, see?' the boy whispered. A panel at the end of the carriage had been removed, and an old bit of board stood propped against the gap from the inside. It didn't show until you were close. 'Come on,' he said, tugging urgently at Deepbriar's sleeve in an attempt to pull him away, 'I don't want him to catch me.'

'You'll be all right with me along,' Deepbriar assured him, grinning, 'I'm a copper, remember? And if he picks a fight it's only one leg that's not working too well, the rest

174

of me's all right. I can deal with a tramp if I have to.'

He reached up to the piece of board and pushed it aside. 'Anybody in there?' A stench wafted out through the opening and Deepbriar took a step back, almost knocking the boy down.

'Anybody there?' he called again, trying to ignore the overpowering smell. It couldn't be Bob Houghton living here amongst such evident squalor; some tramp had taken up residence, as the boy said. Deepbriar almost turned round and left, but then he squared his shoulders, wrinkling his nose. He had to make sure.

'Here.' Deepbriar handed the boy his crutch. 'Pass that to me once I get up there.' With the help of a milk crate to act as a step, presumably left for exactly that purpose, it was possible to grasp the frame of the carriage and heave himself inside. Here the smell seemed even worse. Among a variety of unpleasant odours Deepbriar caught the sickly whiff of decomposition, which made him feel distinctly uneasy. He took out a handkerchief to hold over his nose as he made his way along the corridor, looking into empty compartments, some of them still with seats, others full of rubbish.

The further end of the carriage didn't have compartments, but was an open space, like a proper room. Deepbriar had never seen anything quite like it, and wondered vaguely if it had originally belonged on some foreign railway line, or whether it had been built for royalty. Here there was no jumble, no mess. As Deepbriar approached he could see a chair standing against the side wall, and beyond that a cabin trunk. There was a rug covering part of the worn flooring. Some-body had made themselves comfortable here, everything was neat and tidy, and yet this was where the smell originated. A great cloud of flies rose, buzzing loudly in protest at being disturbed. Deepbriar was relieved to see that they had been gathered on a bloodstained newspaper package that lay on an ancient gate-legged table. One end of a mutton chop, turning green, stuck out where the paper was torn. That accounted for the odour of rotting flesh.

A bench seat ran along the further side of the carriage, and it was here the man had made himself a bed. Deepbriar steeled himself as he approached the still figure. The shape beneath the blankets looked so diminished he was sure the man must be dead. Two corpses within a week was a bit much, he thought, torn between sadness and an illogical feeling of guilt. This stranger had expired here, alone and uncared for. He'd probably suffered a stroke or a heart attack.

Deepbriar reached out a hand, and his

eyes fell on the row of books on a battered table at the end of the seat. A pair of blue overalls lay on the floor. His heart thumping, he pulled back the covers. As he did so, he distinctly heard a moan.

'Bob?' He leant down to view the man's face, and saw eyes sunk so far back that it was like looking at a skull. This impression was heightened by skin the colour and texture of yellow parchment, taut and dry over the facial bones.

It took Deepbriar a moment to be sure, so great was the change that had come over the man, that he was looking at Bob Houghton. He cleared his throat, and when he spoke his voice sounded unnaturally harsh. 'It's all right, Bob, we'll get you out of here.'

'Water.' The word was like a scratch drawn on paper with a dry nib.

Deepbriar looked around. An empty jug and a tin cup stood on the floor by his feet. He picked up the cup and went to lift the kettle that stood on the ring of a camping stove. He drained the few precious drops it held into the cup and brought it back, tipping the vessel with care so none was wasted.

'Fever,' Houghton said. 'Ever since Africa. You—'

'No need to talk,' Deepbriar assured him. 'I have to fetch help, but I'll be back. Just a few minutes.' Taking the cup with him, he threw his crutch through the gap in the side of the carriage and went down after it so fast that he landed on his hands and knees.

He had half expected the boy to be gone, but Tom stood pale faced among the brambles, the tin of bait still clutched tight in one hand, proffering Deepbriar's crutch with the other.

'Good lad,' Deepbriar breathed, getting to his feet. 'The man who's been living in there is very ill. I'm going to have to get help, which means telling the people at the station about him, so you'd better make yourself scarce. You don't want to get in trouble with your Mum and Dad again, or they'll change their minds about the fishing.'

But before the boy could obey a harsh voice came to them from across the tracks. 'Oi, what you up to? Stand still, you blighter, you're not gonna get away with it this time.'

Chapter Thirteen

'Nobody's trying to go anywhere,' Deepbriar called back, one hand pushing Tom towards the narrow path through the brambles, so he was hidden from sight. 'I'm a police officer. I've just found a sick man in one of these carriages. I need you to go and telephone for an ambulance.'

'You what?' The man, bearing the longhandled spanner which marked him as a lengthman, came hurrying over the tracks. 'Don't you go tryin' anythin' on me, my lad. I know all the local bobbies and you ain't one of 'em. If I'm making any telephone calls it'll be to the railway police.'

'All right,' Deepbriar said angrily, stepping out to meet him. A glance behind showed him the boy had reached the alleyway at the back of the houses. 'But if that man dies in the meantime, I'll see you answer for it. So, whoever you're planning to call, you'd better make it quick, or I'll go and do it myself.' He found he still had the empty cup in his hand. 'Before you go, maybe you'll tell me where I can get him a drop of water.'

'There's a tap just down there by the water tower, but I'm doing nothing till I've seen

179

this man for myself,' the man said stubbornly, heading for the carriage.

'Fine.' Deepbriar pushed the cup into his hands. 'You'll need this then. I'll be back in a few minutes.'

'Oi! Come back 'ere!'

But Deepbriar was already heading for the station buildings, hardly needing to use the crutch thanks to the adrenaline racing through his veins.

Having met Deepbriar twice before, the porter needed no persuading. 'I had an idea there might be somebody down there,' he confessed, showing the way to the station master's office.

'Why didn't you tell me when I came looking for him last week, then?' Deepbriar demanded.

The porter looked uneasy. 'Well, if it hadn't been for that other policeman asking after him, maybe I would have done. You told me you were his friend, but how would I know?'

'You say an officer came asking about him? When was that?'

'Wasn't long before you. Could have been the same day, I'm not sure. Not that he said he was a copper, but I could tell. He had a photograph of the man he was looking for, though it looked like it was taken a long time ago. Anyway, I didn't want to get the old chap into trouble. He wasn't doing any harm. It's hard, being down on your luck.' He shrugged. 'Wish I'd done different now, but how was I to know he'd get taken sick?'

'This wasn't quite what I had in mind when I said I would see you on Monday, Constable Deepbriar,' Dr Tordon remarked, coming out of the room where he'd been examining his new patient.

'How is he?' Inspector Prout demanded, elbowing Deepbriar out of the way in his haste. 'Is he well enough to talk?' Reluctantly, as soon as the ambulance was on its way, Deepbriar had informed the inspector that he'd found Houghton, and Prout hadn't wasted any time in getting to the hospital.

'Well, I don't know about that,' Tordon said. 'Mr Houghton is a very sick man.'

'I'm investigating a murder, Doctor. I don't have time for niceties.'

'Maybe if the doctor can answer a question for us, you won't need to bother Bob for a while,' Deepbriar put in. Prout glowered at him, but didn't protest as the constable turned to Dr Tordon. 'How long has he been ill, Doctor? Can you tell?'

The doctor's face split into its ready smile. 'An astute question, and yes, within a little I can give you an answer. He didn't get into that state in less than four days, which means he's been flat on his back since Friday morning, if not longer. It was lucky you found him when you did, Constable Deepbriar; he's seriously dehydrated. Another twenty-four hours and we'd have been too late to save him.'

'So, he wasn't up and about on Friday night, or early Saturday.' Deepbriar said, trying not to sound too triumphant as he eyed Prout.

'Very clever, Deepbriar,' the inspector said sourly. 'Shame you don't have the same sort of alibi, isn't it?' With that he turned and left, his metal-tipped shoes clicking loudly on the lino.

'Alibi?' Dr Tordon murmured, his thick eyebrows shooting up to his hairline. 'Are you suspected of something, Constable?'

'Evidently,' Deepbriar said glumly.

'Hmmph. Never mind, it's our little organ recital this evening. Handel and Bach are very good at cheering people up, I find. And I'd better take a look at that leg of yours, hadn't I, before Inspector Prout decides to put you under lock and key. But first you can have a word with your friend; he was asking to see you. Don't stay too long, he'll be needing plenty of rest.'

'The doctor said you wanted to see me.' Deepbriar looked down at Houghton. It was difficult to hide his shock at his old friend's appearance, even though he'd thought he was prepared for it. He'd never seen a living man look so emaciated.

'I wanted to say thank you,' Houghton replied huskily. 'My life's not been worth much these last ten years, but there's nothing like an encounter with death to remind a man what he's got to lose. I was really glad to see you.'

'Happy to oblige. It's funny to think I expected to be bored, stuck here in Bradsea,' Deepbriar said, his mouth quirking.

Houghton's bloodless lips sketched a smile in return. 'How did you find me?' he asked.

'Classic detective work,' Deepbriar replied, 'by which I mean a large dose of luck, and the help of a little boy who likes train spotting.'

'Good source of information,' Houghton agreed, his eyelids flickering shut.

'I'll come back in a day or two,' Deepbriar said, reaching to push aside the screen, ready to leave. 'We can chat once you've had some rest.'

'No.' A bony hand gripped his sleeve. 'They said there was a policeman here. A local detective inspector, no less. Am I in trouble? And why were you looking for me? You can't have known I was ill.'

'No, I didn't. But all that can wait,' Deepbriar assured him.

'Tell me now.' Houghton pointed at the chair beside the bed, essaying a death's-head grin. 'I shan't sleep unless I know what's going on. Come on, Constable, give me your report.'

'Just like old times, eh, Sergeant?' Deepbriar sat down. 'Here goes, then. To start with I wanted to talk over what you told me on Wednesday. You were right, I must have been pretty wet behind the ears back in '41. It never crossed my mind that we'd been suspected of helping Greensall. That story you told me, the note, and somebody arranging that you'd be kept occupied the night the black-market goods were being moved, it gave me a heck of a jolt. They took a lot of trouble to implicate you, whoever it was.' He grinned. 'To be honest, when I was here before, I thought you were Sherlock Holmes and Dick Barton all rolled into one. I wouldn't have believed you'd have fallen for the tale they used to get you out of the way.'

'I let myself get played for a total fool,' Houghton sighed. 'It was a long time ago, Thorny. I can't think of anything else I could have told you.'

'Maybe I needed to hear it all again, once I'd calmed down it bit. I was out on the promenade looking for you every morning, and when you didn't turn up I started asking around. That's when I discovered that you'd moved. And you seemed to have been pretty careful about telling anybody your new address.'

'Sweeping doesn't pay well. And I was fed up with that dump on Waterloo Road,' Houghton replied.

'That sounds reasonable. The trouble was, somebody else involved in the Greensall case has gone missing,' Deepbriar said. 'Micky Hatherly hasn't been seen in nearly a fortnight. His family are worried.'

'You can't seriously think that's connected to the Greensall case? Not after all this time?'

'I didn't, not at first. But on Saturday something else happened–' Deepbriar broke off, hearing a faint squeak from the other side of the screen, as if somebody had pushed the door open. He hitched his chair closer to the bed and lowered his voice. 'Before I say any more, I'm sorry, but I have to ask you this, Bob. Did you have anything to do with the death of Sidney Greensall?'

Houghton stared up at him, his sunken eyes fever-bright. 'Fair question. I didn't want Greensall dead. I wanted him humiliated, I wanted him made to look like the crook he was, so his posh friends would turn their backs on him. And then I wanted him sent down for the rest of his days. We'd been so near to getting him, Thorny. When his body turned up I felt cheated. You know all this.'

Deepbriar nodded. They had talked it over many times. 'I just needed to hear you say it.

You see, we got things all wrong. That man I found in the river wasn't Greensall.'

'What?' Houghton struggled to lift himself up on his elbows, a look of utter astonishment on his face.

There was a sound from beyond the screen, then with a squeal of unoiled wheels the thing was swung back, and Inspector Prout stood looking down at them both. 'Well, well, maybe you do have some ideas about detection, after all, Constable. Not only have you provided our friend here with an alibi, now, thanks to you, he's given what sounds like an honest answer to the very question I wanted to ask.' Prout gave them one of his unpleasant smiles. 'Doesn't do a lot to help you, though, does it? I think we'd better arrange another little talk, Deepbriar. Let's say this afternoon, at three. And don't be late,' he added, his expression suddenly grim.

Deepbriar stepped around the black maria standing in front of the police station. It was so highly polished he could see his reflection in the shiny black wing, and he grimaced as he noted how badly he was limping. Still, it was easier to push open the heavy door now he was only using one crutch.

He'd had trouble getting away from Mary; telling her about Prout's summons would have worried her. She'd wanted him to take her for afternoon tea at the café she liked so much, and had only been a little mollified when he assured her they would spend the whole of Wednesday together. It felt like a long way off; Deepbriar only hoped he was able to keep his promise.

He wasn't sure why Prout hadn't already placed him under arrest; the inspector seemed totally convinced he was the murderer. There was no concrete evidence, of course; how could there he, since he was innocent, but still he was uneasy as he stepped up to the desk and asked for Inspector Prout.

As he waited, two men came out of a side room. The first was getting on in years, his uniform stretched rather tightly over a large frame that was running to fat, while his head was as near to bald as made no difference; Deepbriar recognized him instantly. It was Constable Hobday, back from leave. As he opened his mouth to greet the man, Deepbriar corrected himself; it was Sergeant Hobday now. 'Good afternoon, Sergeant,' he said, hitching himself forward.

Hobday seemed not to hear, vanishing through another door to the offices at the back of the building. It was the other man who stopped to speak. He was younger than Hobday and wearing a dark-grey tailored suit which must have cost a pretty penny. With a welcoming smile he came across the room, his hand outstretched.

'Thorny Deepbriar! I heard we had you to thank for getting Greensall's body off the beach before it washed away. Good to see you again, Constable.'

Deepbriar shook Vorrman's hand. 'Chief Inspector. I understood you were based at Whellow, sir.'

'So I am. The town's grown so fast that most of our CID people are there these days. Bradsea's become a bit of a backwater, but when I heard the Greensall case had reared its ugly head again I couldn't resist coming to see what was going on. Are you all right? Nobody said anything about you being injured,' Vorrman added, looking enquiringly towards the crutch. He listened with apparent sympathy as Deepbriar explained.

'So, you're mending well. That's good.' The chief inspector nodded, his manner so friendly that Deepbriar could hardly reconcile him with his memories of the man he'd known during the war. 'Inspector Prout's expecting you. I've asked to sit in on the interview. I hope you don't mind.'

It wasn't a question any junior officer could afford to answer with a negative. Deepbriar gave a quick nod and followed as Vorrman led the way to Prout's office.

Perhaps it was Vorrman's presence, but Prout was subdued, and after a few questions about the way Deepbriar had happened across Bob Houghton in time to save his life, he seemed ill at ease, lapsing into silence.

'I'm not sure any of this is relevant to the murder of Sidney Greensall, Inspector,' Vorrman said. 'If there's nothing else you need to ask the constable I think he can probably go.'

The inspector looked less than pleased. 'I've been trying to get to the bottom of what happened in 1941, sir. It does seem as if the body found in the river was wrongly identified. That being the case, I want to track down Greensall's associates, but Deepbriar hasn't been able to give me any names.'

'I told you about Micky Hatherly,' Deepbriar put in. 'Haven't you found him yet?'

Prout glared at him. 'This isn't about Hatherly. There must have been others.'

'Greensall's right-hand man was called Gordy Thwaite. He used to train and manage a few boxers, and one of them became Greensall's minder.'

'Oh yes, I remember,' Vorrman said, 'Pug Parry. Thick as they come, but built like a gorilla. You should find more about both of them in Greensall's file, Inspector.'

Deepbriar watched Prout's discomfiture with something like glee, as he had to explain about the missing paperwork.

'I've had people looking for the stuff that's been mislaid, but nothing's turned up yet,

Chief Inspector,' Prout said, 'so anything you can add might be helpful.'

'I was only involved at the very end. I spoke to Hatherly, on Superintendent Ruggles's instruction, and the man denied that he'd ever given information to Sergeant Houghton or Constable Deepbriar.' The look he gave Deepbriar at this point appeared to be conveying sympathy. He turned back to Prout.

'You seem to be focusing too much on what happened sixteen years ago, Inspector. You're investigating a murder that happened a few days ago, not a suspicious death that happened during the war. When he was killed, Greensall was using the name of Masters. Perhaps his activities during those missing years were the catalyst for his murder. Don't you agree, Constable?'

'It's hardly my place to say, sir,' Deepbriar replied woodenly. In fact, every gut instinct told him that in this, at least, Prout was right. If it was as Masters that he'd been the target, why was Greensall murdered when he returned to Bradsea?

Vorrman grimaced, as if disappointed by Deepbriar's response. He turned back to Prout. 'Surely you're looking into the victim's recent movements? Haven't you got anything from Manchester yet?'

'Is this something we should discuss here and now, sir?' Prout asked, glancing in

Deepbriar's direction.

'Oh, I don't think we need to worry about the constable,' Vorrman replied, the slight smile on his lips not reaching his eyes.

'But according to Superintendent Ruggles he might have been mixed up with Greensall. At the very least, he'd been prepared to tell lies to get Houghton off the hook,' Prout pointed out. 'We have to treat him as a hostile witness.'

Deepbriar was ready to protest, but Vorrman gave him a warning look. 'Like everything else in this case, I'm not sure everything's the way it seems at first glance. I've got a feeling Deepbriar is on the side of the angels. I was thinking he might be of some use to us, since he was so close to the original investigation.'

'Too close, in my opinion,' Prout replied sourly. 'But if you're overruling me–'

'I wouldn't dream of it,' Vorrman said. He rose, going to open the door. 'Sorry, Constable, I think you'd better leave now. I doubt if we'll need to trouble you much more. Concentrate on getting that leg working right, eh?'

Deepbriar loitered, hoping he might get a chance to chat with Sergeant Hobday. As he stood there, his gaze roving over the inner office where the duty sergeant was talking into the telephone, he noticed a board on one wall. As well as several notices about recent changes in regulations, the sort of thing that he used to receive at Minecliff, there were also some photographs. It looked as if Hobday still took pictures of the station staff. Deepbriar was thoughtful as he turned away and struggled back out through the door.

He'd only gone a few yards when he heard somebody hailing him. Deepbriar turned to see Chief Inspector Vorrman. 'Glad I caught you, Constable. Why don't you join me for a drink this evening? I thought we might go to the Old Bull. I'll be there about eight, and I'm expecting somebody else you know to join us. We can catch up on old times.'

Deepbriar couldn't think of an excuse on the spur of the moment. It wasn't until he stood outside cousin Vera's that he remembered he and Mary had promised to go to the organ recital at the church. He turned, ready to go back and see if he could catch the chief inspector and explain, but then he changed his mind. This new Vorrman was a puzzle. Still, he was more forthcoming than Prout; the meeting in the pub might be illuminating.

Chapter Fourteen

'But I thought you didn't like Chief Inspector Vorrman? Didn't you say he and your friend were always at daggers drawn? And wasn't he the one–'

'Yes, I know, love,' Deepbriar said hastily, cutting Mary short before she got into full flow. 'And I'm sorry to miss the recital, but it's not easy saying no to a chief inspector, even when he's not your boss.'

'I suppose not,' she agreed reluctantly.

'I went to the bus station before I came home,' Deepbriar went on. 'There's a trip on Wednesday to those caves you were talking about. It leaves the promenade at nine-thirty and gets back at ten. It's all well organized: they stop for elevenses, we have a proper meal in a café before we visit the caves, then they give us another break for tea on the way back. I thought that might make up for missing this evening. What do you think?'

'It sounds quite nice,' Mary conceded. 'But I still don't see why you couldn't tell Chief Inspector Vorrman you weren't free this evening. You could have met him some other time.'

'Sorry, but it's too late now. Be a love and apologize to Dr Tordon and the vicar for me. Tell them I'll be sure to come next time.'

The Old Bull had been rebuilt since the war. It had become a large place, brash, noisy and too close to the pier. The bar was crowded when Deepbriar arrived. It wasn't the sort of pub he would have chosen for a friendly chat and a drink, but at least among so many people it was unlikely their conversation would be overheard.

'Evening, Thorny.' A heavy hand clapped him on the shoulder and he swung round to see Sergeant Hobday, dressed in a tweed jacket and brown flannels. He held a flat cap in his hand, waving it to waft air at his red face. 'It's been a long time. Chief Inspector Vorrman's already at the bar, we'd better go and tell him what we want or he'll be buying us a half of shandy.'

Deepbriar grinned. 'I'd say there speaks hard experience. As far as I remember, he never even bought a round for us outsiders during the war. I was a bit surprised when he wanted to meet me here.'

'He'll have his reasons,' Hobday said shortly, moving ahead to clear a way through the crush so Deepbriar could follow.

Vorrman greeted both men with a joviality that didn't quite ring true, especially after

Hobday's terse comment, but the chief inspector cheerfully ordered two pints of bitter and insisted on Deepbriar taking the stool he'd been using. After a few stilted remarks about the weather, the three men ran out of things to say, and Deepbriar began to wish he'd gone to the recital at the church after all.

'Are you still keen on photography?' he asked Hobday, since nobody else seemed inclined to break the silence.

'Yes, I do a bit. Not views. People, that's what I like. I had to give it up for a while,' the sergeant went on, 'you couldn't get the paper and chemicals during the war, but it's easy enough now. The local paper did a bit about me last summer.'

'When he was promoted, I suggested he could help us when we needed photographic evidence,' Vorrman put in, 'but he didn't like the idea.'

'It's a hobby,' the sergeant said. 'I prefer it that way.'

'I never found much time for hobbies myself,' Vorrman said, turning to Deepbriar. 'How about you?'

'I used to play a bit of village cricket,' Deepbriar said. 'I seem to recall you bowling a hat trick in the only match I saw when I was here before. You weren't too busy for that.'

'Cricket's different,' Vorrman said, his eyes

lighting up with sudden enthusiasm. 'I remember that game, first of the season. Notched up twenty-four runs, too; not bad considering I was last man in.' He pulled a face. 'Our headmaster was keen on the "manly arts", he had the idea that boxing would turn us into gentlemen.' He lifted his right hand, curling his long thin fingers. 'This was made for throwing a ball, not a punch. I used to get knocked down every time. Even after five years I could barely make a decent fist.'

'Where I went to school we did our fighting in the playground,' Sergeant Hobday put in.

'Same here,' Deepbriar said. 'Though there was one time when a cricket match in Minecliff turned into a bit of a free-for-all. The opposition's bowling knocked our best bat out cold.' He grinned at the memory. 'When the batsman came round he kept trying to smash the ball straight back at the bowler's head.'

'That doesn't sound exactly sporting,' said Vorrman, a little disapproving. 'Not to mention asking to be caught.'

'The bowler was too busy ducking.'

The subject of cricket kept them occupied for quite some time, then gradually the talk came around to police work. 'So, you're joining the plainclothes branch, Constable,' Vorrman said.

'I always fancied it,' Deepbriar admitted.

196

'As a matter of fact, I've been trying a bit of detection, in an amateur capacity, over these last few days, but I haven't got very far. Maybe you can help me, sir. I've been trying to work out why Inspector Prout hasn't arrested me. He seems very sure I had some part in doing away with Sidney Greensall. I reckon he thought I thumped him on the head with my crutch.'

'The possibility did come up, but he changed his mind. He didn't tell you?' Vorrman's mouth twisted wryly. 'Prout hates admitting he's got things wrong. We don't know much else, but we do know Greensall was dead before he was dumped under the pier. The time of death wasn't certain within an hour or two, but it was before the previous high tide. Of course, that doesn't rule you out completely, you might have had an accomplice, but you've become an unlikely suspect.'

Hobday buried his face in his beer, looking increasingly unhappy as Vorrman went on. 'I meant what I said to Inspector Prout during that interview, Deepbriar. I don't see why you shouldn't be kept informed, and if you can help us in an unofficial capacity then that's all to the good. Since Greensall had been living under an assumed name in Manchester for years, I still believe he could have brought his enemy with him. After all, he only arrived back in Bradsea on Wednesday,

I doubt if any of his old mates even knew he was here. Perhaps he was running away from trouble, but he didn't go far or fast enough. Either way, I see no reason for keeping you in the dark.'

'It's good of you to tell me this, sir,' Deepbriar said, his eyes on Hobday as he drained his glass, 'but maybe we'd better change the subject. Can I buy you another?'

'Let me,' Vorrman insisted, 'this evening's my treat.'

For another half hour they managed to avoid talking about the Greensall case. After that, Hobday refused a third pint of beer and left, pulling his flat cap on as he threaded his way out to the street.

I don't think I'd better have another either,' Deepbriar said, consulting the clock above the bar. 'My wife will be back any time now.

'Before you go, there are a couple of things I have to ask you, now the sergeant's gone,' Vorrman said. 'Are you really sure, hand on heart, that Sergeant Houghton wasn't tied up with Greensall during the war?' He silenced Deepbriar's protest with a lifted hand. 'I know he talked a lot about how evil the black market was. But be honest, Deepbriar, couldn't that have been a smoke screen?'

Deepbriar was quiet for a moment. He shook his head. 'No, Chief Inspector. I was with him when he thought Micky Hatherly was ready to turn Greensall in, and I'd never seen him so happy. I don't think he's that good an actor. And another thing I'm sure of. He was a very sick man last week. Whoever murdered Greensall, it wasn't Bob Houghton.'

'All right.' Vorrman shrugged. 'I'll take your word for it, but nobody else is going to. We need to find Micky Hatherly. Until we do, all of us who were in Bradsea when Greensall went missing are under suspicion. I don't want anything like that on my record.'

'You?' Deepbriar was surprised that Vorrman had come out with his concerns so openly. 'You were never implicated. Even Hobday had more to do with the case than you did.'

Vorrman stared moodily into his glass. 'Maybe. But I've not finished moving up the ladder yet, Deepbriar, and I don't want this business hanging over me. You've told me you'll be in Bradsea at least a week yet. Why don't you see if you can find out where Hatherly's gone? It's got to be worth talking to his wife, at least.'

'But I've got no authority here,' Deepbriar protested.

'All the better. That family close ranks at the first sniff of the law, but they might just open up to you.' Vorrman leant a little closer and lowered his voice. 'I can understand you not feeling too enthusiastic about helping Prout at present, but there's no reason why he has to know what we're doing.' He gave a self-deprecating smile. 'Like I said, I still have ambitions, and if that means pulling a fast one on Prout then I can't say it bothers me. And you might have a word with Houghton too, I've got an idea he could know something useful. You can contact me at home if you want. Hobday will tell you where. Think about it.'

'I'll do that. Goodnight, sir. Thanks for the drink.' Deepbriar picked up the crutch and fought his way out of the bar. He'd always thought Vorrman was a self-centred and cold-blooded fish, but this took the biscuit; obviously he was prepared to go behind Prout's back and muscle in on the inspector's case.

Feeling the need for solitude after the noise in the pub, Deepbriar crossed the promenade and skirted the crowd of people milling around the entrance to the pier, trying not to rely too much on the crutch tucked under his arm. When the plaster was first removed it had felt a more familiar part of him than his newly healed leg, and he was eager to shed this extra limb and be himself again.

It was quiet once Deepbriar left the crowds behind, and close to the shelter he paused to look at the sea; enjoying the way the coloured lights strung along the pier threw reflections on the gentle swell.

'Thorny.'

Deepbriar started, turning so fast he almost lost his balance. Sergeant Hobday stood in the shadow cast by the shelter.

'Sorry. I didn't mean to make you jump. I wanted a quiet word. I remembered how you always liked the promenade, I thought you might come this way.' There was a friendliness in his voice that hadn't been there during the time they'd spent in the pub. He came to stand beside Deepbriar, and the two men stood staring out at the ocean in companionable silence for a while.

'It's funny,' Hobday said at last, 'the way good things come out of a tragedy. Those few months, with you and the other youngsters at the station, all of us working long shifts, hardly getting a chance to grab a few hours sleep before we were back on duty. There was something special going on. We were never quite so much of a team, once you'd gone.'

'The Dunkirk spirit,' Deepbriar nodded. 'Don't forget Vorrman was there too.'

'I'm not likely to.' Hobday sounded suddenly tense. 'Listen, Thorny, if I were you I wouldn't stay in Bradsea too long. Your leg's obviously mending well, maybe you could be on your way home in a day or two.'

'Are you warning me off?' Deepbriar was

incredulous. There were several men who might want the ghosts of 1941 left undisturbed, but he hadn't dreamt that Hobday might be one of them.

'Not exactly. It's just better not to get involved with Vorrman. He's learnt to put on a public face, but he's every bit as big a bastard as he ever was, for all his smiles and his fancy manners. There's only one thing that matters to him, and that's how far up the greasy pole Detective Chief Inspector Vorrman can get, and never mind how many other poor devils he pushes off in the process. Don't trust him, and don't cross him. That's it, end of sermon.'

This, from the phlegmatic Hobday, was a long and impassioned speech, and Deepbriar turned, trying to make out the man's features in the uncertain light.

'I'm not as green as I used to be,' he said at last.

'I should hope not.' Hobday sighed. 'I'm wasting my time, aren't I?'

'I wouldn't say that. I'm grateful for the advice. Actually, there was a small favour I was hoping you might do for me.'

The sergeant immediately looked wary. 'I've only got a few months to go before I collect my pension, Thorny. I'm taking no risks.'

'This shouldn't upset anyone. Two things. Is Chief Inspector Vorrman the only officer still serving in Bradsea and Whellow who was here during the war?'

Hobday thought about it then nodded. 'Apart from me,' he replied. 'Thorny, I meant what I said. You'd be best to give him a wide berth. What was the other thing?'

'I wondered if you could let me have copies of a couple of your photographs.'

'You want to be careful, Constable,' Vorrman said, breezing up behind Deepbriar and reaching to open the door of the police station for him. 'If you spend much more of your time here we'll be finding you some work to do. Or has Inspector Prout asked to see you again?'

'No, nothing like that. Just a quick visit today, sir,' Deepbriar replied. 'I've come to have a word with Sergeant Hobday.'

'Oh? What are you two cooking up?' There was a mock joviality about his words that lifted the hairs on the back of Deepbriar's neck, but before he could think of a suitable answer Hobday was there, coming out from behind the desk.

'Constable Deepbriar asked me for a few photographs from the old days, Chief Inspector,' he said. He drew an envelope from his inside pocket, opening it to reveal a thick wad of photos. 'Here.' He held the first picture out so both the other men could see it. 'That's the whole gang of them, all the youngsters who came to our rescue after the bombing. There's young Thorny next to that redheaded lad, I can never remember his name.' He turned the photograph over. 'Pullen. That's it, Dick Pullen.' He shuffled that picture to the back. The next was another group, but this time nobody was in uniform, and there were nearly as many women as men.

'Sorry, I don't know how that one got in there,' Hobday said. 'That's the annual social, 1940. Before your time, Thorny, though you'll know a few of them.'

'I recognize Superintendent Ruggles. Not that I ever had much to do with him. I'd forgotten he was such a powerful-looking man.'

'Boxing champion in his day,' Hobday replied, 'pride of the County Police team. I've heard he still goes to the gym now and then to keep himself fit, even though he's retired.'

'Who's that?' Deepbriar asked, pointing at a man who had one arm tucked protectively around a blonde woman's waist.

'Brian Mason. Sergeant. He was killed by the bomb. I remember him getting his promotion before the war. That's his wife, of course. She was Annie Larch before she married, Chief Inspector Larch's sister.'

The next photograph was a portrait, the head and shoulders of a fair-haired man, a slight smile on his face. 'That's Chief Inspector Larch,' Deepbriar said. The resemblance to Mrs Mason was quite marked, but there was something about the man he'd known that was missing in this picture. It took him a moment to realize it was the permanently haunted expression Larch had worn during the whole of Deepbriar's time in Bradsea. 'He looks different. I suppose this was taken before 1941.'

'No. I took that a few days before he died,' Hobday said, turning the photograph over to read the note on the back. '8 October 1944. He does look different, you're right. He was working again by then, not just sitting behind his desk and going through the motions. We all thought he'd managed to put the bombing behind him. Mrs Mason had come back from Scotland, and that made a difference. She'd taken her two children up there, trying to get away from the war, I suppose, after her husband died. Brian was a good chap, everybody missed him. Same as they did Chief Inspector Larch.'

The door opened and an elderly couple walked in.

'This isn't the time or the place for reminiscences,' Vorrman said, sounding suddenly harsh. 'There are people here needing your assistance, Sergeant.'

'Of course, sorry, sir,' Hobday said. Bundling the photographs into Deepbriar's hand he retreated behind the counter. A young uniformed constable came in. 'The car's here for you, Chief Inspector,' he said, standing to attention as he held the door open.

'Thank you.' Vorrman waited, gesturing for Deepbriar to precede him. Once they were outside he turned briefly. 'Don't forget you're here to make the most of our bracing sea air, Constable,' he said. 'It's not good for you to spend too long indoors.'

Deepbriar watched the car carry Vorrman away and stood waiting for the elderly couple to leave, then he went back inside. Hobday met his look with an unreadable expression on his chubby face. 'What was that all about?' Deepbriar demanded.

'I suppose you never heard what happened to Larch.'

'Rosie told me he died.'

'He committed suicide. And Vorrman pretty much stepped straight into his job. At least, that's when he got made up to Inspector.' Hobday pulled a face. 'When Larch was fit and well he was worth ten of him, best CID officer I ever knew, bar none. And a good bloke, too.'

'Was there a reason for all these?' Deepbriar asked, half taking the big wad of photographs from his pocket.

'Camouflage,' Hobday replied. 'How would it have been if he'd asked to see them and I'd only brought the ones you really wanted? I told you, I'm taking no risks, not when I've only got a few more months to do.'

Chapter Fifteen

Deepbriar leant back on the park bench and went slowly through the photographs. Hobday was right; despite the long hours they had been good days. He lingered a long time over the photograph of Chief Inspector Larch. When he had known the man, there had been a permanent expression of pain in his eyes. When he was spoken to, often a full minute might elapse before he replied.

It would have been no surprise if Larch had chosen to end his life then, but why had he chosen to commit suicide three years later? The man in this picture looked at peace with himself, confident and happy. There was a half smile on his face, as if he'd just shared a joke with the man behind the camera. Yet within twenty-four hours he was dead by his own hand.

Deepbriar knew from recent experience that apparently well-balanced people could he pushed into committing suicide. It had happened in Minecliff only a few months ago; a woman who received a venomous poison pen letter had taken her own life, rather than face evil gossip. What had tipped Larch over the edge?

At last he pushed the photograph back among all the others. He picked out the two he had asked for, clear snapshots of Vorrman and Prout, and for good measure he added the only picture which included Hobday, showing him flanked by the two wartime sergeants, Vorrman and Houghton. Returning the other photos to the envelope Deepbriar slid it into his pocket, then he rose to his feet and hobbled off towards the railway station.

'That's him,' the porter said, pointing at the picture of Chief Inspector Vorrman. 'That's the one who came and showed me the picture. Right, was I? About him being a policeman?'

Deepbriar nodded. 'Yes. Though I'm not sure he was on police business.'

The porter gave Deepbriar a puzzled look. 'Should I have tried to help him then? I mean, the photograph could've been the bloke who was in and out of the yard, but I wasn't sure, so I said nowt.'

'I don't think it mattered.' Deepbriar showed him the one of the three officers, Vorrman, Hobday and Houghton.

'Well blow me! There he is again, and that's our tramp, though he's changed a good bit, poor devil. So, he was a copper too.'

'A sergeant,' Deepbriar confirmed.

The porter shook his head. 'Just goes to show. I was right about him being down on his luck. Doesn't look much like that now, does he, poor devil. Are you really a mate of his?'

'I really am,' Deepbriar replied. 'Why?'

'Because the station master's been talking about clearing his stuff out of that carriage. He reckons we'll be getting orders to put up a fence down there.'

'What will happen to my friend's belongings, then?'

The porter shrugged. 'On the rubbish heap, I shouldn't wonder, seeing he wasn't supposed to be in there. But if you wanted to fetch them I reckon I could square it for you.'

Deepbriar frowned. He wasn't sure what he could do with Bob Houghton's possessions if he rescued them, unless Vera would agree to store them in her garden shed. The books wouldn't last long in there, not if the weather stayed damp. He stumped the end of his crutch on the ground in frustration. 'I'll have to wait till another friend of mine comes down in his car. I've got no way of moving the stuff, even if I can manage to get it out of the carriage.'

'I'll give you a hand if you want,' the porter offered. He gestured at a small trolley. 'We can borrow that, as long as it's back before the morning shift. How about this evening?'

'I brought you some grapes.' Deepbriar put the paper bag on the bedside locker and sank wearily into the chair. Bob Houghton's hair had been given a short back and sides that was severe even by military standards. It accentuated the bony structure of his face, but although he was still desperately thin, his skin had regained a little colour, and his eyes weren't sunk quite so deeply into their sockets.

'Thanks.' The patient ran a hand over his head. 'Reckon they thought I'd got nits or something, damn cheek.'

'You look better.'

'My mouth's still dry all the time, but they tell me I'll live.' Houghton said. 'How's the leg? You look a bit bushed.'

'I'm all right. I was helping the porter move your belongings out of the carriage. It's all in my wife's cousin's shed.'

'That's good of you, thanks.' Houghton proffered the grapes. 'Here, have some of these; they'll help get your strength back. How's the detecting game, Sherlock?'

Deepbriar told Houghton about his drink with Vorrman and Hobday, and his later encounters with the sergeant. 'Did you know Chief Inspector Larch committed suicide?' he asked.

'I can't say I'm surprised,' Houghton replied. 'After the bombing he was in a mess.'

Without a word Deepbriar took the photographs from his pocket and sorted out the one he wanted. He put it into Houghton's hand. 'That was taken not long before he died.'

Houghton was silent for a while, then he looked up at Deepbriar. 'You think something fishy was going on?'

'I think Hobday does, but he's not prepared to talk about it.'

Houghton shrugged. 'Haven't you got enough to do without worrying about Larch?'

'Probably.' Deepbriar put the pictures away and explained why he'd asked Hobday for the photographs in the first place. 'The porter picked out Vorrman, no trouble at all. Evidently, the chief inspector was asking after you, pretty much the same time as me. I don't think he knew you were working for the council.'

'People don't see the man pushing the dustcart. Anyway, you know Vorrman, chief inspector or no, he was always a damn snob, wouldn't give a working man a second glance. The question is, what did he want with me?' Houghton pondered. 'And now he knows where I am, what happens next?'

'I suppose Prout must have told him you're here? There's no love lost between those two.'

'If he has, it's not going to be easy to get out of sight again,' Houghton sighed.

'So there was something behind your move.' Deepbriar hitched his chair forward and dropped his voice to a whisper. 'And don't try any eyewash about wanting a quiet life. I think it's time you told me the truth.'

'Honestly, I didn't come back here with anything more in mind than coming home. This is where I was born. I grew up playing on the beach, fishing off the pier. When I couldn't get a job I decided I'd rather starve here than anywhere else.'

'So what happened?'

'Micky Hatherly. I was down to living on handouts, and I almost bumped into him on the promenade one Sunday. He was out with his wife and his children. They looked so happy. I didn't mind that, not really, I mean, his wife and children having a good time, but it was him. He looked so damned pleased with himself. I wanted to wipe the smile off his face. It only took him a few minutes to ruin my life. If he hadn't refused to sign that statement it wouldn't have mattered when we didn't catch Greensall red-handed. We would still have put him away for twenty years, and right now I'd be looking forward to a decent retirement.'

Houghton looked sheepish. 'I only wanted to put the wind up him a bit. I started following him, letting him see me now and then, lurking around when he was on his way home from work, that sort of thing. I suppose I've changed, because I don't think he even knew who I was. Tell you the truth, I was fed up with it after a couple of weeks. My luck had turned. An old friend had put in a word with somebody at the council depot, and they offered me the job. But then Joe got involved.'

'Joe Hatherly? What's he got to do with it?'

'Unlike his son, he recognized me. And, also apparently unlike his son, *he* still has some very unsavoury business contacts. You know he used to run an illegal book? He's probably still involved with the same racket. Even if he isn't, he's got some dodgy pals. I got a heavy-handed warning to keep away from young Micky, and thought myself lucky not to get a good hiding. It taught me a lesson, and it helped make up my mind about getting out of Clifftop View.'

'So his vanishing act isn't anything to do with you?'

'No, Micky wasn't bothered. And all I wanted was to keep out of trouble. I'm not a copper any more, Thorny. Nobody pays me to risk my neck. I did what Joe Hatherly said and kept away from the whole lot of them, and as soon as I saw my chance I moved to a place where I didn't think Joe's friends could find me. That was nearly two months ago.'

'You say Hatherly Junior isn't involved in any of his father's criminal sidelines. Are you sure?'

'Sure as I can be from what I saw,' Houghton replied. 'Micky found himself a nice girl. Far too good for him, I reckon. It looked to me as if she was keeping him on the straight and narrow. She's not afraid of Joe. That helps.'

'So where has he gone, and why?' Deepbriar demanded. 'Somebody else is looking for him. Reading between the lines, I think Joe got roughed up by some heavies asking after Micky. But what's the connection? Joe admitted to me that Greensall's mob scared him, but they must be long gone.'

'Maybe not. Look what happened to Greensall. He'd been away for sixteen years. He must have thought he was safe, but within a few days of coming back to Bradsea he was dead.'

Deepbriar nodded thoughtfully. 'Chief Inspector Vorrman is thinking the same way. He asked me to go looking for Micky. What I don't understand is why he doesn't make it official. He's based in Whellow now, but he's got the rank to ask for an investigation to be made in Bradsea if he wants. Instead, he tells me some tale about the family being more likely to cooperate with me.'

'He could be right. It sounds as if he thinks they might know where Micky's gone,' Houghton suggested.

'Joe doesn't, I'm sure of it. No, I reckon

the chief inspector's got his own reasons. Something else struck me as odd too. He says that anything I learn doesn't need to be shared with Inspector Prout.'

'He always was ambitious.' Houghton sank back on to his pillows as a bell rang out in the corridor. 'That's the end of visiting time. It always goes so quick.'

Deepbriar rose, helping himself to one last grape. 'I shan't be in tomorrow, but I'll try to come on Thursday. That should give you plenty of time to see if you can come up with something useful.'

'I can tell you how and where to talk to Mrs Micky Hatherly without her father-in-law finding out,' Houghton said.

Before he could go on a nurse came in. 'Didn't you hear the bell?' she scolded, making shooing motions at Deepbriar. 'Visiting time ended five minutes ago. Come along now, our patients need their rest.'

'Fifteen, Woodside,' Houghton called after Deepbriar as he left. 'She's there every Thursday morning, nine until ten.'

The coach stood with its engine throbbing gently, already warm inside from the heat of the sun. Having secured places near the front and settled Mary next to the window, Deepbriar arranged himself in his own seat, wishing there was more room for his long legs. The sea shone brightly, and the promenade looked very inviting. He suppressed a sigh, trying to put himself into a suitable frame of mind; today was for Mary. The bruise around her eye was fading, but it was still there to reproach him.

As the coach climbed steeply up through the town, leaving the busy streets behind, they passed Wellington Rise. Deepbriar stared at Chief Inspector Vorrman's big white villa, standing out among its slightly less grand neighbours. A board caught his eye, outside a run-down boarding house. He frowned, recognizing the name. Where had he heard of the White Swan Hotel? Then he remembered. He'd been on the promenade. The young constable who had reported to Inspector Prout after he'd searched the newly discovered body had mentioned it. Sidney Greensall had been staying there.

Here was yet another coincidence. Or was it? Of all the places Greensall/Masters could have stayed, what had made him pick the shabby hotel right next door to Chief Inspector Vorrman's house?

'What's the matter?' Mary asked, glancing at her husband.

'Nothing. I'm fine,' Deepbriar lied.

'You're not still worried about what the Chief Inspector asked you to do, are you? I doubt if you'll find this missing man by looking out of the window.'

Deepbriar grinned, imagining the outcry

if he caught a glimpse of Micky Hatherly and tried to get the coach driver to follow him, instead of taking them on their sightseeing tour.

'This is supposed to be a day off,' his wife reminded him. 'Not that you ought to need a day off when you're on leave.'

'Sorry, love.' Deepbriar took her hand and squeezed it. 'For the rest of the day I'm not going to think about missing people, I promise.'

The coach was out in the country by this time. Up ahead a road sign pointed the way to Dummel's Bottom.

Mary's lips twitched. 'Not even missing gnomes?' She queried innocently, giving him a quick glance then applying herself to enjoyment of the view.

The day spent with Mary was a success. Deepbriar managed to keep his promise not to worry about Greensall or Hatherly, and they threw themselves into the pleasures of the coach tour. The evening culminated in a singsong on the homebound journey, and they both joined in enthusiastically. Mary's pure voice was much appreciated, especially during the rendition of *Swing Low, Sweet Chariot*, and as they walked the short distance home Deepbriar was inspired to tell her so. They crept quietly into the kitchen and fetched tea and biscuits to take to their room, stifling their giggles like children as they pushed the unwanted extra mattress out of the way and shared their contraband in bed.

As Deepbriar made his way to Woodside the next morning he couldn't help smiling to himself. The previous day had ended in the best possible way. Some crumbs had made their presence felt at what could have been a very inconvenient moment, but they had only served to cause more laughter. Life, Deepbriar concluded, was good. Even the looming threat of Inspector Prout seemed less important.

It was a cloudy day but the rain was holding off. Woodside was a leafy cul-de-sac, well away from the bustling centre of Bradsea. Deepbriar was content, enjoying his morning walk past its lush gardens, breathing in the perfume from the flowers and offering a silent benediction to the song thrush serenading him from the top of a nearby tree. For the first time in what seemed like at least a year, he was capable of something more like a stroll than a hobble. He was still using the crutch, but only for a little added security, very soon now he would be ready to leave it behind.

Number fifteen, Woodside, wasn't a particularly large house. Having arrived ten minutes before the allotted time Deepbriar was at a loss. Did Susie Hatherly come here to do the cleaning? One hour a week didn't seem very long. He looked around, wondering how to loiter without being obvious. Workmen had lifted a manhole cover and dug a trench at the side of the road, leaving their work guarded by a couple of wooden barriers.

Deepbriar stopped by the heaps of earth and looked down at the exposed pipe, then he leant his crutch against the hedge and took out the notebook Miss Caldwell had given him. He read through the details of stolen and damaged gnomes, then lingered over the pages on which he had subsequently written his own notes on the Greensall case. At least one net curtain twitched and he hoped he made a suitably convincing local government official. He would also have to hope the workmen didn't turn up.

At exactly nine o'clock, a woman in a bright yellow coat and a green beret came along the road and turned in at the gate of number fifteen. Deepbriar had never seen Susie Hatherly, but if this was Micky's wife then she wasn't what he'd expected. Certainly the way she was dressed didn't suggest she was there to clean the house. By the time he'd made up his mind to approach her it was too late; the woman had rung the bell, the door opened promptly, and she vanished inside.

Chapter Sixteen

Deepbriar watched the house in Woodside but nobody else arrived, scotching his idea that maybe this was to be a meeting of some women's group. From somewhere nearby he heard scales being played on a piano; it took him a moment to work out that the sound was coming from number fifteen. Was it possible Susie Hatherly was taking lessons? It was an unusual luxury for a young mother from the council estate. And Joe claimed she was short of money since Micky had vanished.

As he pondered, two men in working clothes appeared at the end of the road, each shouldering a shovel. Deepbriar put his notebook in his pocket and walked slowly past number fifteen. A sign in the window told him that his guess appeared to be correct. It advertised piano tuition, with reasonable rates, for all ages.

Remembering his days pounding the Bradsea beat, Deepbriar recalled that he wasn't far from the cemetery. It would be a good place to loiter without arousing the neighbours' suspicions. The scales stopped and the pianist started a reasonable rendition of a Beethoven sonata.

Careful to get the timing right, Deepbriar turned back into Woodside a minute before ten, and the woman in the yellow coat came out of number fifteen just as he passed the house. He slowed down, as if he was finding it hard to get along with his crutch. As Susie Hatherly came alongside, Deepbriar halted and leant against the garden wall.

The woman stepped around him, giving him a quick glance.

'Are you all right?' She seemed genuinely concerned, and her voice was a surprise, kicking the strong working-class accent of the other members of the Hatherly family. Deepbriar wondered if the information he'd been given was wrong, and this wasn't Susie at all. But then, Bob Houghton had suggested that she was too good for Micky.

'Yes, thank you,' he said, 'I've just come a bit further than I should, probably.' He gave a slight frown. 'Sorry, but don't I know you? Isn't it Mrs Hatherly?'

Her demeanour changed instantly. 'Who are you?' she demanded. 'What do you want?'

'Sorry, I didn't mean to bother you, but wasn't it your husband who played such brilliant games last summer? Two centuries–'

'Ohh.' She let out a long breath and smiled. 'I'm sorry. Yes, that was Micky.'

Deepbriar was in motion again, and she

adjusted her pace to his. 'You follow the cricket then?' she said. 'I can't say I remember seeing you at the matches, but I usually have my hands full with the children.'

'Of course. Isn't your husband playing this season?' Deepbriar asked, in apparent innocence.

'Not at the moment, he injured his shoulder.' The answer came too quickly; obviously she had her story ready. Maybe she had learnt to make excuses for his prolonged absence too.

'That's a nice house you've got there,' Deepbriar went on, glancing back the way they'd come. 'I like roads with trees along them, it makes you feel closer to the country.'

'We don't live here,' Mrs Hatherly said quickly. 'I'm taking piano lessons with Miss Foster.'

'Really? That wasn't you I heard when I was going by here earlier?'

'Probably.' She flushed. 'I'm not that good.'

'I don't know, I was quite impressed. It's been years since I played the piano, but I love to hear it.'

'Perhaps you should take it up again.'

'I play the organ in church sometimes, when I have time.'

They chatted easily as they made slow progress towards the council estate, Deepbriar careful to keep his pace slow. She wasn't a bit what he'd expected, and apart from that first abrupt reaction when he'd confronted her, she showed no further sign of nerves. If she was really at her wits end for lack of money, not to mention being worried about her missing husband, she was hiding it pretty well.

Deepbriar didn't notice the elderly woman coming towards them until it was too late. Grey-haired and a little bent, she nevertheless walked quite briskly, and she smiled a greeting as she approached. 'Constable Deepbriar, how nice to see you.'

'Mrs Guest, how are you?' It was too late to do anything to salvage the situation. Susie Hatherly was looking at him as if he'd just crept out from under a stone.

'Your injuries are obviously still troubling you,' the old lady went on, oblivious to the sudden chill in the atmosphere. She turned to the younger woman, 'It's quite a privilege having such a hero in our midst, isn't it?' When Susie Hatherly didn't reply, she looked back at Deepbriar. 'I hope you're continuing the good work. How is the investigation going?'

'Well, I'd hardly call it an investigation,' Deepbriar replied quickly, 'Just looking into a few missing garden ornaments. I can't say I've made much progress. I am on leave, remember.'

'Of course. Well, I must get on. Good morning.'

As the old woman left, Deepbriar turned back to his companion, only to see her hurrying away. 'Mrs Hatherly!' He went after her, as fast as he could, his leg beginning to protest as he attempted to break into a lopsided run. She stopped and turned on him.

'Don't you come near me,' she said furiously. 'Won't you people ever leave us alone?'

'Mrs Hatherly, it's not like that. It's true I'm a policeman, but I'm here on leave, I'm not involved with the local force. I used to know Micky, and when I saw the piece in the paper about him going missing, I visited your father-in-law. Joe's worried, you must be too. I thought maybe there was something I could do to help.'

'There is,' she said, tight-lipped. 'Stay away from me.'

Deepbriar trailed disconsolately towards cousin Vera's, his cheerful mood forgotten. It was too late to wish he'd never shown an interest in the missing gnomes. The damage was done, thanks to Mrs Guest. He made a short detour to Miss Caldwell's house; he would tell her he had more important things to do with his time.

'Constable Deepbriar!' Miss Caldwell opened the front door wide to usher him inside. 'You'll join us for elevenses, won't you?'

'Well, I wasn't meaning to stop–' he began.

'Oh, please spare us a few minutes, if you can,' the woman begged. 'This is most fortuitous, you've come at the perfect time. There's somebody here I'd like you to meet; she's a near neighbour of mine.'

With serious misgivings, Deepbriar went in, expecting to be confronted by another of Miss Caldwell's gnome-owning pensioners. Instead, he found himself shaking hands with a rather pale fair-haired woman, who looked instantly familiar to him. 'Mrs Mason!'

'You know me?' She raised her eyebrows in surprise. 'But I was in Scotland when you were stationed in Bradsea, Constable, and I have to say I don't recall meeting you since.'

'No, we never met.' Deepbriar returned her smile, and obeyed Miss Caldwell's invitation to take a seat. 'I saw your photograph, just a couple of days ago.' He paused. 'I couldn't help noticing how much you look like your brother.'

A shadow passed briefly over her face. 'Yes, David and I were always alike. If you've been looking at photographs I suppose that means you've seen Sergeant Hobday.'

'That's right. There aren't many of the old crowd left.'

'I was telling Mrs Mason how you'd come to my aid,' Miss Caldwell said. 'I know garden gnomes aren't very valuable, but I still think the local police ought to have tried to find out what's been going on.'

'Well, actually that's why I'm here,' Deepbriar broke in apologetically. 'I'm sorry, I've done my best, Miss Caldwell, but I haven't made any real progress. I'm not sure there's anything more I can do.'

'I quite understand,' Miss Caldwell replied, handing him a cup of tea. 'There are far more important things in life than gnomes. It was good of you to try. And now Mrs Mason has something she wants to ask you.' She stood up, the teapot in her hand. 'I shall go and make a fresh pot and cut more fruit cake.' She rested her other hand briefly on Mrs Mason's shoulder. 'Call me when you're finished, dear.'

Mrs Mason seemed about to protest, then she smiled. 'Thank you, you're very kind.'

'Is this anything to do with what's been going on in Bradsea over the last few days?' Deepbriar asked, although he could see no way the discovery of a body on the beach might concern Mrs Mason.

The woman was looking at him uncertainly, as if not sure what to say. 'In a manner of speaking. Constable Deepbriar, before I say any more, I have to ask that, whatever happens, you promise not to tell anybody else about this, not without my express permission. There's something I've kept to myself far too long, and I need to get it out of my system.'

He was a little alarmed. 'Maybe it's a priest you want, Mrs Mason, rather than an off-duty policeman. If this involves a crime–'

'It does, but I have no information that would be helpful in any ongoing investigation.' She paused, then apparently made up her mind. 'I suppose the only thing I can do is trust you to be discreet. I've been going over and over this in my head ever since I heard Sidney Greensall's body had been found. It's about my brother, David. Chief Inspector Larch. Perhaps you've heard that he was supposed to have killed himself. Has anyone told you how he died?'

Deepbriar shook his head. 'No.'

'His body was found at the bottom of a cliff, twenty miles from here. He'd apparently driven there in a police car, which he left standing nearby, and leapt to his death. Based almost entirely on one piece of evidence, the coroner decided that he had committed suicide.'

'What evidence?' Deepbriar asked, an uneasy feeling squirming in his stomach.

She gave him a penetrating look. 'There was a note in the car. It was very short, a few words of apology, and his signature. Everybody knew he'd been ill after the bombing. He was there, at the police station, you know, when the explosion took place. He'd been out working on a case, and he was a few minutes late getting back. If he'd taken just a few more steps he would have been injured, maybe killed, but he was outside the front door, and the walls of the old part of the building are very thick. He escaped with barely a scratch.' Mrs Mason sighed. 'I sometimes thought that made it even harder for him.'

'Sergeant Hobday told me your brother had recovered. That by the time of his death he was working again.'

'He never left work,' the woman said, looking at him in surprise. 'I felt quite guilty about it. If I hadn't been so busy dealing with my own loss, I might have done more for him, made him rest perhaps, or insisted that he ask for treatment. I thought his colleagues didn't understand how sick he'd been.'

'That's not how it was,' Deepbriar replied. 'Everyone at the station knew he wasn't well, but if he'd once gone on the sick list with – well, with mental problems – there's a good chance it would have been the end of his career. While I was there, nearly every man on the Bradsea and Whellow force was working extra hours to cover for him. They all believed that he'd recover, given time.'

'I didn't know.' She stared unseeingly across the room, looking back into the past. 'It's true, by the time I came home he was a lot better, and when I moved in to keep house for him it was almost like old times. Not that any of this makes any difference now.'

'You were telling me how he died,' Deepbriar prompted gently.

'Yes.' Mrs Mason straightened. 'In all these years I've never told anybody this. The verdict was wrong, Constable. David didn't commit suicide. And since he's hardly likely to have left that note in his car and then fallen off the cliff by accident, I think it was murder.'

On Thursdays, the visiting hour at the hospital was during the evening, between seven and eight. Deepbriar ate his meal quickly and arrived breathless at Bob Houghton's bedside at seven-thirty, bringing along a bad case of indigestion.

'About time,' Houghton grumbled. 'Have you spoken to Susie Hatherly?'

'Yes, and much good it did me,' Deepbriar replied, equally bad-tempered. He related a quick summary of the encounter. 'You'd better tell me where she lives, I can't keep waylaying the woman in the street.'

'I thought it might be best to keep away from her father-in-law,' Houghton said, taking Deepbriar's proffered notebook and pencil to write down the address. 'He might turn nasty, particularly if he thinks you're looking into his shady business deals.'

'I'll risk that,' Deepbriar replied. 'Did you ever meet Mrs Mason, Chief Inspector Larch's sister?'

'Yes, of course. I didn't exactly socialize with the Chief Inspector, but Brian Mason was a good friend of mine. I went to their wedding.'

'Would you say she was the hysterical type?' Deepbriar asked. 'I met her today, and she didn't strike me that way, but after the things she told me, I did wonder.'

'I wouldn't have thought so, but I've not seen her in years. People can change. Does this have something to do with the Greensall case? What's she been saying?'

'That her brother's death wasn't suicide, despite the fact that a note was found at the scene. The verdict was based on that one piece of evidence. According to Mrs Mason there was no proper investigation.'

Houghton's brow furrowed. 'So what exactly does she think happened? Is she saying the note isn't genuine?'

'It was in his handwriting. She gave evidence at the inquest to confirm that much. But it was just a scrap of paper with a few words scribbled on it.' Deepbriar took out his notebook and read aloud. *There's no other way, I'm sorry.*

'That was it?'

'Apart from his signature, yes. The paper

was ripped roughly across, as if it was the bottom of a larger sheet. She thinks it was torn from a note he'd written for some completely innocent reason, maybe days or even years beforehand.'

'But he'd not been well; there's no accounting for what a man will do–'

Deepbriar shook his head. 'You saw the picture Jack took in 1944. Larch was pretty much recovered. His sister and her children were living with him, he appeared to be happy. According to what Mrs Mason has told me, the verdict of suicide was a load of baloney.'

'Bloody hell, Thorny,' Bob Houghton breathed. 'Are you sure about this?'

'The night before he died, Chief Inspector Larch told Mrs Mason that he was reopening a case from 1941. He said there'd been a grave miscarriage of justice. She doesn't recall all the details, but he told her a good officer had been forced to resign for something he didn't do. And he said that was only the tip of the iceberg. Larch had grave suspicions about another man, somebody who'd been at Bradsea a long time, and who'd been misusing his position to feather his nest.' Then he dropped his bombshell. 'He might even be implicated in a murder.'

'Of course he didn't name names,' Houghton said, rubbing a hand over his cropped hair in frustration. 'Why the blazes did she wait all this time before she told anybody?'

'She was afraid,' Deepbriar said simply. 'Mrs Mason had two young sons. Her husband was dead, and now she'd lost her brother. She wasn't prepared to risk anything else happening to her family.'

'So why talk now?' Houghton wanted to know.

'Her boys have grown up. One of them's with the Metropolitan Police, the other's in the RAF. But it was only because Miss Caldwell mentioned me being here on leave that she made up her mind to speak about it.'

'What does she think you can do? I mean, no offence, but you're hardly the flipping chief constable!'

'Thanks for reminding me,' Deepbriar said sarcastically. 'She had heard about Greensall, and me being the one who found him. For some reason that brought it all back to her, the things her brother had told her. Maybe he mentioned Greensall's name, and she made the connection subconsciously.'

Deepbriar chewed on his bottom lip. 'What I need is a senior officer who can be trusted, but I only know Prout and Vorrman.'

'Prout wasn't here in 1941,' Houghton pointed out, 'so at least we can be sure he wasn't the one selling out to Greensall.'

'No, but the man's convinced I'm implicated in Greensall's death. I doubt if he'd honour Mrs Mason's request for secrecy. If I went to him there's no guarantee he wouldn't immediately spread the story round the whole station.'

'Do you think it's Vorrman?' Houghton asked quietly. 'He was always a bastard. It doesn't seem likely though; he's so ambitious. Getting caught up with Greensall would have been a huge risk.'

'I don't know,' Deepbriar replied. 'The only people who are still on the force are Vorrman and Hobday. We know Vorrman was asking around, looking for you, though we don't know why. The only other suspect I can come up with is Superintendent Ruggles. I know he's retired, and I heard he moved out of that big house of his, but he's only gone as far as Whellow.'

'That was when his wife died.' Houghton shook his head. 'He was in command of the whole of the Whellow and Bradsea force; he can't have been hard up. Anyway, his wife was really well off. The pair of them were the focus of Bradsea society, the centre of attention. I don't think he'd have been fool enough to get involved with the likes of Greensall.'

'So, does it have to be a copper we're looking for? Maybe Mrs Mason's got that bit wrong,' Deepbriar suggested.

'You told me Greensall's file had been rifled,' Houghton reminded him. 'And back in '41 the note was planted under my locker. How could anybody outside the force have done that?'

Deepbriar sighed. 'Round in a circle and back where we started. When you think about it, that puts Ruggles out of the running, because he wouldn't have had access to Greensall's file once he retired. I don't know what I can do, Bob. Unless I wait until I get back to Falbrough and tell my boss what Mrs Mason told me; I'd trust him to do the right thing. There'll be hell to pay, of course.'

'Yes, and that being the case you'd better be careful. You're likely to be the one with the toasting fork pricking your backside,' Houghton cautioned.

Lowering clouds brought darkness early and there was a brisk breeze blowing. Deepbriar took the quickest route to cousin Vera's, down the alley that would bring him to her back garden. The path ran between high walls, overhung by trees. There was only one streetlight, spilling a small pool of brightness at the far end; it did nothing to illuminate the uneven surface of the alleyway.

Deepbriar thought nothing of it when two men turned in to the alley and started towards him. They came hunched into the upturned collars of their coats, hats pulled low.

It wasn't until he heard the sound of more

footsteps approaching from behind him that Deepbriar began to feel vaguely uneasy. He glanced round. There was another man, big and bulky against the faint lights showing from the street, and as Deepbriar turned to look at him he increased his pace. This galvanized the two figures at the other end of the alley into action. They began to run.

Chapter Seventeen

Deepbriar thought briefly about rushing the man approaching alone from the direction of the street, wondering if he could get past him. He abandoned the idea. Running wasn't an option, his leg muscles simply weren't up to it yet. Instead, he stepped into the darkest shadow, setting his back to the wall and lifting the crutch in both hands, wielding it like a medieval quarterstaff. The two men were coming fast, half-crouching like a pair of bare-knuckle boxers, while the third, a looming threat, had slowed again, maybe thinking he wouldn't be needed. He was the only one who appeared to be armed, with a stout walking stick he was holding across his body.

Getting in the first blow, Deepbriar caught one attacker across the ribs, knocking him sideways and forcing a grunt of pain from his lips. The man staggered and collided with the second, who cursed and half fell against the opposite wall.

Despite this early triumph Deepbriar knew there was no hope of holding off all three of them. The man who had arrived alone was still approaching, very slowly, tapping the stick on his gloved hand. A large man this, more than Deepbriar's match for size, his face totally invisible, as if he had a scarf wrapped around it under his hat. He was almost within range, the stick swinging high.

Deepbriar countered the blow with the crutch, the two wooden shafts crashing together, then as he wrenched his makeshift weapon to the side the walking stick slid up it, the tip grazing his skull as it knocked off his hat. Meantime, another man ducked in and landed a stinging punch on Deepbriar's ribs.

With a dexterity born of desperation, the constable brought the crutch round and thrust the handle at this man's face, following through so the bottom end swept towards the big man. As he ducked away Deepbriar sent the crutch jabbing in, gratified to hear the whooshing outrush of breath as it connected with his solar plexus.

Deepbriar glanced around. No convenient passer-by had appeared. The alleyway remained deserted apart from the four of them. He had gained a brief respite, but already the three were regrouping. There was only one slim chance of escape; above the top of the wall was the bough of a tree, thicker than his thigh. It was only a foot out of reach, an easy jump for a man who had the full use of both his legs.

There was no sound but the harsh breathing of the man he'd winded, who was already moving in again. 'Come on, you fools,' he whispered hoarsely, as he raised the stick, 'get hold of him.'

One of the men gave a low chuckle, evidently relishing the constable's predicament. 'Whatever you say, mate,' he said, bunching his fists and rushing to the attack.

Deepbriar made a feint with the crutch at head height, then abruptly swept it low, tripping the man who had laughed and making the other two dodge out of range. That earned him just enough time and space to make his attempt. Grasping the shaft close to the tip he swung it up into the tree. He twisted it and tugged, relieved to find that the grip had caught fast.

Turning, Deepbriar hauled himself up into the tree, his boots thudding against the wall and seeking a purchase on the bricks. He gasped as the walking stick dealt a solid thump to his back, but it didn't stop his upwards motion and a second later he'd swung himself on to the top of the wall. A bruising blow landed on his calf, and he kicked backwards with all his strength, feeling a savage joy as his boot connected with something soft and yielding.

Deepbriar climbed higher into the tree, not pausing until he was well out of range. He leant against the trunk, with the crutch held ready to repel anyone foolish enough to try to dislodge him.

'After him!' The grating whisper was venomous and urgent. Deepbriar couldn't make out much down below, but he saw the pale blur of a man's face moving closer, and guessed the other two were hoisting him on to the wall. Deepbriar made a sharp jabbing thrust with the crutch. This brought a yelp and the man dropped back to the ground. Curses flew, followed by a muttered argument.

For the moment Deepbriar was out of harm's way, but it was only a matter of time. Once his assailants worked out that all they had to do was climb the wall at a little distance and work their way from either side, it would all be over. Deepbriar considered his options. In all his years in the force, he had never had occasion to use his whistle to summon help; it was no use to him now, lying on his desk in Minecliff's police house. Still, making a noise seemed like a good idea. He pursed his lips and produced a blast that, while it wasn't a patch on the Acme Thunderer, was more than enough to alarm the men below.

They swore, staring up at him, two of them made visible by the dim pallor of their faces, the third no more than an outline and somehow far more menacing. He stood motionless, as if calculating his next move.

239

The sudden cold Deepbriar felt down his spine may have been a trickle of moisture from the earlier rain, dripping off the leaves overhead. Then again, it might have been the realization that the faceless man trying to find a way to dislodge him from his perch was probably a murderer.

Suppressing a shiver, Deepbriar drew in a deep breath. 'Police!' he bellowed, at the top of his not inconsiderable voice. For good measure he followed that up with another shrill whistle.

'Strewth!' One of the faces vanished; a man was edging towards the street, as if he was planning to leave.

A larger shadow moved to cut him off. 'Shut him up! That's what I'm paying you for!' The big man still had the presence of mind to keep his voice down, but it sounded as if he knew he was losing control of the situation.

Deepbriar whistled again, delivering a third penetrating blast from between his teeth. 'Police!' he shouted again. To add to the noise and confusion he beat the crutch down so hard against the bough beneath his feet that he thought he heard the sound of splintering wood.

From the house at the top of the garden he'd invaded came the sound of a door opening. A shaft of light spilled across the lawn and a man's voice called sharply.

'What's going on out there?'

'Climb on the wall where he can't reach you.' The leader of the assault hissed furiously. 'Take him from both sides–'

'Come off it,' another of the attackers whined. 'You never said he was–'

'Shut up, you fool!' the big man rasped, even as Deepbriar yelled yet again. It was enough. The sound of running feet echoed from the high wall as two of his attackers took off.

For several seconds the large man remained beneath the tree, an indistinct darker shadow among many. Deepbriar stared down, but he could make out nothing that might help him to identify the now silent figure. He braced himself, ready to jump; the odds were considerably shorter now. It was too good an opportunity to miss.

'Anybody there?'

Deepbriar had forgotten Vera's neighbour, and the sudden call made him start. He peered into the garden and saw the wavering beam of a torch advancing across the lawn. When he looked back into the alley it was to see the last of his assailants marching briskly away, the stick tapping at each stride. In no time at all he turned the corner into the street and was gone.

Down in the alley, only Deepbriar's hat, lying in a muddy puddle, gave any hint that something out of the ordinary had taken place. The constable waited, concealed by the tree's thick foliage. He felt uncomfortably like a criminal; he'd done nothing like this since he'd gone on scrumping raids as a child. A few minutes later he breathed a sigh of relief when the householder went indoors, shutting the back door and leaving the garden dark and silent.

Deepbriar dropped the crutch then lowered himself to the top of the wall. From there it wasn't too hard to reach the ground, though he swallowed an involuntary yelp as various bruises made themselves felt. He picked up the crutch and rescued his hat, then headed as quickly and quietly as he could to cousin Vera's. Fastening the gate behind him he limped up the path.

Taking refuge in the scullery, Deepbriar inspected the damage. Apart from some scratches to his face, bestowed upon him by the friendly tree, and a few sore spots thanks mainly to the large man's stick, he had escaped unhurt. The same couldn't be said of the crutch, which would never support anybody's weight again. It was only when he saw his trousers that Deepbriar let out an audible groan; they must have caught on the branch. One leg was ripped from knee to ankle. They had been his best flannels, and he doubted if even Mary's skills with a needle could save them. Sadly, he reflected that this would probably mark the end of their recent domestic bliss.

Next morning Deepbriar set out as early as he dared; that wasn't until well after breakfast, since he was trying to keep on the right side of his wife. It was hard to judge exactly where he stood with Mary; he had decided not to tell her about his adventure the night before, concocting an elaborate tale that accounted for the state of his clothes and the darkening bruises, most of them fortunately hidden from the general view. His wife had heard him out without comment, and inspected the ripped trousers with a sigh, and an unreadable expression on her face.

His reluctance to confess wasn't entirely due to his wish to protect Mary from an unpleasant truth. The incident had left him feeling oddly embarrassed. Deepbriar didn't want to have to share his fears with anyone, acknowledging that while they were more logical than the night terrors he'd been suffering, they were somehow just as personal. Even after the hired help had gone, that large bulky figure standing in the shadows under the tree had been undeniably menacing.

It was clear that Mary was looking forward to leaving Bradsea. She had stated more than once that Dr Tordon would surely give him a clean bill of health on his next visit, and that they didn't even need to wait for Charles to fetch them, as they could catch a train to Falbrough, then the bus to Minecliff.

Getting back to a reasonable degree of fitness suddenly seemed much more important. Despite his bruises Deepbriar decided to try walking without a crutch. He had put the broken one alongside its twin in the darkest corner of the scullery, hoping that nobody would notice the damage it had suffered. Cousin Vera had produced a walking stick, left behind by a guest some years before, and with this in his hand Deepbriar set off for the council estate.

'Good morning, Mrs Hatherly.' As the door opened Deepbriar removed his hat, which had cleaned up reasonably well once the mud was dry, and watched a range of emotions chasing across the woman's features. Her knuckles were white as she held the edge of the door, and he suspected she was thinking of slamming it in his face.

'No matter how often you tell me,' Deepbriar said gently, 'I'm afraid I'm not going to forget about this business. If you don't deal with me you could find yourself talking to the local CID. Why don't we have a chat now and get it over with?'

With a sigh she stood back. 'You'd better come in.' She led the way into the kitchen, where two small children, a boy and a girl, gazed open mouthed at Deepbriar, until she shooed them out into the garden. 'Well?'

She rounded on him, her arms folded. She didn't look quite so carefree as she had the previous day, but the constable was convinced this wasn't a woman made sick with worry by an errant husband.

'Did you tell your father-in-law that I'd spoken to you yesterday?'

The question took her by surprise. 'No, I haven't seen him. I expect he'll call in tomorrow night, after work. Would it matter if I had?'

'Maybe not,' Deepbriar replied. He'd never really suspected Joe of orchestrating the attack on him. 'Maybe he'd want you to help me find Micky. He seems a lot more worried about him than you do.'

At this point there was an unexpected diversion as the little girl came running up the garden, crying bitterly, a smear of blood on the sleeve of her blouse. The woman bent to gather the child into her arms. 'Let me see, love,' she said. After inspecting the graze on her daughter's elbow she sat her on the draining board to tend to her.

Deepbriar wandered to the back door. In the lean-to, clean and ready for use, lying in and around a workman's toolbox, was all the paraphernalia of a plasterer's trade, alongside a pair of boots, spotted on the toe caps with pale pink. A bicycle pump and an old inner tube lay on a bench, but the only bicycle was a woman's model. Tyre marks on the floor told him that another bike usually rested alongside.

Back in the kitchen, where Susie Hatherly was applying Germolene to the child's arm, Deepbriar studied a photograph on the dresser. It was a studio portrait of the Hatherly family, obviously taken quite recently. He wouldn't have recognized Micky. The sullen glare the youngster had invariably worn on their previous meetings was gone, and he'd put on flesh; he looked nothing like his father.

Although Deepbriar disapproved of the way Bob Houghton had hounded Micky, he found it more understandable when faced with this photograph; there was a certain smug self-satisfaction about Hatherly junior's smile. And this was the man who, by denying he had ever made a statement to the police, had cost Sergeant Bob Houghton his career and his reputation.

'I shan't be a minute,' Mrs Hatherly said, picking up the little girl and heading for the stairs.

'I'm not in any hurry,' Deepbriar replied. As soon as he was alone in the kitchen he opened the larder. There was no shortage of food; a bowl of eggs stood next to a large slab of cheese, and the meat safe held a shoulder of pork, as well as a plate of what looked like lamb's liver. Whatever Joe might think, there was no danger of his grandchildren going hungry while their father was away. The constable pushed the door closed, and turned to the mantelpiece, having noticed a large envelope propped behind the clock. There were a few words printed on the top of it. He gave a low whistle as he read them, then moved away as he heard the woman coming back downstairs, with the child's lighter footsteps sounding behind her.

Sending the little girl, now clad in a clean dress, back into the garden with a kiss, Susie Hatherly turned back to Deepbriar.

'I don't understand why you're bothering me,' she said. 'Me and Joe have got enough to worry about...' her voice trailed off.

'That's just it,' Deepbriar said. 'You're not worried. Joe is, but not you. Not unless you're a very good actress. Either Micky's run off, and you're glad to see the back of him, or you've known where he is all the time.'

For a second there was anger on her face, then gradually it drained away. 'I don't know where Micky is, but he's safe,' she said.

'Maybe he is, for the time being,' Deepbriar said. 'I've not much time for your father-in-law, but you've not been playing him fair, have you? You told him Micky went missing on his way to work, but all his tools are here. According to Joe you're at your wits' end, not to mention running out of money. But there's plenty of food in the house, and you can still afford to have your piano lessons. I doubt if he's been giving you enough for that.'

'I don't think that's any of your business,' Susie Hatherly countered, her cheeks flushing pink.

'You're right, it isn't. But if you care about your husband then you'll hear me out. Micky must have had a very good reason for wanting to disappear, and I think I know what that reason was. If I'm right, then I'm not the only one who'll be keen on finding him. I believe somebody threatened Joe, not long after Micky disappeared. It could be they wanted to know where Micky had gone.'

She shook her head, as if in disbelief.

'I think it's only a matter of time before that same person comes here,' Deepbriar said. 'I don't want to scare you, but it's true. If the police make the hunt for Micky official this man might get desperate. Believe me, you don't want him to come calling, not when you've a couple of young children in the house. Help me find Micky before things get worse than they already are.'

'Micky's done nothing wrong,' the woman insisted. 'He's gone away for a while, that's all. I never asked the police to look for him, did I? When Joe suggested putting a notice in the paper instead I let him think I didn't like the idea, that we ought to make it official, but really it was just the way we planned it. Micky didn't want us to be charged with wasting police time.'

'As far as that goes you're right, neither of you have committed a crime,' Deepbriar conceded. 'But you haven't answered the big question.'

'I told you, I don't know where he is,' she said, looking at him squarely.

'That's not what I was going to ask. I need to know why Micky vanished. Who scared him so badly that he decided to disappear? It wasn't Bob Houghton, was it?' She looked blankly at him. 'The man who sweeps the promenade.' Deepbriar said. 'I understand he started following Micky around, until Joe warned him off.'

'That old chap. I never knew his name.' She gave a small shrug. 'He never bothered us much. The children didn't seem to mind him either, even though he looked a bit grim. No, it wasn't him. Though when Joe told us what he'd done to get rid of him, Micky was worried in case the old man told the police. We don't want his father dragging us into anything.'

'If it wasn't the road sweeper that gave him a fright then who was it?' Deepbriar persisted.

'I don't know.' She met his look, unflinching. 'That's the truth. Micky said what I don't know can't hurt me.'

Deepbriar refrained from pointing out how wrong she was. 'There must be something.'

She shook her head dumbly.

'He was right to be scared,' Deepbriar said. 'You've heard about that body turning up on the beach?'

'Yes.' The woman's face was suddenly very pale.

'I'm pretty sure Micky knows who killed him. It's likely that same man committed murder during the war. If you and Micky don't want to be looking over your shoulders for the rest of your lives, then I need to know who that person is, so I can find him before anybody else gets killed.'

Chapter Eighteen

Susie Hatherly stared at Deepbriar, wide eyed. 'I don't know who it is,' she whispered, 'Micky's always been afraid of someone. It all got worse a few weeks ago. We...' she checked herself, her gaze sliding away from his. 'He decided to go away.'

'Not he,' Deepbriar corrected her, 'You got it right the first time, didn't you? The pair of you are emigrating to Australia. The trouble is, it takes time for the papers to come through.'

'Nobody's supposed to know.' Her voice was trembling. 'Not even his dad.'

'Running away isn't the answer. You have to help me find Micky,' Deepbriar urged. 'He'll never be safe until this man's caught.'

Susie Hatherly was biting on her lip, tears brimming in her eyes. 'There's nothing any-one can do. I think it might be a policeman,' she said, 'somebody high up.'

It was only what Deepbriar had been expecting, yet her statement hit hard. If Chief Inspector Vorrman was the murderer he'd have his work cut out to make an accusation stick. He might have to do something drastic. A senior officer could use his position to

251

sweep the whole thing back under the carpet, and he might even produce false evidence that would put Deepbriar's head on the block, and there was no telling what might happen to Micky.

'Micky's working,' Susie Hatherly dropped the words into the silence. 'He sends me money in the post every week.'

Deepbriar felt a sudden surge of hope. 'Have you kept the envelopes?'

'No. But the postmark is always Firstall.'

It wasn't the best of news. Firstall was a market town, ten miles inland. The postmark would appear on thousands of letters every day.

'Has he got any friends there? Or maybe he worked for somebody in that area before?'

She shook her head. 'I don't think so. Is Micky really in danger?'

'Somebody's afraid your husband will talk, Mrs Hatherly. And whoever that person is, he's going to want to make sure Micky's mouth is kept permanently shut.'

'I have got something.' She opened a drawer and pulled out a small brown envelope. It looked like a pay packet. 'This was wrapped around the last lot of money he sent me.'

Deepbriar stopped on the corner of Dry Lane. He took the little envelope from his pocket and stared again at the rows of letters and numbers. They were in pencil and some of them had already rubbed away to nothing. Only one figure had been written in ink, right at the bottom. It could be a week's pay: £8/2/10.

The first line in pencil read RC, then 107114, and what Deepbriar could only think of as a squiggle. Below that came BL, 72118, again followed by the same unrecognizable hieroglyph. The lower lines weren't so easy to read, but it looked as if the next one began with an 5, and the last with an R. They too were followed by five or six numbers, and the mysterious symbol.

Lower down, the pencil marks had all but vanished, but it looked like amounts of money, probably adding up to the total written in ink. The payment was clear enough, but payment for what?

Deepbriar carefully tucked the envelope inside the back of his notebook. As he left the council estate, he pondered on the assault of the previous evening. The small man had protested that he'd not been told their intended victim was – what? A police officer? And that had prompted a response from his boss; only a few words but enough to be sure this was an educated man, certainly not working class like the two hired thugs.

He wasn't quite sure why his steps turned

towards Miss Caldwell's house; she would be at work. When he arrived he hesitated for a second, then turned in at a gate three doors further along the street.

'Constable Deepbriar, what a nice surprise.'

'Mrs Mason...' He flushed in acute embarrassment. Pain had suddenly shot up his leg, rendering him almost speechless. 'Sorry–'

'Is something wrong? Are you unwell?'

'Cramp.' He ground the word out between clenched teeth.

She ushered him in, making sympathetic noises as he almost fell through the door. 'Come and sit down. Miss Caldwell thought you might be overdoing things.' Once he'd collapsed into a chair she whisked out of the room and returned a moment later with a glass of water. 'I've stirred a bit of salt into it, that's supposed to help. And the kettle's on for elevenses. A cup of tea, that's what you need.'

Deepbriar drank the salt water and returned the glass. 'Thank you.' He kneaded the cramped muscles and the pain eased a little. 'I'm really sorry, Mrs Mason. I feel a proper fool.'

'Don't worry about it. Since the boys left home I don't get a lot of company, and I was hoping to see you again anyway. There's something I wanted to say. Oh, there's the kettle. Just a minute.'

She vanished again. Deepbriar leant back with a sigh of relief as the pain faded to a dull ache. On the wall directly in front of him were several family photographs. 'You must be very proud of your two sons,' he remarked, when Mrs Mason returned with the tea tray. 'You've obviously done a fine job.' The most recent pictures showed two young men with their mother's fair colouring, both in uniform.

'Yes,' she smiled, 'they've turned out well, but I can't take all the credit. They were well-behaved boys, although I'll admit it wasn't always easy, with no man in the house.' She handed him a cup of tea, looking a little troubled. 'I'm glad you came, Constable. I don't think I should have spoken so freely yesterday. I've put you in an awkward position. It might be best if you forget the whole thing.'

'Truly?' Deepbriar asked. 'I've been going over what you told me, and I agree with you about your brother. I don't believe he committed suicide. It may not be too late to find his murderer.'

She made a little gesture with her hands. 'Is there any hope of discovering the truth after so long?'

'If it hadn't been for Sidney Greensall's body turning up on the beach, sixteen years after his funeral, then I'd probably say no,'

Deepbriar replied. 'But I'm sure that case is all tangled up with what happened to the chief inspector.' He began ticking off facts on his fingers. 'First, in 1941 a man was found dead in suspicious circumstances. The body was identified as that of Sidney Greensall. With their resources already stretched to breaking point and no real evidence of foul play, the police didn't waste much manpower on trying to find out how he died. Rightly or wrongly, they were probably only too pleased to be rid of a local villain. An officer who was suspected of being in Greensall's pay was got out of the way, and the case was conveniently forgotten.

'Second, in 1944, your brother dies. You've told me he was about to look into mistakes that were made three years earlier. He must have been referring to the Greensall case, I'm sure of it. I think that's why he was killed, but because his death was made to look like suicide there was no investigation.' Deepbriar grimaced. 'It's hard to make any excuses for allowing that crime to go unexamined. Perhaps somebody had a particular interest in preventing an investigation.

'Lastly, all these years later, another body turns up. There's absolutely no doubt it's murder, and we know the man's identity. Obviously, Sidney Greensall didn't die sixteen years earlier. There's no mistake this time.

'Mr Larch was planning to find out which officer had been accepting bribes from Greensall during the first years of the war. That's why he was killed. Probably the only man who would know the truth about what happened in 1941, apart from that bent copper, was Greensall himself. He came back to Bradsea, and within days he was murdered. It all points to the same man being responsible for those two deaths.'

'So my brother was killed to keep him quiet?'

'That's right.' Deepbriar frowned. 'Whoever this other officer is, he couldn't allow an investigation. Sergeant Houghton had been framed for complicity in Greensall's black market activities. Your brother was a good detective, everybody says so; once he'd recovered his health he'd have discovered the truth. Mrs Mason, I want you to think back. Is there anything else he said that might be of use? A name perhaps, or anything about the reason for his suspicions. The smallest detail might help.'

She shook her head. 'I've gone over it so many times. Wouldn't he have left some sort of record?'

'Maybe not, if he was investigating his own colleagues. I'm afraid I'm not on the best of terms with your local hobbies, so there's no way to find out,' he said, feeling suddenly depressed. 'It was bad timing on my part, turning up back in Bradsea the same time as Greensall. Anybody looking into his murder would be bound to treat me as a suspect.'

'It's hard to imagine any of the men David knew and worked with...' her voice faltered. 'How can you begin to sort out who it was?'

'Finding out where the most likely suspects were at the time of the murders would be a start. I'm discounting the first death, the man whose body was mistaken for Greensall's may not even have been murdered, though if he was I'd suspect Greensall, rather than the man who killed Chief Inspector Larch and Greensall himself.' Deepbriar ran a hand over his hair. 'We need to start with your brother. After so long, I don't suppose there's much hope of finding witnesses who saw him on his way up to the cliff.'

'It's a bleak place, and there's no view, except out to sea,' Mrs Mason said. 'Why would David go there?'

'Probably because somebody arranged to meet him. I wish I could look through the station reports for that week.'

'The piece of paper they said was a suicide note should have been kept, shouldn't it? I'd like you to see that. Everybody took it at face value, but it was all wrong. David would have written me a proper letter if he'd really intended to commit suicide.' She gave a shaky laugh. 'We talked about it, you see, when I came back from Scotland. Evidently, not long after the bombing, he'd spent the whole of one weekend thinking about ways to end his life, and he'd actually got as far as writing to me, telling me how sorry he was. That was what stopped him. He decided he was being selfish, when I'd just lost my husband. When he realized I might need him, he thought he'd better go on living, for my sake, and for my boys.'

Deepbriar struggled to find something to say. 'All the lads at the station thought a lot of him,' he volunteered at last.

'Yes.' She sighed. 'Which brings us back to how we might find out more from the old records. Jack Hobday was particularly kind when my husband died. If it's just a matter of taking a look at some files, don't you think he might help?'

'I doubt it. He's close to retirement, he doesn't want to rock the boat.' Deepbriar drank the last of his tea. 'Though, talking of retired police officers, do you know Superintendent Ruggles?'

Mrs Mason looked surprised. 'We never mixed in the same social circles; his wife was connected to a local aristocratic family. They didn't have much to do with the likes of us. Why do you ask?'

'If you were friends, a man in his position might be useful.'

She shook her head. 'You've convinced me

that my brother was killed by one of his colleagues. I know it's silly, somebody as senior as Superintendent Ruggles isn't likely to be the murderer, but I'd rather not trust anyone who was here in Bradsea when David died. That's why I never talked about my suspicions, not in all these years, because I was afraid somebody at the station might have been involved. Then Miss Caldwell told me you were one of the young officers drafted in after the bombing, and that you'd not been back to Bradsea since. It was a relief being able to tell somebody the truth at last.'

Deepbriar nodded. 'I wish I could be more help. We need somebody in authority on our side, but you're right, we can't take the risk. I'm afraid Inspector Prout wouldn't take me seriously. Either that or he'd spill the beans. Never mind; I do have a lead. There's a man who was involved with Greensall back in 1941. Of course, nothing's ever simple; it would be easier if he hadn't taken it upon himself to disappear.'

The woman looked alarmed. 'You don't think there's been another murder?'

'No, I think he's safe enough for the moment. He's gone into hiding. Almost certainly because he's scared of the man we're looking for. I'm doing my best to track him down.' It didn't seem the right time to voice his innermost fears; if Greensall's murderer found Micky first, their witness could end up dead, and the whole case would come crashing down around his head.

Deepbriar dug into the shopping bag for the books Houghton had asked him to fetch from among his belongings. 'You're looking a lot better.'

'That's more than I can say for you,' Houghton replied, looking up at him sharply. 'You're doing your best to hide it, but there's something not right with the way you're moving. What've you been up to?'

'I don't suppose you'd fall for the line I spun to Mrs Deepbriar,' the constable said, grimacing as he sat down. 'On my way home last night, I think I may have had a run-in with our murderer.'

This information seemed to galvanize Bob Houghton, and for the next five minutes he was the man Deepbriar had known sixteen years before. He fired questions at him, digging at Deepbriar's memory to gather every possible piece of information about the attack.

'You didn't report it,' Houghton said, once he'd finished.

'I've seen enough of Inspector Prout for the time being,' Deepbriar replied. 'Anyway, never mind that, I've seen Susie Hatherly again, and this time I think I might have got something. Micky's working. She doesn't know where exactly, but he's been sending her money.' He reached to his pocket.

'Good evening, Bob.' Both men looked up, startled, at the man who loomed over them, a basket of fruit in his hands. Deepbriar pushed to his feet.

'Well, if it isn't Chief Inspector Vorrman,' Houghton said, sinking back against his pillows, a distrustful look on his face. 'On your way to visit somebody are you?'

'I came to see you. For old times' sake. Sit down, Thorny, we're both too big to stand here taking up all this space; the sister might turn one of us out.' He placed the fruit on Houghton's locker then turned to look for a chair, going to fetch one from beside an empty bed. Deepbriar and Houghton exchanged glances.

'Thorny?' Houghton mouthed.

'Don't remember him ever calling you by your first name before, come to that,' Deepbriar muttered.

'How are you getting on?' Vorrman asked, once he was seated.

'I'm all right,' Houghton replied grudgingly. 'Look, what exactly are you doing here? You can't pretend the two of us were ever friends.'

'Maybe not, but we were colleagues for quite a few years. At our age there doesn't seem much point carrying on an old feud, does there?' The chief inspector looked from one man to the other. 'We're all aware that the Greensall case is about to rear its ugly head again. And the two of you have a very good reason to want it solved. Everybody knows you've been asking questions, Thorny.' He gave a little laugh. 'You're quite a large presence at any time, but on crutches – well, let's just say you've been hard to miss.'

Deepbriar kept his peace, wondering how long it would take for him to get to the point.

'What's that to do with you?' Houghton demanded abruptly. 'Greensall was found in Bradsea, it's not even your case.'

'No, but we all know what Prout is making of it; his investigative talents leave a lot to be desired,' Vorrman replied. 'He came close to putting our friendly village bobby here under arrest, even though he knew he couldn't be the murderer. Well, not without an able-bodied accomplice. Following the same flawed reasoning, of course, I gather he's only waiting for you to be released from hospital so he can pull you in for questioning.'

'But Bob wasn't involved in Greensall's death any more than I was,' Deepbriar protested. 'He was ill. Dr Tordon told Inspector Prout he couldn't possibly have been up and about at the time of the murder.'

Chief Inspector Vorrman shrugged. 'That's merely one man's opinion. I daresay some other doctor could be persuaded to tell a different story if the case came to

263

court.' He gave a humourless smile. 'If I were you I shouldn't be in too much of a hurry to leave here, Bob.'

'You still haven't answered my question,' Houghton said harshly. 'What's your interest in all this?'

'Call it a sense of justice.' Vorrman's dark eyes scanned first Houghton, then Deepbriar. 'Even if you prove you weren't responsible for Greensall's death, both of you suffered because of what happened back in 1941. The whole case was botched.'

'Don't tell me you believed Bob was innocent all along, sir?' Deepbriar stared at him. 'You were the one who spoke to young Hatherly. It was thanks to you that Ruggles decided we'd faked the information that was supposed to bring Greensall in.'

'I always had my doubts,' Vorrman replied. 'But it was only a gut feeling, and I didn't see any point in making a fuss. I believed it was just another case we didn't have the manpower to investigate. Either that or our superiors didn't want to risk showing the force in a bad light. Now I'm not so sure. Looking back, the whole affair was hushed up very quickly.'

'I don't understand why you've decided to talk to us now,' Houghton said. 'Are you offering to help?'

'Let's just say I think it's time we pooled our resources. How about it?'

Chapter Nineteen

Detective Chief Inspector Vorrman sat at his ease, a half smile his lips as he waited for an answer. Deepbriar, all too aware of the other man's seniority, fidgeted on his chair, unwilling to speak. He was grateful that Houghton felt no such constraint.

'Give me one good reason why we should throw in our hand with you,' Houghton demanded.

Vorrman shrugged. 'I could give you several. First, neither of you has any authority in Bradsea. I'm sure Constable Deepbriar has done an admirable job so far, but before long he's bound to tread on somebody's toes and get himself into trouble. More importantly, I have more resources at my disposal than the two of you. Access to the records, for example.'

'He's got a point, Bob,' Deepbriar said.

'I accept that he'd be a useful ally, Thorny,' Houghton looked sceptical. 'But it's not as easy as all that. You see, Chief Inspector, while a constable with no position here won't want to risk going home with another black mark on his record, I've got nothing to lose. I trust Thorny, because I know he's as innocent of any involvement in Greensall's death as I am. Likewise, I know neither of us was making a profit out of the black market during the war. The trouble is, I just don't see how you're going to convince me that you're equally innocent. I didn't like you when we worked together, and I don't like you now.'

Vorrman appeared to be undisturbed by Houghton's blunt comments. He nodded, 'And there's a serious shortage of suspects, which means as far as you're concerned I'm at the top of the list. But try looking at it from my point of view. I can be equally sure that I'm not guilty, whereas the evidence Prout has gathered still points at you. Despite that, I'm prepared to take a chance. I think we need each other. Isn't it worth setting our previous disagreements aside? As an earnest of my good intentions I'll give you some information, free and gratis. You might like to know that Greensall's closest associates during the war have been eliminated from the enquiry. Pug Parry has been in Wormwood Scrubs for the last three years, and Gordon Thwaite died in 1949. Manchester haven't turned up anything on Hubert Masters either. It seems our Sidney was living the quiet life.'

'On his ill-gotten gains, presumably,' Deepbriar mused.

'Which brings us back to the black market,

and Micky Hatherly,' Vorrman said. 'How's the search going, Constable?'

'Don't tell him anything,' Houghton said.

'Oh come on, Bob, give me a break,' Vorrman's mouth quirked in a wry smile. 'I think Thorny's capable of making up his own mind.'

'Just as long as you both know where I stand,' came the harsh reply. 'As far as I'm concerned you're the prime suspect, and I wouldn't give you the time of day.'

'There's nothing to tell,' Deepbriar put in quickly, before Vorrman could respond. 'I've spoken to Mrs Hatherly twice, sir, but I'm no nearer finding her husband. I'm certain she doesn't know where he is.'

'Let's hope whoever killed Greensall comes to the same conclusion,' Vorrman said, getting to his feet. 'If you won't believe in my good intentions, at least I hope you'll accept that I don't want anyone else getting killed.' He gave them a brief nod and put on his hat. 'Goodnight.'

'Slimy bastard,' Houghton hissed, as Vorrman's tall bulky figure disappeared from sight.

'We've got nothing on him, Bob. There's no proof that he's the murderer.' Deepbriar had been doing his best to visualize Vorrman as the man who'd led the assault on him, but he couldn't make up his mind. It might have been him, it might not. He sighed. 'If he accepts you weren't in with Greensall, maybe he's got another suspect.'

'Maybe he knows it wasn't me, because it was him,' Houghton replied darkly. 'Unless we're missing something, the only people who had access to the files, both in '41 and in the last few months, are Vorrman and Jack Hobday.'

'There's one thing we haven't considered,' Deepbriar was suddenly thoughtful. 'Can we be absolutely sure Joe Hatherly didn't put Greensall out of the way? For Micky's sake?'

'He can't have tampered with Greensall's file. Besides, Joe's a small-time villain, I doubt if he's capable of murder. I take it Micky hasn't turned up yet.'

'No.' Deepbriar gave Houghton an account of his talk with Susie Hatherly.

'So, at least Micky's wife is sure that he's alive and well.'

'For the moment,' Deepbriar said. He brought out his notebook and handed the envelope to Houghton. 'I can't make head nor tail of this. Micky used it to wrap up some cash. It looks like a pay packet, but it doesn't tell us who he's working for.'

'What are these figures? The ones lower down are money, obviously. Add up to £8/2/10. Not exactly good wages, but enough to keep his wife and children fed.'

'More than the standard agricultural

wage,' Deepbriar nodded, 'but if he's doing unskilled work he must be working more than a forty-seven hour week to earn that much. Any idea what the rest of it means?'

Houghton shook his head. 'Make a copy I can keep, will you, Thorny? Maybe something will come to me. Since you didn't show this to Vorrman, I take it you're not falling for his old pals act. You don't trust him.'

'Not with information about Micky Hatherly, I don't,' Deepbriar said, frowning as he tried to copy the exact shape of the figures and symbols on to a page of his notebook.

'One thing Vorrman was right about,' Houghton cautioned, taking the piece of paper from him. 'You're a bit noticeable. Be careful if you get a lead on Micky; you don't want anybody on your tail.'

The nightmare put in another appearance that Friday night. Deepbriar sat bolt upright, staring at the lighter patch marking the position of the window while he waited for his heartbeat to return to normal. At his side Mary was breathing deeply; he was relieved that he hadn't disturbed her. He climbed out of bed, dragging on his dressing gown. Picking up his notebook, he crept from the room. It was too early to go to the shelter. The sun wouldn't be up for another hour, so he made himself comfortable in an armchair in the guest lounge, turned on the table lamp at his side, and settled down to think.

Without sufficient facts, it was all too easy to speculate; intuition was all very well, but the basis of good detective work was logical deduction. Deepbriar opened the notebook at a pristine new page, and wrote down the first of many headings. He had to get his thoughts in order.

The evidence of his own eyes, and Dr Tordon's medical opinion, ruled out Bob Houghton as the killer of Sidney Greensall, and when Chief Inspector David Larch died, Bob had been in Africa. Jack Hobday and Chief Inspector Vorrman had both remained in Bradsea for the duration of the war, and either one of them could easily have tampered with Sidney Greensall's file. He put their names under a second heading, leaving space to add comments below each one.

After a moment's hesitation he added Superintendent Ruggles to that list. After all, Mrs Mason hadn't been prepared to trust Ruggles, despite his seniority. He too had been in Bradsea in '41 and '44, and although he was no longer a serving officer, he still lived in the area. It was possible he'd tampered with Greensall's records before he retired, or he could have visited the station more recently and gained access to the filing room on some pretext or other. Deepbriar made a note beneath the man's name. He would see if he could find out if Ruggles made a habit of calling in at the station.

By the time the dawn crept into the room, making the electric light look pale and sickly, Deepbriar had filled several pages with notes. Having consciously set aside his personal prejudices, the results surprised him. Sergeant Hobday was almost as likely a murderer as Chief Inspector Vorrman. Superintendent Ruggles might have committed the crimes, although Deepbriar had failed to come up with a motive, unless, contrary to everyone's belief, he'd been short of money during the war.

Deepbriar turned off the lamp and stretched. He sat back in the chair, his hands clasped comfortably across his stomach, and fell asleep, and it was there Mary found him two hours later, snoring softly.

Miss Caldwell stamped a date in the two books Deepbriar had chosen. 'I know you said you wouldn't be looking into the business of the missing gnomes any more,' she whispered, 'but I believe I may have discovered something, if you're interested.'

'As a matter of fact I was hoping for a quick word with you,' Deepbriar replied, looking at the clock on the wall. 'Will you be leaving as soon as the library closes?'

She nodded. 'Ten minutes.'

They walked together to a seat on the promenade, Miss Caldwell congratulating Deepbriar on having dispensed with the crutches.

'I'm glad to be rid of them,' Deepbriar admitted. 'What did you want to tell me?'

'I've tracked down the owner of the gnome from the beach. And she's quite sure there were no marks on it before it was stolen, because she'd only had it a few days. That set me thinking, and I went back and talked to some of the other owners. It's funny, but a lot of the gnomes were quite new when they were taken. Do you think that means something?'

'Maybe,' Deepbriar nodded. 'You know, Miss Caldwell, I don't think you ever needed my help; you have quite a talent for investigation.'

'It must be all the detective stories I read,' she replied, smiling. 'I must say I've quite enjoyed myself, but I'm no nearer discovering who's been taking the gnomes, or why. Perhaps it will have to be one of those unsolved mysteries, like the Mary Celeste. Of course, you're involved in something much more exciting. Once the newspapers began writing about that man on the beach being murdered I'm afraid the gossips have talked about nothing else. Your name keeps cropping up.' Her eyes were alight with interest. 'You said you wanted to talk to me. Dare I hope there's something I can do to help?'

'It's possible. Tell me, if a man wanted to get a job in this area for a few weeks, but needed to keep a low profile, where might he go?'

'Well, there are always seasonal jobs in hotels. Or the funfair in Whellow.'

'Both too public. This person is afraid of being seen. It's possible he could be somewhere near Firstall.'

'That's different. Firstall's a market town, not a resort,' Miss Caldwell mused. 'He'd probably look for work on a farm. They take on casual labour during the harvest, though not nearly as much as they used to, of course, and it's been a very wet month, so some of the crops have probably been lost. If that's what he's doing, your man might need some experience. And he would need to be reasonably strong. Does that fit the bill?'

'I'm not sure about either the experience or the strength,' Deepbriar demurred. 'I don't know enough about him, but I might be able to find out.' He showed her the little brown pay envelope, and she studied the letters and figures with interest.

'No,' she said after a few minutes. 'Nothing comes to mind. I'm sorry.'

'It doesn't matter, you've already been a

help, Miss Caldwell. I know I said I'd given up on the gnomes, but I'll keep in touch; something might still crop up. The case of the Mary Celeste has always bothered me, I don't like unsolved mysteries.'

The map he borrowed from cousin Vera sent Deepbriar's spirits plummeting. There were dozens of farms around Firstall, and Micky Hatherly could be working at any one of them – or none, if Miss Caldwell's guess was wrong. He spent a disagreeable five minutes persuading the map to concertina back into its old folds, then sat staring gloomily at the empty fireplace. Mary was having her afternoon rest, and heavy clouds were darkening the sky outside. It was nearly three o'clock on a Saturday afternoon; about this time lots of people would be happily anticipating the moment when they'd receive their week's pay. Micky Hatherly was probably among them.

Deepbriar thought with longing of his bike. Sometimes when the weather was bad he'd grumbled about having to cycle the beat around Minecliff's neighbouring villages, but right now he'd give a lot to be fit enough to borrow a bicycle for a spin out to Firstall. It would be a futile gesture, of course; he'd about as much chance of stumbling across young Hatherly by chance as he had of winning a fortune on the football pools.

'Are you staying in all afternoon?' Cousin Vera asked, breezing into the parlour with a feather duster in one hand and a dustpan and brush in the other. She gave him a rather pointed look. 'Didn't the doctor say you needed plenty of exercise?'

Deepbriar wandered rather aimlessly around the town, then made his way to the station, with the vague idea of meeting Joe Hatherly as he returned from work. A bunch of holidaymakers streamed off the train, and Deepbriar stood aside and watched them, waiting for the familiar figure in the grubby overalls. He didn't appear. Half an hour later a second train arrived, a lot less crowded. Joe Hatherly wasn't on that one either.

His curiosity aroused, Deepbriar headed to Cockle Close. At Joe's house none of the windows was open, not even a crack, and all the curtains were drawn. It seemed he'd wasted his time, but Deepbriar knocked on the door anyway, and when there was no reply he peered through the letterbox. A pair of work boots lay haphazardly at the foot of the stairs, and a worn and rather grubby jacket hung on the newel post. Something prickled at the back of Deepbriar's neck. He banged on the door again. 'Joe! It's me, Deepbriar.'

By this time, a few neighbours had appeared at their doors and were looking in his direction. Deepbriar turned to the nearest, a huge woman in a wrapover pinafore, her arms akimbo, her beady eyes watching him cynically. 'If it's money you're after, he's not in,' she offered. This sally roused a laugh from several of the onlookers.

'I didn't come to collect, I came to pay him,' Deepbriar said with sudden inspiration, speaking loud and clear. He thumped the knocker again. 'You hear, Joe?' More heads appeared at doors and poked out of windows. Deepbriar fetched out his wallet and selected a ten shilling note. 'I've got something for you. Shall I leave this with one of your friends?'

The door opened a crack and one eye peered around it. 'What's this about money?' Joe Hatherly growled.

'I think we'd better talk in private, don't you?' Deepbriar suggested pleasantly, returning the note to his wallet while the crowd of neighbours watched with great interest.

Joe said something unintelligible and moved back. Deepbriar stepped into the shabby hall, and Joe slammed the door shut behind him. A faint ironic cheer sounded from outside, and Deepbriar grinned.

When Joe turned round, the sight of him wiped the smile off Deepbriar's face. The man had a black eye, his lips and jaw were grossly swollen, and his nose looked as if it was broken. 'What happened?'

'What do you think?' Joe glowered from

his one good eye, and led the way to the kitchen, with a limp far more noticeable than Deepbriar's. He winced as he lifted the kettle, and Deepbriar took it from him, filled it with water and put it on the stove.

'Thanks,' Joe said grudgingly, slumping on to a wooden chair. 'Mugs are in the sink. Haven't got around to washing up.'

Deepbriar said nothing as he rinsed the crockery and brewed tea, while Joe sat with his head in his hands, the picture of misery.

'Why, Joe?' Deepbriar asked, handing the man a mug of strong tea. 'Was it to do with Micky?'

Joe Hatherly nodded. 'A man can't tell what he don't know, can he?' His hands were shaking as he wrapped them around the mug. 'He kept on askin' the same ruddy question. Where's Micky, where's your son. I told him what I told you, I don't have a clue. He didn't believe me at first. Then once he realized I was telling the truth he went mad. I thought he'd kill me. Maybe he would've done an' all, if a couple of me mates hadn't come along. When he saw them he took off.'

'Just one man?' Deepbriar was incredulous. 'Blimey, Joe, who was it, Sugar Ray Robinson?'

'Could've been, the way he used his fists. Pair of bloody sledge hammers. Boxers hands they were, I'd bet he's done some bare-knuckle fighting in his time. I didn't get to see the rest of him. It was black as bloody pitch, and he had his face all wrapped up in something. He was a big bugger, though. Bigger'n you by an inch or two, an' wide with it.' Joe gave a slow shake of his head, it seemed all his old belligerence had been knocked out of him. 'I tell you, Mr Deepbriar, he didn't give me even half a chance. I never want to meet 'im again, an' that's a fact.'

'When was this?'

'Last night. I'd backed a good horse, see, an' I was celebrating. I had a few pints at the Lord Nelson, and I was walking home. He come at me when I was on that bit of waste ground behind the football pitch. I never had a chance. He'd knocked me down almost before I knew 'e was there.'

'You didn't see his face, but you must have heard his voice.'

'He whispered. Even when he lost his temper.' Hatherly shuddered. 'It was enough to freeze your blood. Like that bloke on the pictures. You know, the one who does them horror films.' Deepbriar nodded. He had the feeling he'd heard that whisper himself. 'Common sort of man was he? Like one of the roughs from the fair?'

Hatherly looked up sharply, his one good eye meeting Deepbriar's look. 'Now you come to mention it, I reckon he was a bit of a toff. I dunno, he didn't say much, but ... 'ang on,' he said accusingly, 'do you know who this bloke is?'

'No, but I think I've met him. I was luckier than you, I only got a couple of bruises, and they don't show.'

'Christ.' This revelation seemed to strike Joe dumb, and he buried his nose in his tea.

A sudden thought occurred to Deepbriar and he leant urgently across the table. 'Joe, what about Susie? If this man didn't get anything useful out of you, maybe he'll go there next.'

'I thought of that.' There was pride in his voice, the first sign of his old assurance returning. 'I sent a message with one of me mates as soon as they'd got me 'ome. Told her to take the kids and skip off to visit one of her relatives for a few days. Comes from a big family, she does, aunties and cousins all over the flippin' place. She can stay out of sight till this blows over.'

'That's good.' Deepbriar remembered why he'd come. 'Joe, I think I'm getting nearer to finding out where Micky's hiding. Has he got friends anywhere near Firstall?'

'Not that I know of. Why?'

'What about when he was young? He must have had a job before he was finished with school, something to make some money in the holidays.'

'He ran a few errands for a bloke who had

279

a shop on the High Street,' Joe replied. 'It was wartime, there wasn't much. The pier an' the funfair was all shut down.' A familiar expression crept hack over his battered features; he was hiding something.

'Ran a few errands for you, too, did he Joe?' Deepbriar guessed. 'Gambling doesn't stop because there's a war on, does it? If you don't watch yourself you'll get nicked one of these days, but you needn't worry, I'm after bigger fish. Are you sure Micky never went to work on a farm?'

'Micky, on a farm? Are you kidding? He's a town boy. I dunno what tree you're barkin' up, Mr Deepbriar, but it's the wrong one.'

Chapter Twenty

Deepbriar decided to check that Susie Hatherly had taken her father-in-law's advice; he didn't like to think of her encountering the man who'd made such a mess of Joe's face. When he got to the house he found it shut up and apparently deserted, and he got short shrift when he asked the neighbours where the family had gone; evidently, it wasn't unusual for families to do a moonlight flit from the council estate.

The early evening was turning dark, the skies overcast and threatening. Deepbriar checked his watch. If he was quick he could call in at the hospital and still get back to cousin Vera's in time for the evening meal, though he'd be running things a bit tight. As he walked he tried to get his thoughts in order, but the clarity of the morning had gone. He was sure he'd missed something; there was a clue hovering at the back of his mind, if only he could latch on to it. That was all the more reason to talk to Bob Houghton.

A sudden deluge started when Deepbriar was fifty yards from the hospital gates, and he lumbered into a clumsy run. His muscles protesting, he took refuge in the corrugated iron lean-to provided for staff bicycles. All around him people were scurrying for shelter, figures made indistinct by the downpour and the failing light. The rain fell ever harder; everyone wore hats pulled low, or carried umbrellas angled into the wind. Deepbriar found himself thinking again of the man who'd led the assault on him, trying to conjure him up in his mind's eye. With nothing but the shape and size of the man to go on, he still had the feeling he might know him if he saw him again.

A black hat caught Deepbriar's attention, bobbing above the heads of the small crowd gathered in the porch above the hospital's front door. The man was tall, and it looked as if he might be wearing a dark coat. Deepbriar abandoned his refuge and ran out into the rain, now reaching monsoon proportions. By the time he reached the entrance he was almost soaked to the skin, and the man had vanished.

Deepbriar hurtled through the door and stood staring around him. There was no sign of the man in the black hat, but there were damp footprints on the floor, all of them leading upstairs to the wards. With water dripping from his clothes and his boots squelching unpleasantly, Deepbriar followed the diminishing trail, moving faster than he'd done for many weeks.

He turned into the men's ward far too quickly, and was completely unprepared when one foot skated from beneath him. The tip of the walking stick found no grip on the wet lino, either; it slid to one side, and he fell spectacularly, with a thud loud enough to make the whole room vibrate. A second later the stick, which had skittered across the room, completed the perform-ance by crashing musically into the bottom of a radiator.

A nurse came running from the little office at the end of the ward as several visitors hurried to Deepbriar's aid. One of them was a tall elderly man, rather frail in appearance and wearing a heavy overcoat that hung loosely on his spare frame. His damp black hat was still in his hand as he bent to retrieve Deepbriar's trilby. 'You came quite a purler,' he said solicitously. This, undoubtedly, was the mysterious figure Deepbriar had been pursuing.

'I'm all right, thank you,' Deepbriar replied, a little breathless and shamefaced.

'Really, all this noise!' The sour-faced staff nurse gave Deepbriar a look that would have withered a cactus. 'This is a hospital, dedicated to the care of the sick. My patients require peace and quiet.'

'I'm sorry, nurse, it was the wet floor,' Deepbriar said lamely. rubbing an aching buttock.

'And who brought in all the water?' she retorted tartly. With a click of her tongue and a ferocious glare the woman turned on her heel, leaving an uncomfortable silence behind her. Deepbriar crept to his friend's bed, and gradually the quiet hum of conversation resumed. Bob Houghton greeted him with a grin. 'Thought they'd be carting you off to set some more bones,' he said. 'What's the rush?'

'I don't have long, I have to get back for my meal,' Deepbriar replied lamely. He grimaced as he sank wetly on to the chair.

'Come off it, you came through that door like a bloodhound on a scent!'

Reluctantly, Deepbriar admitted what had happened, looking ruefully across the ward at the visitor who was nursing the black hat on his knee. 'It was a stupid mistake. Listen, Bob, I think the man in the alley has got to be our murderer.' He explained about Joe Hatherly's escape. 'I don't know, maybe he was exaggerating, but this bloke's pretty scary.'

'I suppose Joe didn't get a look at him?'

'No more than I did. It's ruddy annoying. He was within arm's reach. If only I'd thought of knocking his hat off!'

'Three against one's no joke. It sounds as if you did well getting out of it with just a few knocks,' Houghton said.

'I can't help wondering if that was all he

had planned for me,' Deepbriar replied thoughtfully. 'Maybe I've been upsetting somebody. Chief Inspector Larch talked about reopening the Greensall case, and look what happened to him. As for Greensall, he came back to Bradsea under an assumed name, after he'd been away for sixteen years. Within days, he was murdered. And if I'd turned up dead in the sea maybe Inspector Prout would have assumed that I'd been fool enough to get caught out by the tide again. It doesn't take much water to drown a man once he's unconscious.'

'You really think he wanted to kill you?' Houghton didn't sound convinced.

'I wouldn't rule it out.' Deepbriar took his notebook from his pocket, relieved to see that it hadn't got wet. 'I've been trying to make two and two add up to four, or maybe it's five, I don't know any more. Take a look at this and see what you think.' Having opened the book at the relevant pages, Deepbriar handed it to Houghton, and sat in silence while his friend studied the notes he'd made that morning.

'So, Hobday, Vorrman or Ruggles,' Houghton said at last. 'No fresh suspects.'

'Not unless you've got any ideas.'

'Can't say I have.' He tapped a finger on the notebook. 'Look, Thorny, I reckon you've taken some of this too far. What's Superintendent Ruggles doing in here? We both agree he had no motive. The whole case hinges on finding out who was taking bribes from Greensall; why would a man as well off as Ruggles take the risk?'

'Greensall had quite a few friends among the local gentry,' Deepbriar pointed out.

'Yes, but a police superintendent! Ruggles wouldn't be so stupid. If this is definitely about money, and I can't think of any other possible reason, then Ruggles is out of it. He had a top job, and everybody knew his wife was loaded.'

'If you remove Ruggles from the list it doesn't leave much.'

'I think we can eliminate Jack Hobday too,' Houghton said. 'If he had more than his pay to spend during the war, he never once showed any sign of it, and I can't see him having the nouse to keep it that quiet.'

'I agree he's the least likely of the three,' Deepbriar said. 'And to be honest I can't match him with the man in the alley, he carries too much weight around his middle.'

'That leaves us with Vorrman.' Houghton dropped his voice. 'I found out something that might swing things where he's concerned. You see that chap over there, the one with his arm in a sling? We got chatting this afternoon, turns out he used to play cricket with our least favourite chief inspector, and he heard a bit about that legacy. It seems it was less than a thousand pounds. A nice enough sum of money, but once he bought that house there wouldn't be much left. You saw that suit he was wearing when he came in here. How can he afford to live like that? It's not as if he's a bachelor; he's got a wife and a couple of kids too.'

'But if he's the guilty party he's been taking a big risk, splashing his money about.'

'He's always been an arrogant bastard.' Houghton handed back the notebook. 'As for the man in the alley, Vorrman's the youngest, and the fittest. It must have been him.'

'It's all spinning through my head so fast it's making no sense,' Deepbriar complained, running his hand over his hair. 'I'm missing something, I know it.'

'Ruggles has retired, he's an old man,' Houghton persisted. 'And you've agreed it's not Jack. That leaves Vorrman. He's the one.'

'He looks the most likely,' Deepbriar agreed, still not wholly convinced. 'Let's give it a rest.' He glanced out of the window. 'The rain's blown over. It's been a pretty bad August this year, let's hope September's better. Have they given you any idea how much longer you've got to stay here?'

'Only a few more days, so they say. I'm allowed to go for longer walks now, not just round the ward. I reckon I could get downstairs if I put my mind to it. I'm a lot stronger than I was. Dr Tordon says he wants me to put on some weight, but I've always been on the skinny side, ever since I got out of the army.'

'You could do with a bit of fattening up,' Deepbriar agreed, patting his own ample stomach; he'd always thought his own physique was about right, especially for a policeman. A bit of weight lent a man authority. 'What will you do when they discharge you? Have you got a place to stay?'

'I've got an appointment with the almoner; it's being sorted out.' Houghton's expression discouraged further enquiry, and Deepbriar let the matter drop. A few minutes later he made his excuses and left, promising he'd call in again soon. The rain had stopped but the streets were awash. He managed to convince himself that that was why he didn't take the shortcut down the alley, despite knowing he was cutting things fine if he was to get back before his dinner was on the table.

'Morning, Thorny.' Sergeant Hobday resumed his comfortable position, leaning one elbow on the counter and propping his head on his hand. 'When the door opened I thought for a minute I was going to have some work to do.'

'Peaceful Sunday, eh?' Deepbriar said. 'That's the sort I like.'

Seated in the office behind Hobday a

solitary uniformed constable was pecking tentatively at a typewriter, but otherwise all was quiet.

'It's a rarity, so don't tempt fate. What brings you back here? I'd have thought you'd avoid the place, what with our Mr Prout getting all worked up over you finding Greensall.'

'It's a bit disconcerting being his prime suspect,' Deepbriar agreed. 'I was hoping I might find you on duty. I came in for a chat. Mrs Deepbriar wanted to go to the early service, since she's helping her cousin with the dinner. There's something about Sunday morning at home that makes me uncomfortable, a man always gets the feeling he's in the way. Anyway, I couldn't face hanging around with the smell of roast beef making my stomach rumble.'

Hobday laughed. 'Good enough reason. You're in luck; the inspector was here a while ago, but he got called out. I doubt if we'll see him again for a few hours.'

'Suits me.' Deepbriar said, fetching a chair from against the wall. 'It's funny being back in Bradsea. Do you ever see any of the other lads who were here in the war? I heard from Dick Pullen two years ago. He's moved down south. He's teaching young lads to drive. Always liked motors, didn't he? He reckons we'll all be riding around in cars one of these days instead of walking the beat. Daft idea, if you ask me.'

'It wouldn't suit me; I never fancied learning to drive,' Hobday remarked. 'How about you?'

Deepbriar grimaced, remembering his only experience behind the wheel. 'My new boss reckons I should have a go, but I prefer my bike.'

'Me too. Or Shanks's pony. Chief Inspector Vorrman's supposed to be buying himself a car. Got more money than sense, that man.'

'I was wondering about that. Is that right about him getting a legacy?' Deepbriar asked.

'So they say. And it must have been a tidy sum.' Hobday sighed. 'Some people have all the luck. Only thing I ever inherited was my Dad's flat feet.'

'I thought you got them pounding the beat,' Deepbriar grinned, 'like the rest of us.'

'Chief Inspector Vorrman got lucky there too,' Hobday said enviously. 'I heard he only did a couple of years on the beat before he moved up here and got his stripes. There was talk about him having posh connections. You can tell he's from down south, of course, the way he talks. One thing's for sure, he's never been short of cash.'

'I don't suppose you see him much, since he took over at Whellow,' Deepbriar said casually.

'I dunno about that.' The sergeant lowered his voice so the young constable couldn't hear. 'It really gets Inspector Prout's goat, when he comes sticking his nose in. Quite funny sometimes.'

'I thought the inspector wasn't amused when he sat in on that interview,' Deepbriar nodded.

'It's about time for a cup of tea,' Hobday said, glancing over his shoulder at the constable who was still tapping at the type-writer, then turning back to Deepbriar. 'Be a good chap and put the kettle on, Thorny. The youngsters we get these days can't make a decent brew unless you stand over them.'

'I'll see to it.' Deepbriar said equably. 'Three sugars?'

'Four. And the lad here has two. Oh, and you'd better make one for the youngster up in the CID office, black with one sugar. Reckons it helps him stay awake.'

A few minutes later, a tray in his hands, Deepbriar was ready to return to the front office. He leant his shoulder against the door, and as it cracked open he heard voices. He paused, hoping one of Hobday's superiors hadn't turned up; the public weren't sup-posed to be allowed to roam around the station unaccompanied, and the sergeant might be in trouble if his boss decided to get officious.

'So Inspector Prout isn't in?'

Deepbriar's brows furrowed. There was something familiar about that deep bass, though it was a voice he hadn't heard in many years. With a sudden shock, the identity of the man came to him. It was Superintendent Ruggles.

Chapter Twenty-one

Deepbriar was unashamedly eavesdropping, thankful that he'd made no noise when he pushed the door ajar.

'Constable Wardle's upstairs in the CID office, Mr Ruggles,' Sergeant Hobday was saying. 'Would you like to go on up? Or I could call him?'

'No, it was Prout I wanted.' Ruggles was short to the point of rudeness. He'd always been that way with junior officers, Deepbriar recalled, but that was nothing unusual in the police force. It was as much to do with class as rank. With Ruggles, they'd never expected anything else; the man had habitually kept his subordinates at a distance.

'He may be back in a few hours, sir, but I can't give you an exact time,' Hobday offered. The sergeant's tone was all it should be, respectful and attentive. 'I'm very sorry, when you've given up your Sunday morning to come over from Whellow. You're sure I can't help?'

Deepbriar felt a twinge of rebellion. Back in 1941, Ruggles had put a black mark on his record without giving him a chance to defend himself. Since the superintendent had retired from the force he no longer had any authority here; he was due the same respect as any other citizen, but there was no need for Hobday to be so deferential.

He found he badly wanted to match a face to the voice. As a very junior constable he couldn't recall ever speaking to Superintendent Ruggles personally, but he'd never forgotten the man's formidable presence. Sixteen years had passed since then; he was eager to see how much the superintendent had changed. He hoped Ruggles was wearing a black hat and coat; that might make it easier to visualize him muffled to the ears and wielding a thick walking stick. The thought made Deepbriar impatient. He shifted slightly, but he couldn't see through the gap between door and jamb.

'I suppose...' Ruggles paused. 'I never approved of the office grapevine, Sergeant, but it has its uses. What can you tell me about recent developments in the Greensall case?'

'Sir?' Hobday sounded flummoxed and Deepbriar drew in a sharp breath. Ruggles had no right to ask for that information. While a discreet query to a high-ranking friend might have been passed off as justifiable curiosity, his request put the sergeant in an impossible position.

'Come on, man,' Ruggles said impatiently. 'We all thought Greensall was dead. When that body was found in the river I was in charge of this station. In the light of recent events it's obvious that some serious mistakes were made. If there's to be an inquiry I need to know about it. Up to now, Inspector Prout has kept me fully informed, it's simply bad luck that he was called away.'

There was a brief, charged silence, then Hobday spoke, his voice a little higher than was normal. 'Before we discuss this any further, Mr Ruggles, perhaps you'd like to join us for a cuppa? Constable, go and check if that kettle's boiled, there's a good lad. You can go upstairs and have yours with Constable Wardle, keep him company for a bit. I'll shout if I need you.'

Deepbriar backed away from the door and retreated to Rosie's cubby-hole, putting the tray down and picking up the sugar bowl and spoon. When the constable entered he was apparently stirring sugar into one of the mugs. 'What's up?' he asked innocently. 'Sergeant Hobday getting impatient, is he?'

'No, we've got another visitor,' the constable sounded nervous. 'It's Superintendent Ruggles.'

'I thought he'd retired,' Deepbriar said, all innocent interest as the younger man reached to open a cupboard.

'That's right.' The constable offered no further comment as he removed the sergeant's mug from the tray and replaced it with two china cups and saucers, then began rummaging through a drawer. 'Blooming tea-spoons, I can never find them,' he said gloomily, 'you wouldn't think they'd get nicked from a police station.'

'Here,' Deepbriar offered, fetching one from the sink and giving it a quick wipe with the tea towel. 'I suppose I'd better stay out of sight. I'll just drink my tea quick then scoot out by the back door. I don't want to get anybody into trouble.'

'Right, thanks. I'll let Sarge know you've gone.'

'Fine, but don't tell him while the super's here,' Deepbriar cautioned.

The constable nodded, most of his attention on the arrangement of the milk jug, sugar bowl and tea strainer. As he picked up the tray with exaggerated care, Deepbriar gave him a friendly nod of farewell, taking a mouthful of tea that was hot enough to scald, as if he was in a hurry to be gone. A few moments later he heard footsteps on the stairs; Sergeant Hobday and the ex-super-intendent were alone.

At one time Deepbriar's scruples might have prevented him from returning to listen at the invitingly open door, but with the threat of a murder charge hanging over his head, he found he'd become less nice about his manners.

With his eye to the jamb Deepbriar could just make out the large figure seated on the bench that ran along one side of the room. He hadn't known quite what to expect. Mr Ruggles was wearing a stone-coloured mackintosh. One large hand lay in his lap, holding a light brown hat that boasted a bright feather in its brim; the rather foreign accessory didn't look as if it would sit well above Ruggles's blunt features. Sixteen years had lightened the iron-grey hair and drawn a few more lines on the man's face, but he was still the same large commanding figure Deepbriar remembered. Bob Houghton had maintained that Ruggles was getting on in years, but this wasn't an old man.

As for the encounter in the alleyway, Deepbriar tried yet again to conjure up the figure of his assailant, but he found the memory was becoming hard to retain. The man had been big, with an aura of menace that may have made him seem even larger than the reality. Glancing at Sergeant Hobday, who had retreated behind his counter, Deepbriar simply couldn't imagine him as a potential murderer. He grinned to himself. He'd give a lot to hold an identity parade, with the three suspects dressed in identical black outfits. Maybe that way he'd be able to sort out the leader of the assault. After a while Deepbriar leant back against the wall. From this position he could hear the two men without any risk of being seen.

'Does Chief Inspector Vorrman intend

taking over the Greensall case?' Ruggles asked abruptly.

'Not that I know of, sir,' Hobday replied. A china cup rattled against the saucer. Evidently his hands were none too steady as he poured the tea; Hobday had no appetite for this conversation. Deepbriar felt a brief twinge of sympathy for the sergeant. He'd been so intent on keeping his head down during his last few months in the force.

'But he's been here.'

'He's called in once or twice, but that's nothing unusual. You can't blame him for being interested, sir. The same as the rest of us, he was here all those years ago, when we thought Greensall had copped it. It's a funny old business, isn't it, him turning up like that when we all thought he was dead and buried. Still, I daresay Inspector Prout will get to the bottom of it.'

There was a brief silence before Ruggles spoke again. 'Other people from the past have been putting in an appearance too. You'll know about Houghton.'

'Yes, sir.' The sergeant sounded surprised. 'I've been meaning to pop in and see him, just for old times' sake. It's sad seeing a man brought that low. He's had some bad luck over the years.'

'Yes. I've been a little concerned for him myself. I've made it my business to know who calls to see him. Perhaps you can tell me why Deepbriar visits him so often.'

'Thorny? He and Houghton were mates, sir. He was the youngest of those bobbies they sent out from county after the bombing. Bob Houghton took him under his wing, seeing Thorny was a bit on the green side. I don't think there's anything sinister in it.'

'So it's just coincidence that they've both turned up here at the same time?' Ruggles sounded sceptical. 'You'll have bumped into Deepbriar yourself, I imagine, since Inspector Prout sees him as a possible accessory to murder.'

Deepbriar closed his eyes for a second. It took a conscious effort to remain silent, not to let a pent-up breath come sighing from deep inside. Not murder then. Vorrman's hints had been right; Prout had accepted that he didn't murder Greensall.

'He's been interviewed a few times. It looked a bit suspicious first off, what with him being the one who found the body. I know it's not my place, sir, but I must say I don't think Deepbriar's involved. He's very well thought of back in Falbrough.'

'But if Houghton's the guilty party, it's hard to rule him out as a possible accessory, Sergeant.' Ruggles said, mildly enough.

Deepbriar didn't expect Hobday to respond. He was surprised when the sergeant continued. 'I heard Bob Houghton was ill.

Evidently he was flat on his back that Friday night, which means he couldn't have been taking part in a murder.'

'The opinion of a doctor at the cottage hospital may not hold much sway with a judge and jury. Let's forget about Houghton for the moment. What else can you tell me about Deepbriar? Where's he staying?'

Deepbriar listened as Hobday gave Ruggles the address.

'Not far away then,' was Ruggles's only comment. 'So, he's still in the force?'

'Yes. And he's just got a move to CID. I think he's pretty chuffed about it. You know he was sent here to convalesce? Got himself hurt tackling a murderer; there's been talk of him getting an award.'

'Really.' There was another pregnant pause. 'Maybe I've misjudged the man. I admit I thought he and Houghton were probably on the fiddle back in 1941, Sergeant,' Ruggles said. 'It wasn't exactly trumpeted about at the time, but I expect the whole station knew about it.'

Hobday mumbled something that Deepbriar couldn't catch, and he wondered if the sergeant had guessed he was listening.

There were sounds of somebody walking across the room and the faint clatter as a china cup and saucer were returned to the tray. 'I don't suppose there's been any more news from Manchester?' Ruggles asked casually. 'We may all be worrying unnecessarily. Greensall's murder could be an outside job.'

'We've heard nothing,' Sergeant Hobday replied, his tone wooden. 'And Mr Prout had my lads looking into any suspicious strangers hanging around town that day. They drew a total blank. I gather the inspector's given up on that line of enquiry.'

'A professional killer, a man who knew his job, would be able to blend in with the holidaymakers,' Ruggles said thoughtfully, 'but I think Prout is right. This case hinges on what happened during the war. Just one more thing, Sergeant. The man who made a false statement and then retracted it. What was his name, Hatherly? I heard a rumour that he'd gone missing.'

'That's a fact,' Hobday told him. 'And you're not the only person who's wondering why. Chief Inspector Vorrman was asking, and I think Deepbriar's looking for him, too.'

'Is that so? I hope Inspector Prout's following the same line. If Hatherly knows something relevant it's important that we get to him first.'

'I think Thorny's just keen to clear his name, sir,' Hobday said. Deepbriar was touched that the sergeant had tried to defend him, even if the attempt was lukewarm.

'And Chief Inspector Vorrman, as always,

has an eye on the route to further promotion,' Ruggles said. 'I dare say he'd like to prove that I'd made an error of judgement when I refused to pursue the case more rigorously back in 1941. The fact is, I'm beginning to wonder if I was misled. That's why I want to know exactly how this case progresses, Sergeant. If I made a mistake then it needs to be put right. You've been candid with me, Sergeant Hobday, I appreciate your cooperation. Thank you.'

The words were generous enough, but Deepbriar decided sourly that he didn't care much for Ruggles's tone.

'That's all right, sir. I'd be grateful if none of this goes outside these four walls, though. You being retired and all I probably shouldn't have said quite so much.'

'I'm always discreet, Sergeant,' Ruggles said frostily. 'You can tell Inspector Prout I'll call and see him tomorrow morning.'

The hinges on the heavy front door creaked, and after it closed there was a deep silence.

'Bugger,' Sergeant Hobday said expressively.

Deepbriar grinned, and went quietly back to Rosie's cubbyhole, where he threw the dregs of his cold tea down the drain. He wondered whether he should leave, but before he'd made up his mind he heard somebody coming along the corridor.

'You were listening,' Hobday said accusingly.

'Was I? You know what they say about eavesdroppers, Sergeant. Maybe I've just been sitting here drinking my tea.'

'And maybe pigs can fly,' the sergeant retorted. 'Look, keep out of my hair, Thorny. All I want–'

'Is to keep your nose clean until you retire,' Deepbriar finished for him. 'Fine, I won't come bothering you again. But just this once, Jack, between you and me and these four walls, what do you really think?'

'I think something around here smells, but I'm not a flipping bloodhound. I'm not even a flipping detective. It's no business of mine. Sidney Greensall was a villain, and the world's better off without him. Maybe it doesn't matter who finished him off.'

'What about Detective Chief Inspector Larch, though,' Deepbriar put in suddenly. 'Don't tell me you haven't wondered about that so-called suicide. You were the one who told me he'd got over what happened to his mates. He was back at work. You don't honestly believe he went and killed himself just a couple of days after you took that photograph. And did you know he'd told his sister he was going to reopen the Greensall case?' This was an exaggeration, but Hobday's stubborn refusal to get involved was galling, and Deepbriar wanted to sting him into some reaction.

When it came it wasn't at all what he expected. Hobday turned on his heel and left the room, slamming the door behind him.

'Toasted crumpets,' Mary said, putting her head round the door.

'Sorry?' Deepbriar was miles away, his head full of pencil marks on a worn scrap of brown envelope. They'd begun to swim in front of his eyes, and he'd let the vital clue slip to the floor.

'Tea. Hot toasted crumpets,' his wife reiterated.

'Whatever you like, love, I don't mind.' Deepbriar replied with a sigh.

'I asked you if you wanted some half an hour ago; they're ready and getting cold. Are you feeling all right? You can usually be relied on to smell hot crumpets from half a mile away.' She bent to pick up the scrap of paper that lay on the rug by Deepbriar's feet. 'Is this rubbish?'

'No!' He almost snatched it from her. 'It's evidence. If I can work out what it means I might be able to find Micky Hatherly.'

'Oh well, if you've got more important things on your mind than eating, we'll have our tea without you,' Mary said huffily, turning away but pulling up short as her husband grabbed her hand.

'Mary, don't go. I'm sorry, I didn't mean to snap. I was thinking.'

'Obviously,' she replied, removing her hand from his grasp. 'Don't let me stop you.'

'Mary!' He rose to his feet and went after her. 'You've always been good at crossword puzzles, maybe you can sort it out.'

She rounded on him, arms akimbo. 'I might try, Thomas Deepbriar,' she said, 'if you can give me one good reason why I should.'

Her use of his given name brought him up short. 'Have I been that bad?' he asked.

'Worse,' Mary replied bluntly. 'So I suppose if I want to get any sense out of you I'd better have a look at this clue of yours.' She took it and scanned it for a moment. 'Where did this come from?'

Deepbriar explained about Micky Hatherly and the money he was sending to his family. Mary nodded thoughtfully, then went to the door.

'I won't be a moment. I just need a word with Vera.' Two minutes later she was back. 'It's what he picked,' she said.

'What?' Deepbriar stared at his wife, as lost as if she'd suddenly started talking Chinese.

'Fruit. Look, RC for redcurrants, BL is probably blackcurrants. The others could be strawberries and raspberries. And the numbers afterwards are the weights. That says

107 pounds, 4 ounces. The handwriting's awful, the abbreviation for ounces is just a squiggle, but it's not that difficult. Vera says there's only one place it could come from, if it's near Firstall, and that's Low Valley Farm. It belongs to a man called Marsden.'

Deepbriar took the envelope from her. Now he knew the answer, it was obvious. 'I thought it was 107114, squiggle, not a hundred and seven pounds, four ounces. You're a genius! And say thank you to Vera for me.' He reached for the local map and scanned it, tracing routes with a finger. Suddenly he snatched up the map, folded it inexpertly and pushed it into his pocket. 'Got to go, love. I shan't be long.'

'Go? Go where?' she called after him. 'What about the crumpets?'

There was no reply except the click of the front door closing.

Chapter Twenty-two

People were already leaving the hospital as Deepbriar walked in through the gates, then he heard the clang of the bell, and the rest of the visitors came flowing out. He attempted to talk his way past a staff nurse, but she was adamant. 'Visiting time is over,' she said firmly. 'I can't possibly let you in.'

'I don't suppose Dr Tordon is on duty?' he asked without much hope, unconsciously turning his hat over and over in his hands.

'He is not,' the woman replied tartly. The last handful of visitors were leaving, and the staff nurse stood ready to close the door. 'You can come back tomorrow evening,' she said. Deepbriar was about to turn away, when he noticed a large figure walking slowly down the stairs. He stepped forward to gain the man's attention. 'Mr Ruggles.'

The ex-superintendent hesitated for only a moment, a slight frown on his face before it showed a look of enlightenment. 'Deepbriar, is it?'

'That's right, sir.'

Ruggles nodded. 'This is convenient. I have been talking to your friend Houghton. I was hoping to have a word with you.

Come along.'

They sat in Ruggles's car, parked where the town ran out of both houses and road. The promenade ended in a wide patch of waste ground, giving them a view back along the beach. It was a quiet spot, ideal for confidences. As Ruggles stared out to sea, Deepbriar gave his companion a sidelong glance; they were almost equal in size and build, but the older man had a hardness about him that made him formidable. Deepbriar didn't find it difficult to imagine this man killing another, yet the very thought made him feel as if he had slipped into some strange alternative world, like Alice falling into Wonderland.

'What I said to Houghton this afternoon, I'd better repeat to you,' Ruggles said, still staring out at the breaking waves. 'I owe you an apology, Constable. During the war, when you were among those young officers posted to Bradsea, I made a false judgement. It wasn't entirely my fault, but I have to take the blame. I allowed myself to be imposed upon. As a result, Houghton left the force and Bradsea lost a good sergeant. In your case, I was wrong to condemn you unheard, and I'm sorry. What damage was done by the remark I appended to your file, I am unable to say, but I regret it. After such a long passage of time, I don't know if I can make any suitable reparation, but I assure you I shall do my best.'

'Sir?' Whatever Deepbriar had expected, it wasn't this. 'You say you were misled.' He hesitated, unsure how to put his suspicions into words. 'It was Sergeant Vorrman who interviewed Micky Hatherly, after Sergeant Houghton had made his preliminary report. As far as we were concerned, that's when it all started to go wrong.'

'When Vorrman reported back to me, he made it quite clear that Houghton was involved in something illegal. And later he presented me with a piece of evidence that made the case impossible to ignore.' He gave Deepbriar a sharp look. 'You know about that?'

'If you're referring to the note that was supposed to have been found under Sergeant Houghton's locker, I only heard about it when I met up with Bob again,' Deepbriar replied.

'I had no reason to distrust Sergeant Vorrman. He wasn't a popular officer, but he generally got the job done. It was the sergeant who suggested the course of action I took regarding both you and Houghton. In my own defence, at the time a speedy resolution to the case seemed expedient. We were seriously undermanned, with very few experienced officers, some of whom weren't functioning at their best.'

Deepbriar glanced in Ruggles's direction

again; he was probably thinking about Chief Inspector Larch, but it didn't seem like the right time to bring up the question of Larch's suicide. 'An enquiry would have proved us both innocent,' he said.

'Probably.' Ruggles sighed. 'It wasn't exactly my finest hour, Constable, but I allowed the case to be forgotten. After Greensall's supposed death the black market activity in Bradsea dwindled to almost nothing. Sergeant Vorrman took over the investigation and he arrested several small fry from Greensall's organization. That was the end of it as far as I was concerned.'

'What changed your mind, sir? If you're sure it was Vorrman—'

'I have no evidence that would stand up in court. There's no proof that Sergeant Vorrman was taking money from Greensall, nor can I prove that Chief Inspector Vorrman, sixteen years later, was responsible for the man's death.' Ruggles pulled the starter and the motor throbbed into life. He took a grip on the steering wheel, which looked suddenly small between his large hands. 'I had hoped that Inspector Prout would turn up something useful, but I gather he's at a dead end.'

He turned his head and looked at Deepbriar, giving him a long penetrating stare. 'I want justice, for everyone involved, Constable. From what I've heard, there's a man who worked for Greensall who could provide us with the solid evidence we need, and you're close to finding him. That's probably the best hope we have. I suspect you're a better detective than Prout will ever be.'

Deepbriar was silent for a moment. 'With respect, sir,' he said at last, 'thanks to you, I've lost count of the times I've been turned down for a transfer to the CID over the last sixteen years, and never once been given a reason why.'

'My mistake,' Ruggles said, as he let in the clutch. 'I've admitted I was wrong, and told you I'm sorry. What more can I say? Except that solving this case isn't going to harm your career; I'll see you get all due credit.' He dug two fingers into the top pocket of his jacket and brought out a small card. 'My telephone number's on there. What you have to do is find out where that missing witness is hiding. When you do, let me know and I'll give you whatever help you need. But be careful, we don't want the wrong man going after him.'

At Deepbriar's request, Ruggles dropped him by the pier, and he walked slowly back to cousin Vera's, where he was met with cold buttered crumpets and an equally cold welcome from his wife.

Deepbriar couldn't sleep. He lay staring at the dim shape of the window, wondering how he could get to Low Valley Farm.

'What's the matter?' Mary sat up in bed and reached for the light pull over the headboard.

'Sorry, did I wake you?' he asked.

'No, I've got indigestion.'

Deepbriar looked at her in concern and began to get up. 'Shall I fetch you some bicarb?'

'Stay where you are; it'll go in a minute.' She pulled a fluffy bedjacket over her shoulders and looked at him, a little frown between her brows. 'Have you been having nightmares again?'

'I haven't been to sleep.'

'Honestly, Thorny, what is it now? I thought you said finding Micky Hatherly would solve the case.'

'It's all very well knowing he's probably working on that farm,' Deepbriar told her, 'but I can't think how to get there. It's miles off the bus route. And even if I find him, suppose he doesn't want to talk to me? If he takes to his heels I'm in no shape to go after him.'

'You'll need some help, then,' Mary said simply.

'Yes, but who from? I've been wondering if I should have told Superintendent Ruggles the whole thing. If only I was sure about Vorrman; if he's not the murderer then Ruggles is the prime suspect. The only person I can really trust is Bob Houghton, but he won't be out of hospital for several days. I don't think Inspector Prout would keep it to himself, otherwise he'd be the one to tell. If only I was fit,' Deepbriar added gloomily. 'I could borrow a bike.'

'A car would be better,' his wife replied. 'The answer's obvious. You'll have to ask Charles. He never needs any persuading to help you, especially if there's some sort of action in the offing, and if there's any running involved, he can do it.'

'That's a brilliant idea. Thanks love.' He leant across to kiss her cheek. 'What would I do without you?'

'What, you mean apart from starve and have no decent clothes to put on?' She snugged down beside him. 'Any chance we can get some sleep now?'

When Deepbriar woke up he couldn't remember what he'd been dreaming about, although he knew his sleep had been troubled. After breakfast he walked to the nearest telephone box and called Minecliff Manor. It was the colonel who answered his call.

'Sorry, Thorny, the son and heir's away. He and Elaine are visiting friends in Scotland, and they won't be back until Thursday,' the colonel said. 'Anything I can do?'

Knowing that the old man hadn't driven more than ten miles from home for years, Deepbriar reluctantly told him that there

313

wasn't, and hung up. There was only one thing to be done. He turned his steps towards the police station.

Inspector Prout looked far from overjoyed to see Deepbriar. He ushered him into his office but didn't bother to shut the door or offer him a chair. 'It's Monday morning and I've already had one piece of bad news, Constable,' Prout said. 'This had better be good. And don't take long, I'm expecting somebody.'

'I think I've located Micky Hatherly,' Deepbriar said. 'He knows the identity of the officer who was in Greensall's pay.'

'Hatherly! Now look here, Deepbriar, I've only got your word for it that he ever had anything to do with Greensall. There's nothing in the file. As for bent coppers, that case was supposed to be closed when Sergeant Houghton resigned. If he'd been innocent he'd have insisted on being the subject of an enquiry.' Prout's mouth twisted in an unpleasant smile. 'We won't mention your own little faux pas.'

'But half the papers on the Greensall case have gone missing,' Deepbriar shot back. 'You could try asking Sergeant Hobday. He'll tell you Micky Hatherly was involved, he was the one who gave us the first tip off. Hatherly's the key to finding the murderer. He worked for Greensall. All the evidence suggests he knew the identity of the police officer who was taking bribes to protect the black market; he's still afraid of him, that's why he ran off.'

'This is all just conjecture,' Prout said dismissively.

'But one word from Micky Hatherly will give us the answers. The police officer who was taking bribes got worried when Greensall came back to Bradsea. Maybe Greensall was trying a spot of blackmail, I don't know, but he decided he had to put his old friend out of the way. Hatherly probably knows the killer's identity, and I think I know where Hatherly is. Don't you want to know?'

'All right, Sherlock, amaze me,' Prout said sarcastically. 'And when we discover that this Hatherly went missing because he's had a row with his wife, or because the bailiffs are after him, then I'll be happy to charge you with wasting police time!'

'You'll go and see him yourself, sir?' Deepbriar asked. 'I need to know you'll follow this up. Because if the murderer gets to him first—'

'For God's sake!' Prout slammed his palm on the desk. 'Stop trying to tell me how to do my job, Constable! Where is this Hatherly?'

Deepbriar felt a flush rising to his face. 'I think he's working for a man named Marsden, picking fruit. He's at a place called Low Valley Farm, about five miles from Firstall.'

Prout grabbed a sheet of paper from his

desk and made a note. 'All right, I've got that. You say you think that's where he is. I don't have time to go on a wild goose chase. How did you get this information?'

'His wife admitted that he'd been sending her money every week, and that the envelopes were always postmarked Firstall. And she gave me this.' He handed over the pay envelope.

'RC 107114? What the hell's that supposed to mean?'

'Redcurrants,' Deepbriar explained. 'He picked one hundred and seven pounds and four ounces. Then there's blackcurrants, strawberries and raspberries. The bottom line shows how much he was paid.'

'And from this you've deduced who Hatherly is working for? Don't tell me; you're some sort of handwriting expert.'

'I don't need to be. There's only one fruit farm anywhere near Firstall.' Deepbriar bit his lip. 'Sir, I know you and I got off on the wrong foot, maybe that's not surprising, I know how it looks, me being the one who found Greensall's body, that's the sort of coincidence that looks too unlikely to be true. But I'm afraid Micky Hatherly's living on borrowed time. I'm as sure as I can be that he's at Marsden's farm. His wife told me he'd always been afraid of somebody from his past, and she said she thought it was a policeman. In fact, the threat of trouble got too much; they're planning to emigrate. They were waiting for the papers to come through. Something must have happened, though, and Micky went on the run.'

Prout gave an exaggerated sigh. 'All right, Deepbriar, I'll look into it. It'll give me something to do while I'm waiting to hear if Houghton's going to make it. But if he doesn't, I reckon this case will soon be closed.'

'Sir? What do you mean? Has something happened to Bob Houghton?'

'Haven't you heard? He took it into his head to go walkabout late last night; he fell down the stairs and cracked his skull. What really annoys me is that if I hadn't let that damn doctor fob me off, Houghton would have been questioned days ago. Obviously, he wasn't nearly as sick as he was making out. A man who was at death's door a week ago can't have suddenly found himself fit enough to go waltzing around the hospital after dark, can he?'

'Is he badly hurt?' Deepbriar asked, appalled at the news.

'Nobody's telling. I gather they'll know more in a few hours. Now look, Deepbriar, you've said your piece. You can clear out now.'

Deepbriar nodded. 'Yes sir,' he said mechanically, his thoughts far away as he

317

left the room. He was wondering what could possibly have made Houghton tackle the stairs in the middle of the night. There was only one reason that made sense.

The public telephone box at the hospital was in the front hall. Perhaps Bob had solved the mystery of Micky's whereabouts. But who did he want to call? Cousin Vera didn't have a telephone, so it couldn't have been his old friend. And he wouldn't have wanted to talk to anybody at the police station. That left ex-superintendent Ruggles. He had given Deepbriar his telephone number, and asked to be told if Hatherly was found. Obviously, he had made the same request of Bob Houghton.

Deepbriar was halfway along the corridor when he heard Prout bellow from behind him. 'Sergeant, hasn't Mr Ruggles arrived yet?'

Deepbriar turned round, and saw Prout's young sergeant pop his head out of a doorway. 'Yes sir, isn't he with you? He came about five minutes ago, I was going to show him in, but he said he'd find his own way.'

Prout sighed. 'Then where is he? I said I'd make time to see him, but I don't want to hang around all morning.'

'He didn't come back past me, sir, he must've gone out through the back door.'

Prout noticed Deepbriar then. 'Are you still here, Constable? I thought I told you to get out.' He turned back into his office and slammed the door.

Deepbriar hurried down the stairs, trying to get his thoughts in order. As he reached the swing doors somebody gave one of them a push from the other side, knocking him off balance.

'Sorry.' The man who'd come rushing through dropped the file he was holding, to thrust out a hand and grab Deepbriar before he fell. 'You all right?' Chief Inspector Vorrman asked, as the constable regained his footing.

'Fine,' Deepbriar replied. 'It was my own fault, I'd forgotten about the one way system through these doors. I was miles away...' He broke off, watching as the other man bent to pick up what he'd dropped, seeing his long thin fingers closing on the file. In that instant it all became clear. He'd found that missing piece of the puzzle.

Chapter Twenty-three

'Chief Inspector, I know this is going to sound crazy,' Deepbriar said, taking off his coat and rolling it into a bundle, 'but do me a favour. Make a fist and punch me.' He held the coat against his ribs, and jabbed a hand at it. 'Right here, as hard as you can.'

Vorrman started to protest, his eyebrows lifting, then with a little shrug he obeyed. Deepbriar knew even before the blow struck him that he'd been right; the chief inspector had told him about his abject failure to learn to box. Nobody could ever describe him as having fists like sledge hammers, yet those were the words Joe Hatherly had used about the man who attacked him.

'Do you want to tell me what that was in aid of?' Vorrman asked, rubbing his knuckles.

'It's Mr Ruggles,' Deepbriar said urgently. 'He was the one who was taking bribes from Greensall, and he's just found out where Micky Hatherly's hiding. I think he's on his way there now. If we don't get to Micky before he does, there's likely to be another murder.'

Unlike Prout, Vorrman believed him. 'Come on,' he said, leading the way to the back door. 'His car was out here, maybe he hasn't left yet.'

The yard behind the station was empty except for a police car. Vorrman ran to the corner of the road so he could see down to the promenade, with Deepbriar hurrying behind him.

'There,' the chief inspector said. At the far end of the road, where it turned to go out of town, a man stepped out of a telephone box, striding across the pavement to his car. 'That's him. We're going to need transport. You're quite sure about this, Constable? You've got some sort of proof?'

'Joe Hatherly was beaten up,' Deepbriar said, as they hurried hack to the police station, 'by a man who was trying to discover Micky's whereabouts. I should have seen it sooner. When we were in the pub you told me you'd never been any good at boxing.'

Vorrman gave a wry smile. 'While Ruggles was a police champion, in his day. I was beginning to come to the same conclusion about our esteemed ex-superintendent. If we get to Hatherly in time, perhaps we can finally wrap up this case.' He hesitated as they reached the car. 'Can you drive, Constable?'

'No, sir, I'm afraid not.'

'Then we'd better hope there's somebody on duty who can.'

Three minutes later they were pulling out of the yard, with Constable Norris in the front seat alongside the driver. 'Use your bell if you need to, Johnson,' Vorrman ordered, 'we're in a hurry. Exactly where are we going, Deepbriar?'

'The Firstall road, sir, a place called Low Valley Farm.'

Chief Inspector Vorrman bent over a map, tracing their route. 'Low Valley Farm is down a long winding lane, and it doesn't look as if there's any other way out.' He was silent for a moment, staring at the road ahead. 'Why do you think Ruggles stopped at that telephone box, Deepbriar?'

'I've been wondering about that, sir. Calling for reinforcements perhaps? Micky's not likely to go with him willingly.'

'But he won't want to charge in mob-handed, not in front of witnesses. Suppose he put a call through to the farmer?'

'To flush Micky Hatherly out, you mean?' Deepbriar nodded, his eyes widening. 'That's a brilliant idea.'

'Mine, or his?' Vorrman asked sardonically. 'No, never mind, Constable, let's just hope my guess is right. So, Ruggles won't drive up to the farm. He'll have left a message to bring Micky running, then he'll lie in wait somewhere.'

'Micky's got his bike with him, but it won't be much of a contest if it comes to a chase.'

'We have to keep the two of them apart if possible. If Ruggles gets desperate there's no knowing what he might do.' Vorrman returned to the map. 'There's a road here that goes quite close to the farm. It might be possible to take a short cut across the fields.'

'Excuse me, sir,' Constable Norris put in. 'I know the area quite well. There's a footpath from the Cromwell Road to Low Valley.'

'Look, sir, isn't that Mr Ruggles's car?' It was the driver, Johnson. They had breasted a hill and, about two miles away, on the other side of a shallow valley, a small black dot was about to disappear from view.

'He'll be turning into the lane in a couple of minutes, Chief Inspector,' Norris said eagerly.

'Right. Direct Johnson to the start of that footpath, Norris. You and I will go to the farm that way, and see if we can intercept Hatherly. If Ruggles did send him a message, with luck Marsden won't have been in too much of a hurry to deliver it. Deepbriar, you and Johnson are to drive on towards the farm. Use the car to barricade the lane if necessary. I don't want Ruggles making a break for it.'

'Nobody's going to pass us down here,' Johnson remarked a few minutes later. The road ran between high banks topped with hedges, and it wasn't very wide. 'Downhill all the way, pretty much, from here to the farm.'

'Slow down,' Deepbriar suggested. 'In fact, how about turning the engine off? We don't want him to hear us coming. And stop just before that next corner.'

They coasted to a standstill, the only sound the faint tick of cooling metal. Deepbriar eased quietly out of the car and advanced cautiously down the lane to peer round the bend. A car was parked in a field gate about a hundred yards ahead.

'He's there,' Deepbriar said softly, coming hack to Johnson. 'We'll wait until we hear him start the motor.'

'Let's hope there's time for the chief inspector to join us,' Johnson said.

'What's the matter, don't you fancy the idea of arresting your former boss?' Deepbriar asked, grinning.

'Not particularly. Have you seen the size of him? Superintendent Ruggles won the police boxing championship five times. If–' he broke off at the sound of a motor rumbling into life, his hand going immediately to the starter.

They took the corner slowly, to see Ruggles's car accelerating away from them. Deepbriar's breath caught in his throat. A cyclist, head down and pedalling hard, was coming up the hill. He was tucked in by the steep bank to leave room for the car to pass him safely.

'No-o-o,' Johnson protested, as the car they were following swerved violently. There was a rending crash, the car ploughing its bumper into the bank. Both the bicycle and its rider were tossed into the air. Hatherly was thrown clear over the bonnet and on to the car's roof. He lay there for a split second then slid bonelessly down the boot to land in the road.

Deepbriar was out of the police car before it stopped, cursing his stupidity. This was his fault. He'd expected Ruggles to force Micky into his car and deal with him elsewhere, but he'd misjudged the situation.

Ruggles too was moving, he was already in the lane, leaning over Hatherly's unmoving form. He glanced up at Deepbriar, and for a second the constable wondered if he'd plead innocence and claim it had been an accident. Then he saw what the man held in his hand. Dwarfed in the meaty fist, the pistol was aiming at the unconscious man's head.

'No!' Deepbriar shouted. He felt rather than saw the driver, Johnson, moving up behind him. 'Leave him alone. There's more of us on the way, sir. Put that thing down, please. You can't kill us all.'

'They'll hang me anyway,' Ruggles said harshly. 'The little coward deserves to die.'

'He's not worth it, sir,' Deepbriar said,

searching for something that would get through to the man. 'Let him go and you might not have to face a murder charge. Nobody's going to blame you for getting rid of scum like Greensall.'

The other man grimaced, hesitating. 'When Greensall contacted me a month ago I knew I had to get rid of him for good this time. Hatherly was supposed to help me, but instead he made a run for it. He ruined everything. If he'd been there to help me, the body could have gone in the river and never been heard of again.'

'Unless he turned up in the same place as the man we mistook for Greensall back in '41. Who was he?' Deepbriar had seen what Ruggles hadn't. Constable Norris was coming up the road, advancing in a stealthy creep, as if he was playing Grandmother's Footsteps. He had to keep Ruggles's attention.

Ruggles was silent for a second, then he shrugged, as if he could see no harm in satisfying Deepbriar's curiosity. 'Just a tramp. Luckily, he hadn't been on the road for long, he still had plenty of flesh on him. It was quite a struggle getting him into Greensall's clothes. We made a good job of him, though. We cut his hair, even trimmed his fingernails.' He laughed briefly. 'It was a waste of time. Once the fish had finished, his own mother wouldn't have known him.

Don't come any nearer, Deepbriar, I'm a good shot. I can drop you quite well from here.'

'Boxing and shooting,' Deepbriar commented. 'All the manly arts, eh? There's one thing I don't understand. You were a high-ranking officer. Why risk it all for the sake of a few pounds from a lowlife like Greensall? Everyone knew Mrs Ruggles had plenty of money.'

'Leave my wife out of this!' Ruggles's face reddened, his features contorting. 'People like you couldn't begin to understand. My wife was a lady. It wasn't her fault those penny-pinching relatives of hers didn't grant her a decent allowance. She deserved the very best of everything, it's what she'd grown up with, it was hers by right. What did it matter if a few crimes went unpunished? As soon as you put a man like Greensall in prison two more would just spring up to take his place.'

Deepbriar kept his eyes fixed on the gun. He had located Vorrman now. The chief inspector was at the top of the bank, working his way along under cover of the hedge. He was much closer than Norris.

'You're right,' Deepbriar agreed. 'And I'm sorry, I didn't mean any offence. Hadn't we better see if we can get your car off the bank?' He took a tentative step closer, seeing Vorrman still moving out of the corner of his eye, wanting to make Ruggles turn further from the chief inspector.

'Stay where you are!' Ruggles brought the gun up so it was pointing at Deepbriar. He jerked his head at Johnson. 'You. Back your car into the field gate and turn it round. Don't try anything clever or you'll have two deaths on your conscience. I assure you I'm quite capable of shooting Deepbriar before I finish Hatherly. Go on, move.'

Deepbriar heard Johnson's footsteps on the road, then the car's engine firing, but Ruggles's attention never strayed, his eyes and the gun levelled at Deepbriar. 'Why did Greensall have a hundred pounds in his shoes?' Deepbriar asked, frantically trying to keep Ruggles occupied. He could feel sweat running down his back, and his heart was pounding as if he'd just run a mile.

'The bastard threatened to tell the whole story if I didn't hand over some cash, so I gave him the hundred to keep him quiet and told him to come back for the rest a couple of nights later. That bought me a bit of time. I'd planned to put him in the sea off the boat jetty, but some damn dog came along and started barking. I had to leave the body under the pier without searching it properly. If only he'd stayed in Manchester, nobody would ever have suspected me.'

'But that's not true, is it, Mr Ruggles? Chief Inspector Larch was on to you. At least, he knew Bob Houghton had been blamed for something he didn't do,' Deepbriar said rashly.

'My word, I did get you wrong, didn't I, Deepbriar. So you worked that out too? Who knows where you might have ended up, but for me. It's just as well I blighted your career. You might have been another interfering know-it-all like Vorrman by now. Still, maybe you'll be given an award for bravery, how would you like that?' He smiled, with no hint of humour in his expression. 'It's likely to be posthumous, of course, if you're fool enough to try anything.'

Chief Inspector Vorrman had slid down the bank and was standing in the road. He was slowly lifting his right hand, his long fingers curled around a large stone. Deepbriar was having trouble breathing.

'Down!' Vorrman yelled, his arm swinging as he lunged forward in the classic style of the fast bowler. Deepbriar obediently flung himself sideways. Vorrman's aim was good; the stone struck Ruggles between the shoulder blades, pitching him to the ground. Ruggles's grasp on the gun was loosened but he shifted his grip as he fell, capturing it between finger and thumb.

Deepbriar was too far away. As he scrambled back to his feet Ruggles was already on his knees and the weapon was back in his hand.

Chief Inspector Vorrman had continued his run, his long legs propelling him straight at Ruggles. Deepbriar felt as if he was caught up in one of his nightmares, unable to move because his legs were encased in concrete.

It can only have taken a couple of seconds, but it felt like a lifetime. Ruggles glanced sideways, and saw this new adversary. He hesitated, the gun wavering indecisively, then Vorrman was upon him, blocking the older man from Deepbriar's view.

'Sir, Mr Ruggles, don't do it!' Deepbriar shouted. 'He's got a wife too. Think how Mrs Ruggles would have felt if–'

The sound of the shot reverberated around the sunken lane. Chief Inspector Vorrman stopped in his tracks, then took half a step backwards. 'Oh God,' he said softly.

Deepbriar was running now, hands out, reaching, expecting the man to collapse into his arms. Then he saw Ruggles. The man had turned the gun on himself, and the bullet had removed most of his face. Ruggles staggered, a gargling sound coming from what was left of his mouth. After what seemed an eternity he fell, and was mercifully silent.

'God,' Deepbriar echoed. Behind him he could hear Johnson being violently sick, while Constable Norris was trembling, knees beginning to buckle and his face turning a nasty shade of grey.

'Constable Deepbriar,' Vorrman said evenly, 'get the youngster out of here.' He tipped his head towards Norris. 'We'll need an ambulance.'

'Sir,' Deepbriar acknowledged, taking the young man by the arm and steering him down the road, away from the body. 'You heard the chief inspector. An ambulance. Go and use the telephone at the farm, lad, quick as you can.'

Norris nodded, still looking a bad colour but steadier on his feet. Deepbriar went back to join Vorrman, who was bending over Micky Hatherly. Blood was welling from a deep cut on Hatherly's chin, and the side of his face had been scraped raw where he'd hit the road.

'His pulse is strong.' the chief inspector said, taking his jacket off and draping it over the man's chest. 'Not much we can do for him until the ambulance gets here. Johnson, you might as well drive up to the top of the lane. Stop anybody else coming down.'

The man obeyed, looking grateful to get away. Deepbriar went to Ruggles's car. He found a coat on the back seat and took it to drape over its owner's shattered head.

'That's a big improvement, thank you, Constable,' Vorrman said, a slight shake in his voice now the crisis was over.

'You all right, sir?' Deepbriar asked.

The other man grinned. 'I'll live.'

'Then maybe you won't mind satisfying my curiosity.' Deepbriar hesitated, knowing he was about to take a huge liberty.

'Well?' Vorrman prompted. 'It's all right, Deepbriar, I've got an idea you just saved my life. I'm ready to be magnanimous.'

'I'm sorry, sir, but I've heard a lot about that inheritance of yours. It made everybody so jealous, but I've been told it wasn't all that much. I was wondering if you wanted to tell me how you can afford to run that big house, and buy suits like the one you've just ruined.'

At this Vorrman actually laughed. 'As you so aptly reminded Ruggles, I have a wife, Deepbriar. And Mrs Marjorie Kay Vorrman's maiden name was Rothfield.'

Marjorie Kay Rothfield! Even Deepbriar recognized the name of one of the most famous romantic novelists of the age. 'Flipping heck!'

'Precisely. I'd be grateful if you'd keep that to yourself. My wife prefers the quiet life, so we let people think our money came from my legacy, which, as you pointed out, actually wasn't very large. I assure you, the tax man keeps a close eye on our income, every penny is accounted for.'

'I never doubted it, sir,' Deepbriar said, hoping he didn't sound as foolish as he felt.

'I can't say I'm sorry to be leaving,' Mary

said, as Major Brightman opened the door of the Colonel's old car for her.

'It'll be nice to get home,' Deepbriar agreed, lifting their suitcases into the boot. 'Though I'm not looking forward to house hunting. We can't hang about, either. The new village bobby will be wanting to move in, he's already had to wait two months.'

He stared across the promenade. In a couple of weeks Bob Houghton would be back there, pushing his barrow and his broom. It looked as if he would receive an apology, and some kind of compensation, too, if Chief Inspector Vorrman got his way. Bob hadn't said a lot when he heard, except that he wanted to keep his job, if the council were prepared to wait for him to recover. With the whole story exploding on the front of the daily papers, Deepbriar didn't think there was much doubt about that.

The next band of rain was on its way, the sky growing darker by the minute. Along by the bandstand a familiar shape was sniffing around a lamppost. The first heavy drops of rain began to fall. 'That black dog,' Deepbriar said, half to himself. 'I wonder where he lives. If...' he broke off, then began to laugh.

'What's so funny?' The major came to stand beside him, staring down the road, where the dog was beating a retreat with its tail between its legs as the downpour started in earnest. He frowned, unable to see the cause of Deepbriar's merriment.

'I'll explain in a minute,' he said. 'I'm sorry, but I've got to pop round to the library for a quick word with Miss Caldwell. It's been staring me in the face the whole time.' He shook his head in disgust. It had taken him far too long.

He had seen the dogs out at Dummel's Bottom. They must have left a powerful scent on the newly manufactured gnomes. Then there were the marks on the gnome that was found on the beach, the exact distance apart of a set of strong canine teeth. The day he'd found Greensall's body, he'd even watched the thief trying to bury the evidence of his crime in the shingle, but failed to come to the obvious conclusion.

Deepbriar was smiling as he went into the library. He must remember this day, if he ever became complacent about his abilities as a detective. It hadn't been until the very last minute of his stay in Bradsea, that he'd finally solved the case of the vanishing gnomes. Even then, he'd only been enlightened by the sight of the culprit slinking off home to get out of the rain.

The publishers hope that this book has given you enjoyable reading. Large Print Books are especially designed to be as easy to see and hold as possible. If you wish a complete list of our books please ask at your local library or write directly to:

Magna Large Print Books
Magna House, Long Preston,
Skipton, North Yorkshire.
BD23 4ND

This Large Print Book, for people
who cannot read normal print,
is published under the auspices of

THE ULVERSCROFT FOUNDATION